THE BIG JOB - LARGE PRINT

A STELLA REYNOLDS MYSTERY

LIBBY KIRSCH

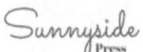
Sunnyside Press

Sunnyside Press
PO Box 2476
Ann Arbor, MI. 48106

www.LibbyKirschBooks.com

The Big Job/ Libby Kirsch -- 1st ed., large edition

ISBN-13: 978-1-7337003-8-2

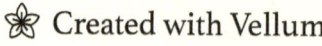 Created with Vellum

For Tom. Thanks for always being so supportive.

1

"Standby, Stella."

She'd heard photographers say the same thing to her in different states across the country for years, but nothing else about this day was familiar. Stella Reynolds blotted her forehead with her fingertips and smoothed a hand over her long, auburn hair. Her chest felt tight, her stomach fluttered, and she pressed her lips together. It was ridiculous, but she couldn't ignore the signs: she was *nervous*.

A nasal, confident, familiar voice behind her calmed her enough to take a deep breath. She listened to Vindi Vassa, a coworker from what felt like another lifetime, as she wrapped up a live shot for her station in San Diego to Stella's left.

"Preston Harrington has always maintained his innocence and has refused to cooperate with police or prosecutors..."

More reporters—some half-dozen—stood in front of the Palm Springs, California, courthouse, covering a whopper of a murder trial smack dab in the middle of paradise. Local stations from nearby San Diego and Los Angeles were there, along with CNN... and Stella.

The thought made her stomach flutter again and she gulped. Irritated at herself, she then shook her head hard.

"Hey. Are you okay?" Kelly Wozniack stuck his head out from behind the camera and looked at her over his glasses. "It's just a teaser—you know that, right? Five seconds—ten, max—and then we're done until three."

"Yeah, I know," Stella said, grimacing when her breath stuttered in three hops. She closed her mouth. Breathless for a pre-recorded tease! What was wrong with her?

"Okay, well, any time you're ready. I'm rolling." He didn't put his head behind the camera, though—just continued to stare, like he knew a car accident was about to happen and didn't want to miss it.

Woz was about her height at five-foot-nine but

wider than a MAC truck and just as noisy. His loud breathing echoed through the parking lot, and in the desert heat, he had long ago sweat through his shirt. His messy, grey and black hair was curly and longish, sticking straight out from his head like he had a hand on one of those static electric balls at a science museum.

She squared her shoulders and took a cleansing breath. "Three, two—"

"Wait," Woz interrupted, "we don't do that countdown thing out loud. You just have to count in your head and then start."

Stella blinked. It was a small thing, really, but she'd been saying, "Three, two, one," before every pre-recorded standup for years. She'd been told long ago that the short countdown gave the editor enough tape to grab the edit. Now she felt tiny beads of sweat reform at her hairline. "Right, count to myself. No problem."

It was a problem, though. It took her three tries to say her six-second line correctly. Finally, she got it out. "A murder in paradise, and now the trial begins for the man accused of killing his business partner, all while the world waits for what could be a life-saving, game-changing drug." She looked up at him, her eyebrows raised.

Woz hit a button on the camera and said, "It's okay; they probably won't even use it."

She barked out a laugh at the absurdity of her day, which, although it was only noon in California, had started more than nine hours earlier in Ohio.

Lucky Haskins, her boyfriend of several years, had taken her to the Columbus airport for an early flight that morning. She had planned to fly to New York City for her new job as a network reporter for NBC News, where she would spend the week in training at their offices near Times Square, and then get her first assignment. Instead, she'd gotten a call from her new manager as she'd stood on the curb by Lucky's car.

"Change of plans, Stella. Can you rebook onto the five-ten flight to Palm Springs? Our reporter covering the Harrington trial fell ill."

"The five-ten to Palm Springs?" she'd repeated. "Uh..." Stella had scrunched her face together, wondering if she should head into the airport to make the change or call from her phone.

"If you can't do it," Sher Patrick had snapped, "tell me now. We've got a storm system moving into the Plain states, though, and I don't want to pull my roaming reporters."

"Uh," she'd repeated. She hadn't been sure the

logistics of switching her flight at this late hour, but before she could say as much, Lucky had held his phone in front of her face. She'd squinted to focus, and then said, "No problem, Sher. I'm headed that way now." Lucky had booked her onto the flight on the app on his phone.

After six hours on a plane and a quick introduction to the photographer she'd be working with that day, she was now taping a tease for the evening news and preparing for her first network live shot in the field.

"News starts at six thirty Eastern, three thirty Pacific," Woz said, "so you've got three hours to figure out what you're going to say."

"Do they just want a video wrap or a sound bite?" She had no idea what he had shot from opening arguments and didn't know how she was going to wade through hours of court video in time for the news.

Woz shrugged and Stella hid a grimace. Was he intentionally being difficult, or was he just unaware of how unhelpful he was? She let out a deep breath and squared her shoulders. After all, Woz was only going to be her partner for the day, not the year.

He lumbered up the steps to the satellite truck and opened the door, waving her in with a grunt.

As she stepped into the small room, Stella felt at home at last. News feeds from across the country played on the half-dozen monitors facing her. Rows of blinking, square buttons and lines of audio and video input and output jacks stared back at her. She rolled a wheeled desk chair to the editing computer, inserted the disc Woz handed her, took a notebook out of her briefcase, and sat back to listen.

The case had been making headlines since Dr. Drew Chambers, a founding member of the startup, Luna C Engineering, had been brutally murdered at their offices in Palm Springs. The company had designed a revolutionary new drug for anxiety and depression called Wondred, which was touted as a game-changer in the mental health industry. No side effects had been reported during years of trials. The company had been waiting on FDA approval and was on the verge of going public when the murder happened. Millions of dollars had already been lost and millions more were at stake as the company's future was tied up in the murder trial.

The camera locked on Preston Harrington, who sat stone-faced, staring straight ahead toward the judge. He was so tall that his long legs barely fit under the desk; he had wavy brown hair, an off-putting, seemingly permanent frown, and wore an unusual, fuzzy, green sweater.

Stella's lips crowded to one side of her face. It was ninety degrees outside and Preston Harrington was wearing a sweater? It was likely a last-minute idea by his lawyer to make him appear friendlier and more approachable, but the effort had been wasted. No amount of sweater-softening would reach the subconscious of the jury—not with a scowl etched across Preston's face.

The judge finally called court to order, and the prosecutor stood to address the jury. Gail Abingdon walked behind the defendant and reached out, as if to put her hands on his shoulders, but then she stopped theatrically and dropped her hands to her sides.

"Preston Harrington isn't like your neighbor. He's not like anyone you know. He's cold, he's calculating, and he's a killer. He couldn't take the insult of coming in second—of being constantly outshone by the victim. Dr. Drew Chambers not only designed the product industry insiders say will revolutionize the way doctors treat patients, but he was also the face of the company—the media darling. Who was Preston Harrington? He was a no one, a never was, a hanger-on, and in his jealousy, he finally snapped."

Harrington glared through the entire twenty-five-minute barrage of accusations.

The prosecutor's speech was methodical—scholarly, almost—as she laid out the state's case: Preston Harrington killed his business partner in a jealous rage the day before the company was to go public. After Gail Abingdon sat down, Stella turned her eyes back to Preston Harrington, interested to hear how his lawyer would paint the same set of facts. Instead, the video went to black. She looked over at Woz in surprise. "Defense didn't speak?"

"Nah." He leaned against the counter and wiped his brow with a handkerchief. "The judge dismissed everyone after Abingdon spoke—said we'll start back up in the morning for the defense's opening arguments."

"That's weird," Stella said. "It's the first day of the trial and she only has the jury hear one side of the case?"

"I know. At this rate, we'll be here for weeks."

You'll be here for weeks, Stella thought, wondering when she could book her flight to New York.

2

_____

"What does he look like?"

Stella groaned. With her cell phone pressed against her ear, she turned away from Woz to answer Lucky's question. "I promise you there's nothing to be jealous about." She kept her voice low, aware that the photographer was only feet away.

"Are you avoiding the question?" Lucky asked playfully.

"Don't be ridiculous."

After a pause, he said, "Seriously, now I'm worried. What does he look like?"

"Lucky! He's... old... and I don't know, kind of sweaty, and too close for me to say any more!"

"Okay, okay, Bear, don't get frustrated. You

know I trust you. It's just hard when you're thousands of miles away, working long hours with a stranger."

"Well, don't worry about *this* stranger!" Stella glanced back at Woz in time to see him pick his nose. "Seriously. I'll call you tonight, okay?"

"I'll be watching! Break a leg."

She tucked the phone into her bag at her feet when a shadow fell over her.

"You must be Stella."

She looked up at the deep, gravelly voice and was nearly blinded by the sun when the stranger stepped back. Raising a hand to shield her eyes, she squinted, still seeing star bursts of light. "Yes?"

"Hi. I'm Terry Henshaw. I'll be working with you today on camera."

Terry had soulful, brown eyes, a permanent five o'clock shadow, and the sweetest dimples she'd ever seen. His faded blue jeans looked soft enough to touch, and his tight, white T-shirt made it clear that he spent more time at the gym than away from it.

He cocked an eyebrow, and her face turned scarlet. "Oh. Hi."

"How was your trip in?" He rested his arm on the tripod and leaned in, like he really wanted to know her answer.

As she summarized her day, she tamped down her guilty thoughts—after all, she hadn't *really* lied to Lucky, since she hadn't met Terry when they'd spoken a few minutes ago.

Woz was the satellite truck operator—nothing there had changed—but she should have realized there would be another person working with her on the story. Woz had to stay behind the control panels of the truck when they were live, so that meant a second photographer was on site every day.

She flipped open a nearby laptop, but before she could do more than look for the icon for the news program she would use to write her story, Woz called out from inside the truck.

"How clean are your hands?"

Her nose wrinkled. "What?"

Woz looked pointedly at his computer. "I just want to make sure your hands are clean if you're going to use my equipment."

Terry snorted and Stella struggled to keep her expression neutral. "Ah, yup. I'm good to go." She held her hands out toward the sweaty, grimy, slightly dirty man to show him they were still glistening from a recent pump of hand sanitizer.

"Listen," he frowned, and Stella bit her lip—so much for not smirking. "I don't know you or how you operate. I just want to make sure you treat the equipment with respect, so it'll last." Stella nodded and turned back to the laptop, but Woz wasn't done. "We just got this satellite truck and the computer, for that matter, last year. You should've seen the piece of crap I was working with before that. I promised myself I'd take care of this stuff and that's what I intend to do."

Stella held up her hands again. "All clean, promise."

She brought the admittedly pristine laptop into the truck and typed out her story before walking out to the parking lot. After asking for the number for the newsroom, Woz recited it and Stella dutifully tapped it into her phone. A minute later, the executive producer was on the line.

Sher Patrick didn't even say hello. "I just got off the phone with Jolene, and she thinks she'll be ready to jump back in tomorrow. You need to stop by the hospital to fill her in on what happened today—I want her to hit the ground running tomorrow. With a little luck, we can have you on the first flight to New York in the morning. I'll have Peter book it before he heads home tonight."

Jolene Colbourne was a rising star at NBC. Stella had watched her coverage of the Drew Chambers murder and subsequent arrest of his business partner for the last two years on the evening news. Stella would be glad to hand this story back to her.

"I've got you heading up the C-block," Sher said, referring to the block of news after the second commercial break of the half-hour. "Your hit will come about six forty-seven, and I don't want you to even think about going longer than forty-five seconds. You must hit your marks. Local news isn't always very precise, but we are."

"Forty-five seconds, got it."

"It goes without saying, Stella, that network news is a whole different league. We don't have room for mistakes—you don't have six live shots later tonight to fix anything. You get one shot, so make the most of it; every word counts. Your job is to set the scene for our viewers and tell them things they can't glean from the video. Your job is to be excellent."

Sher disconnected without waiting for her to answer. Stella's heart rate, which had slowed to normal over the previous hours, crept back up to mid-workout levels. Set the scene? Tell viewers what they can't glean from the video? Stella, *herself*, was gleaning everything from the video— she'd been at 20,000 feet when Gail Abingdon made her opening statements, after all.

She tried to steady her breathing, so before walking back to the satellite truck, she paused to take it all in: the sun, the palm trees, and the heat. It was just another live shot, that's all.

She then saw, however, what Terry was working on as he knelt by the truck. His dimples flashed before he turned to a metal briefcase lying open next to him. He extracted a large light with black, metal flaps on each side and screwed it to the top of a small tripod.

Her photographer was setting up lights. It was three o'clock in the afternoon in the middle of the desert in Palm Springs, California, and the sun was shining overhead, but Terry had lights going up for their live hit still more than thirty minutes away.

Stella was used to the photographer grudgingly using the truck headlights for an eleven p.m. live shot. She knew network was a different level, but knowing it and seeing it in action were different things, and it did nothing to calm her nerves.

The parking lot was quiet—the local news reporters were on extended lunch breaks before their five o'clock live hits. Working on East Coast deadlines in the West Coast time zone would add an additional challenge to the job, and she heaved a sigh of relief that this was just a one-day gig.

"Go ahead and get in place," Terry said, moving from the lights to the camera, "so I can get a light check."

The temperature rose by at least five degrees when she stepped in the circle of light. Between the sun beating down from the sky, two lights in front of her, and two lights behind her, she had to pull her shirt away from her sticky back within minutes. Terry wasn't done, though. While she fanned herself with her notebook, he unzipped a small, round bag and caught a reflective light panel neatly in the air when it popped out. He angled the shiny material toward her and she squinted against the onslaught of light that hit her square in the eyes.

"Sorry." He changed the angle of reflection so she could see again. "Gorgeous."

She smiled and then smothered a laugh as Terry stared appreciatively not at Stella, but at the playback monitor at his feet. "We should always be so lucky to have this kind of natural light. Woz!" When he yelled, the other man lumbered out of the truck.

"Looks good. Maybe move the key light back a bit?"

While they fussed around with the placement of the lights, Stella blew out a deep breath and resisted the urge to fan herself again with her notebook. "How long?"

"Music starts in about ten minutes." Woz looked at his watch. "That means *we're* about thirty-five away. Damn C-block." He shook his head and headed back to the truck.

Stella stepped out of the spotlight and headed for the satellite truck, too, figuring she'd stay cool in the air conditioning while she could. Woz, however, held out a hand to stop her.

"EP likes everyone in place at the start of the news. She wants to make sure all the signals are strong, and sometimes they have to change the order at the last minute, so be ready. Our hit's not supposed to come until six forty-seven, but if something fails in Florida or the signal gets lost in Texas, they'll take us early, sometimes without warning. Are you plugged in?" he asked.

Stella shook her head and held out her hand for the IFB box, that magical, brick-sized contraption that allowed her to hear what was going on in the studio in New York through a tiny earpiece.

Woz wrinkled his nose. "What?"

"Do you have the IFB box?" She felt as confused as *he* looked.

"Oh, right." He shook his head. "I forget what a newbie you are." She pursed her lips, but he ignored her. "We don't use IFB boxes. It never works out well with the satellite truck—sometimes there's reverb. You just dial into the IFB line with your cell phone."

Stella stared down at the end of her IFB plug, which was easily twice the diameter of the headphone jack on her cellphone. "Just one problem: it won't fit!"

With a loud, wheezy breath, Woz disappeared around the side of the satellite truck, emerging seconds later with a small plastic bin. He rummaged through it for a moment and then handed her an adapter. She dutifully connected her IFB into the adapter, pushed the end into her cell phone, and dialed the number he recited.

"I don't hear anything." Panic settled into her chest. No IFB? She'd rather board a plane knowing the pilot was blind than try to wing a live shot without being able to hear her producer.

"Well, you wouldn't, would you?" Woz said unhelpfully. She narrowed her eyes and he blew out a heavy sigh, as if she were asking him to explain gravity. "At your local news station, as soon as you plug in, you might hear *Oprah* or *The Ellen Show*. There's nothing on at NBC News headquarters

right now, though, is there? You'll hear other reporters do mic checks and Sher might ask you a
question or two, but until the newscast starts,
there's nothing to hear."

"Right. Right, of course." Stella nodded and
smiled until Woz left for the truck and then she let
herself zone out. What *else* didn't she know, that
she didn't know? She'd never expected a learning
curve when she took this job, yet here it was, and
she felt like the total newbie Woz assumed
she was.

The next half-hour passed in a blurry haze of
squinting, sweating, and deep, calming breaths
that did nothing to slow her racing heart.

All too soon, they were five minutes away. Sher
asked for a mic check, they were two minutes
away, and then, through her IFB, Woz said, "Four-
point-eight-million."

"Excuse me?" Stella looked into the camera, as
if she could see him through the lens.

"I said: four-point-eight-million. That's how
many people usually watch our network news
every night, and now they'll be watching you.
Neat, huh?"

Terry shrugged, as if to say *no big deal,* and then
lifted the reflective panel higher. The temperature
rose a few degrees.

She gulped. No big deal—only 4.5 million more people than she'd ever been live in front of before. She heard the news anchor back in New York, *Hank-freaking-Smith* introduce her story, and then *Hank-freaking-Smith,* the same guy she'd watched since she was small and first realized what news was, said *her* name.

She thought about the nearly five million people tuning in to watch and their collective ten million eyeballs trained on her, and... she froze.

3

"I mean, I've literally never seen anything like it!" Woz didn't even pretend to lower his voice. "She froze solid, like ice. Like... well, you know, something that's super cold." He laughed. "Exactly, like an igloo. Craziest thing I've ever seen. All I'm saying is where'd they get her from?"

"Shut up, man. Give her a break." Terry shot a sympathetic look at Stella and continued to coil a cable around his arm. Woz shrugged and walked around the truck.

The fresh silence reminded Stella of another that had seemed to last much longer: her own inability to speak during her live shot.

Worse still was the ominous silence of her cell

phone. It hadn't rung once since *Hank-freaking-Smith* took the story back to New York and made a smooth excuse about technical problems with the satellite signal.

She looked up at the sky. All was sunny and clear in Palm Springs—there was absolutely zero reason for a bad signal. Chances were that her boss knew that just as well as your average viewer.

At any other job, the minute Stella did anything wrong, the news director had been on the phone with her instantly to chew her out. The lack of anyone yelling now was infinitely worse. What were they saying about her in New York?

No tears threatened, as she was too stunned to feel anything, yet. She stared at her cell phone, her eyes widening only a fraction when it chirped. It was a text from Lucky.

Well, you *looked* good.

She barked out a laugh. The sudden release of tension was enough to make her eyes well up and her breath catch in her throat. Even her boyfriend couldn't put a positive spin on things.

Terry disappeared into the truck, and Woz ignored her as he repacked the light kit. Stella figured she might as well help clean up while she waited for the call that might end her network career before it had really started. As she reached for

Woz's laptop, however, intending to bring it into the truck, another set of hands got there first. She looked up in surprise and locked eyes with a stranger.

His several layers of clothes were in tatters and wet with sweat, his hair greasy and unkempt. She started to release her hold on the computer, confused, when she heard Woz yell, "Oy! Get out of here!"

Her grip tightened, but so did his. A slight struggle broke out—this time, *Woz* stood frozen in shock—as Stella and the stranger tussled over his computer. Her grip was better, but the man was motivated. After several moments, she felt her fingers slipping, but before the stranger could wrestle the computer away, his eyes widened. She ducked instinctively as a stick came flying through the air, missing her by inches and smacking the man's arm with a thwack.

Now holding the laptop to her chest with both hands, her heartbeat thundering in her ears, she turned to see what fresh threat loomed. A second man, apparently homeless, as well, towered over her.

He was missing a leg and had used his crutch to crush the would-be thief. He held out a hand and said, "Annie, are you okay?"

"I—I'm not Annie," she said. After he pulled her upright, she pointed at the man hurrying away. "Do you know him?"

He shook his head and turned in the opposite direction, crutching off past the satellite truck to the street. A three-legged dog followed close behind.

"Hey!" Finally unfrozen, Woz took a step toward the man on crutches.

She held out his computer. "Leave him be, Woz. I think he just saved m—" She'd been about to say "me," but realized nothing was going to save her after that live shot. "Your computer," she amended. "He just kept that man from stealing your computer. Let him go. Here."

He accepted the laptop without a word. Stella took off her suit jacket, laid it neatly over the handrail to the satellite truck steps, and started unlocking the legs of the closest light stand. She was still in shock over her live shot, and it hardly registered that she had nearly been shellacked by a flying crutch while fighting off a homeless man.

"Hey guys," Terry said, bounding down the stairs of the satellite truck. "Does anyone have dinner plans?" He'd been inside the truck for less than a minute and had missed the whole thing.

She shook her head—dinner with anyone

didn't sound appealing just then—but before she could explain, Woz mumbled, "Union..." He cleared his throat and tried again. "Union rules say you can't touch the equipment."

"Oh, right. Sorry." Her shoulders slumped. First, a horrible live shot, and then she'd broken union rules just trying to help.

Woz squinted at her. "Why didn't you let that guy have the computer?"

"Well... it wasn't his, was it? It wouldn't have been right, and... like you said, you just got it—it's almost brand new." He looked at her incredulously, and she added, "I just... it wouldn't have been fair."

She walked toward the satellite truck and heard Terry say, "What did I miss?" before she stepped inside, plopped into a seat, and rested her head on the shallow table, waiting for this day to end.

After what felt like an hour, Woz wheezed his way back into the truck. "Sher should be calling soon."

She nodded and watched him switch off all the monitors and decks before finally powering down the generator. The silence that followed was almost immediately broken by a buzz from her phone.

She bit her lip, realizing this could be her last conversation with a network-level executive producer. "Hello?"

"Stella, rough bit with the IFB. Woz said it won't happen again. In the meantime, we want you back in New York for training ASAP, obviously. I want you to fill Jolene in on what happened in court today and then catch the first flight out tomorrow. This has been one giant cluster-you-know-what since Jolene got sick. It's time to get back to normal."

Sher disconnected and Stella looked over at Woz wonderingly. "What happened with my IFB?"

"The connection failed a few seconds before they took your signal, remember?"

"Uh huh..." she said slowly. "Why did you cover for me?"

He scratched his head and plopped down opposite her. The truck shook and shifted under his weight. "I'm not sure." He scrutinized her for a moment before continuing. "I feel like I psyched you out just before Hank tossed to you, which, you know, I was trying to do. I just never thought you'd actually freeze up. So, I just wanted to make it right. If you mess up again, though, you're on your own, capisce?" He wheezed as he heaved himself out of the chair.

Stella smiled slightly. It had still been a terrible afternoon with her worst live shot ever—which was really saying something—but she wasn't out of a job. That, at least, was something to celebrate.

She gathered her bags and stood. "Well, thanks, Woz."

He tapped his computer. "You, too."

She walked out of the dark truck and into the sunshine. "Bye, Terry!" He looked up and waved, his eyes sparkling in the bright day.

She could have happily gone straight to her hotel room and slept for twelve hours, but instead, she walked to a nearby coffee shop and sat at a table to charge her phone and read the newspaper. When the owner of the coffee shop started giving her the side-eye for nursing her latte for so long, she packed up and headed back to the parking lot in front of the courthouse. Woz and Terry were long gone, but she and Vindi had dinner plans that night to catch up on the last several years of their lives since working together in Bozeman, Montana.

Reporters from at least five local TV stations, plus the CNN reporter, were all gearing up for an hour's worth of live shots and updates of stories about what happened in court that day. Stella found a bench under the shade of a palm tree and sat back to watch her old friend at work.

Vindi was still as gorgeous as ever. Although her frame was slight and she stood no more than five-foot-two, she exuded the confidence of a heavy-weight prize fighter. Her dark hair had grown out and now fell halfway down her back, but she still had the perfect accessories at her neck and ears. While Stella was sweating again in the desert air, Vindi's olive skin was smooth and flawless, and her makeup appeared to have been applied by a professional.

Across the lot, Maria Garcia, a well-known reporter at CNN, was tagging out from her live hit. The media darling had risen to prominence during hurricane coverage just a year earlier in Florida, when she had clung to a signpost while winds battered the street on which she stood. At the time, she'd been working for a local news station when CNN snatched her up. Now she was practically the face of the network, reporting on all kinds of major stories.

Stella smiled when Maria Garcia looked over, but the other reporter only stared, assessing Stella for several long moments, before she turned back to her cameraman.

Finally, Vindi finished for the night and waved

Stella over. She gathered her bags and the two women headed to Vindi's car.

"Did you get fired or what?"

She glared at her friend. "No." When Vindi turned to stare at her, she dropped her attitude. "I probably should have, though."

"What happened? You looked like a deer in the headlights, like you've never done a live shot before."

"I don't know. It just—it..." Stella sighed. "Hey, we have to make a quick stop before dinner." She filled Vindi in on the Jolene situation.

"So she's still in the hospital, but she'll be covering the trial tomorrow?" Vindi entered the address into her GPS and turned the car around.

Stella shrugged. "That's what she told my executive producer. I'm supposed to go fill her in on what happened today."

Vindi shot her a disbelieving look and Stella shrugged again.

They chatted all the way to the hospital about what each had been up to since they'd last spoken, covering everything from families to jobs before finally getting to the meaty issues of relationships. Vindi told Stella with relish how she'd left her latest boyfriend after discovering he had been cheating with a virtual woman.

"What does that even mean, a *virtual* woman?" Stella squinted at her old friend. "So there wasn't actually another woman?"

Vindi's eyebrows were drawn together and she scowled at the road. "While he may not have physically touched anyone else, the things he typed online..." She shivered. "It's almost worse, if you ask me." They drove in silence for a few minutes and then Vindi shook herself. "Things with Lucky are still good?"

"As good as they can be when you're living in separate towns."

"John's doing well," Vindi said, keeping her eyes on the road. "He's really settling into his anchoring job in San Diego."

"Oh?" She tried not to sound too interested; she could talk about her ex-boyfriend without things being weird. "He's at the CBS affiliate, right?" As if she didn't know.

"Mmhmm." A small smile flitted across Vindi's face—she obviously wasn't fooled by Stella's nonchalant tone. "No serious girlfriend that I can tell, though. We talk every once in a while—mostly about you," she added with mock outrage. "To be honest, it's getting old."

Stella turned to look out her window. The truth was she and John had stayed in contact, too, with an email here and a voicemail there. It was as if neither was ready to completely let go.

"Hmm," Vindi said, not missing the reaction.

"You have arrived at your destination," the mechanical voice of the GPS system effectively ended the discussion, and Stella jumped out of the car as soon as Vindi parked.

"Palm Springs Mental Health and Wellness Center?" Vindi ducked to read the sign at the top of the building but made no attempt to get out of the car.

"I didn't realize...." Stella stared at the sign over the main entrance with trepidation. "Oh. Well, I guess Jolene's inside. Come on."

4

"How long are you in town for, anyway?" Stella turned around to see what was taking Vindi so long to get out of the car. She was antsy to get this over with so she could enjoy her night.

"Until the jury hands down their verdict." Vindi dug around in her purse for a moment before finally climbing out onto the asphalt. She slung her bag over her shoulder and jangled her keys before slamming the door. "Preston Harrington is from the San Diego area, and our viewers are thirsty for information on the case. I've been lobbying hard for this assignment for months, and my news director finally relented last week. I think we're even staying in the same hotel —well, at least for tonight."

"So, it'll be fun—just like the old days, huh?" Stella nudged Vindi in the side with her elbow. The two had briefly shared an apartment in Bozeman many years ago.

"We're not sharing a room again, are you crazy?" The smile died on her lips as she looked up at the mental health hospital looming in front of them. "I-I just mean I'm far too old to have a roommate," Vindi added feebly.

They walked through the automatic doors into the lobby and stopped for a moment to get their bearings. The wide, open room had more plants than hard surfaces. Warm, yellow-brown wood floors shone under the fluorescent lights above, the walls were painted a cheerful, yet soothing teal blue, and a forest of plants, including trees and flowers, rimmed the perimeter of the room, giving it an earthy, Zen feeling.

"Can't hide that antiseptic smell, though, can they?" Vindi muttered as they made their way to the help desk.

Three older women wearing identical burnt-orange smocks and smiles turned as they approached.

"Can I help you, dear?" the woman in the middle asked.

"Yes, I'm looking for the room number of a... uh, a friend of mine." She'd never met Jolene, though, and suddenly she wasn't sure if she was allowed into the hospital to visit a stranger.

The woman smiled kindly and said, "What's her name, dear?"

"Jolene Colburne."

The woman on the right tapped the name into her computer and then swiveled the screen toward the woman in the middle. She nodded and said, "She's on the fourth floor." She got out a map and a highlighter and proceeded to give Stella directions. All three then turned to someone behind Stella, ready to give them their undivided attention.

"Isn't that just what you'd expect in a place like this?" Vindi muttered as they walked toward the elevators.

"It's like all three shared one brain," Stella said out of the side of her mouth. Her friend's peal of laughter echoed through the lobby and they both ducked guiltily into the elevator. They rode up to the fourth floor in silence. When the doors opened, Stella grunted when she ran into Vindi from behind.

"What's the matter?" She pushed against the doors so they wouldn't close on her and then edged around Vindi to see her friend reading the sign posted on the opposite wall.

No yelling, shoelaces, cell phones, or pictures allowed.

"You know what? I'm going to wait in the car." Vindi spun to catch the elevator doors, which were trying to close again. "Jolene Colburne doesn't want a bunch of strangers in her room."

"Vindi," Stella looked at her old friend through narrowed eyes, "she's not contagious! Anyway, she knows I'm coming—my boss told her I'd check in after work today."

"Nope, I just don't feel right about this. I'll see you back at the car. Take your time!" Without waiting for Stella's response, Vindi stepped back into the elevator and repeatedly pressed the button for the lobby until the doors closed.

Stella looked down at the map still clutched in her hand and followed the path of the highlighter to the correct wing of the fourth floor. Jolene's door was open, and she tapped lightly, standing uncertainly at the threshold. The word "hello" was on her lips, but she didn't speak, suddenly nervous to go in. A nurse walked past her through the door and spoke to Jolene.

"It looks like you have a visitor tonight, you lucky girl! Who's come to see you?" The nurse nodded encouragingly, and Stella took a few tentative steps into the large, open space.

If the nurse hadn't used Jolene's name, Stella would have sworn she was in the wrong room. The woman lying in the hospital bed shared only a passing resemblance to the Jolene Colburne she had watched on the news for the past year.

The woman shifted slightly in the hospital bed and cleared her throat before running a self-conscious hand through her hair. "Who are you?"

Stella smiled, and her voice was too loud when she answered. "I'm Stella Reynolds? Sher told me to fill you in on what happened in court today?" The sound of Velcro unsticking ripped through the room and the nurse wound a blood pressure cuff around Jolene's arm. She sent a pointed look at Stella and then at the chair next to Jolene's bed while she pumped the cuff full of air.

Stella self-consciously walked through the room and perched at the edge of the hard, synthetic fabric-covered chair. "I'm sorry, I..." A loud beep sounded in the room and she gulped before continuing. "Sher told me you thought you'd be back for court tomorrow?" She tried not to make it sound like a question but failed.

Jolene's face fell when the nurse clucked her tongue.

"Jolene, you said your boss was in the loop." The nurse released the dial on the pump with a *pfffft* and then added, "One-twenty over eighty. Good girl." With a *riiiip,* she took the cuff off Jolene's arm, hung it back on its hook behind the bed, and marked the chart hanging nearby. The pencil scraped against the paper, and then the nurse hung the chart back on the wall.

Blood type, blood pressure, and drug dosage was all laid out in graphite marks. Stella looked away when Jolene spoke.

"I... I was going to," she finally said to the nurse, "but it got busy..." she trailed off, leaned heavily against the pillows, and turned toward the window.

The nurse beckoned Stella outside. When they were alone in the hallway, she said, "She's tired. Her parents are coming tomorrow to bring her home."

"Bring her home?" Stella turned to look across the room at the other reporter. She didn't look well, but she didn't necessarily look ill, either—just tired. "No. No, she's supposed to be covering this court case we're all—my boss is expecting her back in court tomorrow."

"Not Jolene. She's going home to rest, doctor's orders."

~

"ALL I CAN TELL YOU, Sher, is what the nurse told me: Jolene's parents are coming to take her home. I don't know why or what's wrong, and the nurse says she can't release any information about Jolene to anyone, except her family." Stella paced the far corner of the fourth floor hallway, whispering into her cell phone to a stranger about a stranger.

"This is an unexpected twist," Sher said. Stella heard a tapping sound that might have been a pen banging against a table in New York. "I guess we'll keep you there for now, Stella, but don't get too comfortable. Plan on staying out there to cover the trial for a few days and we'll reassess what's going on then."

She stared out the window, and though the call was over, she kept her cell phone pressed tightly against her ear, still processing what her boss had said. Not a lot of faith in her from New York.

Suddenly, Sher spoke again—although not to Stella, this time. "Jimmy, start working on staffing levels and see who we can move over to Palm Springs. We need a solid reporter on the trial—

and after tonight's live shot, I don't think that's Stella."

A man's voice, small and tinny, responded, "She won't last the week."

Stella moved her cell phone away from her face and looked down at the screen, finally ending the call, herself. Her stomach clenched. *She won't last the week?* That's what her new bosses thought of her?

"Miss?"

The nurse was so close that she jumped in surprise before wincing as her cell phone slipped out of her fingers and crashed to the floor. She swooped down, but it was too late: streaks of broken glass cut diagonally across the screen.

"Hi, hon. I came to tell you that talking on cell phones isn't allowed, but I guess that won't be a problem, anymore," the nurse said with an apologetic smile. "Visiting hours are just about over—I thought you might want to say goodbye to Jolene?" Stella bit her lip and the nurse nodded encouragingly again. "It's been a rough day for her; I'm sure she'd love a friendly smile before bedtime."

Stella forced herself to follow the nurse down the hall, peeling off just outside Jolene's room to take a deep breath before walking in.

"Well, I guess I'm heading to the hotel for the

night," she said brightly. In the ten minutes she'd been in the hallway, however, Jolene's condition had deteriorated further.

The other woman ran a hand across her face while muttering under her breath, "They're watching, they're watching... they are always watching."

Stella looked behind her for the nurse and then saw, with alarm, that she was alone. "No—no one is watching, Jolene. It's just you and me in the room."

The other reporter wrapped her arms around her bent knees and rocked softly back and forth in the bed. "They're watching," she said, her gaze vacant, her eyes locked on nothing. "They're watching... always watching."

"Okay, well..." Stella backed slowly toward the door.

Suddenly, Jolene sat upright and stared straight ahead at the wall. In a clear, loud voice she might have used on the evening news, she said, "Preston Harrington is innocent. The San Diego native is hiding something, but it's not guilt. In this case, not all is as it appears."

Stella was frozen by the door, her eyes open so wide for so long that they started to water.

Jolene then slid back down against the pillows.

"Jolene, do you know something about the case? Can you tell me anything about it?"

The woman was back to muttering, though, and after a moment, Stella quietly left the room. As she waited for the elevator, she tried to shake off the uneasy feeling that had settled in her stomach. Jolene was very ill, but the clarity in her voice at the end was alarming. *Was* Preston Harrington innocent? Was Jolene taking some insider knowledge about the case with her when she left town tomorrow?

More pressing, at least to her, was whether she would even be around to find out.

5

"That's the widow," Vindi nodded to a woman sitting in the front row of the courtroom.

Day two of the Drew Chambers murder trial was slated to start in five minutes. Stella had wedged into the back row with the rest of the cameramen and reporters, and Vindi whispered information about all the key players she'd gotten to know over the last two years of covering the crime.

The widow, Sloan Chambers, had shoulder-length, brown hair and wore a grey, silk skirt and maroon cardigan set, her pearls and expression both oozing privilege and power from the front row. She glared at Preston, who stared calmly back, and finally stood and walked regally to the exit with another woman—her lawyer, if Stella had to guess.

"She makes an appearance every day but can't stay and watch until after she testifies," Vindi said as the door closed quietly behind the widow.

"For the prosecution?" Stella asked, and her friend nodded. By law, witnesses for the prosecutor couldn't stay in the courtroom during the trial before taking the stand.

"She's a doctor, too. Did you know that? There are more PhDs in this trial than lawyers." Vindi gestured to a man sitting directly behind the defense table. "Preston's brother, Sawyer—another doctor—will probably stay for the whole day."

While Sloan was clearly a force to be reckoned with, Sawyer looked like a puffy lump of sweating cotton. He and Preston shared the same sharp nose and cheekbones, but that was where the similarities ended. Where Preston was all angles, Sawyer was squishy and slumped. His pants looked to be a size too big, as if he knew he was going to gain weight and had planned his shopping accordingly.

"What's the deal there?" Stella motioned toward the brothers.

Vindi shrugged. "It's hard to say. Sawyer's been to every court appearance, every briefing, every, well, everything, but it's strange. The brothers don't talk much—at least not in front of the cameras."

"That's kind of..." Sweet wasn't the right word, so Stella finally settled on, "Brotherly."

"Maybe, but don't forget Sawyer is an investor in the company, too. He gave them their seed money before they found other investors."

"I just read that he owns a ten percent stake?" Stella said.

Vindi nodded. "Yup. He wants this trial to end quickly, just like Preston, so they can get back to work and make millions," Vindi said. Both women settled back into silence, waiting for court to start some twenty minutes after the scheduled start time.

"All rise." The bailiff's voice rang out from the front of the room as the door from the judge's chambers opened and Judge Catherine Jenkins stepped into the room.

She had short, blond hair which was still damp, and her billowing, black robes caught on the chair as she tried to sit down. She pulled the robes free, sat with a flourish, and then asked both tables of lawyers if they were ready. When they agreed, the judge wasted no time calling the jury in.

The group of fourteen men and women filed into the room from a side door. The twelve members of the jury sat in two rows along the left side of the courtroom and two alternates sat just to their right, near the defendant's table. The group skewed older, with lots of grey hair, and they oozed both money and irritation at being there. Nine women and five men wedged themselves into their seats and Judge Jenkins smiled at them warmly.

"Good morning, ladies and gentlemen. I'd like to remind you of the rules of conduct today." While she rattled off a list of rules, the lead prosecutor, Gail Abingdon, scribbled furiously on her legal pad. As the judge droned on, she tore off the top sheet and passed it to the lawyer next to her.

Stella watched with interest as the note then made its way past two more lawyers and back one row to Maria Garcia, the reporter for CNN. Maria quietly unfolded the note, her eyes widened, and then she folded the paper and slipped it into a pocket.

Stella turned to see if Vindi had caught the exchange, but she was staring at the jury with a glazed expression.

She turned back to Maria. Was it her imagination, or was the other reporter sitting taller in her

seat, thrumming with energy hard to find anywhere else in the courtroom? What did Gail
Abingdon have to say to the reporter? Whatever it
was, it couldn't be good for any of the other reporters in the room.

She glanced around the courtroom in time to
see two members of the jury yawn as the judge
continued to list off what they should and
shouldn't do during the trial. Stella stifled one,
herself—she'd slept poorly the night before, unable to stop worrying about Jolene and her own
job security.

The sound of a chair squealing against the tile
floor brought her back to the present.

Preston Harrington's lawyer stood and turned
to the jury. "Good morning. I'm Niles Yarley, the
lawyer representing Preston Harrington. I want to
tell you some things about Preston that the prosecutor over there doesn't want you to know."

Yarley wasn't much to look at—he had shaved
his head bald or nature had done it for him—and
he was short and squat with wide hips and shoulders. When he spoke, however, the whole room
seemed to strain forward to hear him better. His
voice was quiet but carried across the space like
that of a preacher.

"Preston Harrington has lost his business partner, his chance at a Fortune 500 company, his peace, and nearly his sanity in the last two years. He is a shell of the man he used to be, and his family hardly recognizes him. He had no reason to kill the person helping to make all of his dreams not only a possibility but also a reality, and the state has no evidence tying Preston to the crime. Where's the murder weapon? Where's the DNA?"

He shook his head and meandered toward the jury box. "What you will hear over the next days or weeks is that Preston was jealous, but jealous of what? Drew Chambers wasn't a good husband and he had no children. Drew Chambers wasn't happy. *Preston Harrington was.* He was in the middle of launching an exciting business not as a silent, useless partner, as the state would have you believe, but as a valued, important thought leader in a product launch that required and depended on his ideas and business acumen. Preston Harrington loves his family. It breaks my heart to see them separated like this during the trial."

Yarley had the jury on the hook and he knew it. He walked closer to them and leaned against the narrow rail that separated them from the rest of the courtroom.

"You'll hear Preston had money troubles. Sure he did: he was pouring his life savings into a revolutionary product that will help millions and change the face of medicine, after all. Yes, he was broke, but only in the short term. Preston and Drew had just secured funding from a major player in the medical-technology field, so money was not a concern for either Drew or Preston. It must have been for someone else, though. Someone killed Drew Chambers, and the state is failing—*failing*, I say—at their job of finding out who."

Yarley heaved a beleaguered sigh, stood tall again, and moved toward the center of the line of jurists. "It is not my job to solve the crime but to prove to you, beyond a reasonable doubt, that Preston had no reason to want Drew dead. Just the opposite, in fact: his death has railroaded the product launch, which is now in serious jeopardy. In fact, I submit that Preston Harrington wants to know far more than anyone else who really killed Drew Chambers, because he wants that person behind bars or dead."

The jury gasped, and as the judge banged her gavel for order, Yarley turned back to the defense table with a small, satisfied smile.

∼

HOURS LATER, Stella and Woz were the only members of the media left in the rapidly emptying courtroom. She didn't have a live shot that evening; with that massive storm sweeping over the middle of the US now spawning tornadoes, half of the evening newscast would be devoted to storm coverage. Woz had sent back video from the morning's proceedings, and on the East Coast, *Harry-freaking-Smith* had already read a small story about the trial in the C-block, just before the final commercial break. Now the local stations were halfway through their evening newscasts as Stella and Woz packed up for the night.

"It's kind of sweet, isn't it?" she said, putting her notebook in her bag. "I mean, you hear about sisters being close all the time, but brothers—it just seems—"

"They don't look too chummy, though, do they?" Woz grunted. "Sawyer just kind of sits there, glaring. Preston, too."

Stella nodded and shrugged. He had a point.

Woz, still sweating despite the cool, indoor air, grunted as he took the camera off the tripod and shook off Stella's offer to carry the microphone. "Union," he muttered and then coughed. Stella smelled coffee and orange Tic Tacs on his breath.

She shrugged and walked ahead of him, wondering if holding the door for him was also against union rules. He walked through without comment, so she supposed not.

Outside, Stella put on her sunglasses against the blinding sunshine, and they crossed the street and walked down a block to the satellite truck. Once Woz was packed up, they made plans to meet in court the following morning. Stella turned back toward the courthouse to walk to her hotel and flinched at the roar of the truck's engine coming to life. She hustled across the street to the sidewalk.

As she stepped up onto the curb, she caught sight of a maroon cardigan and pearls at the side exit of the courthouse. Curious, she stopped, held her phone in front of her face, and looked beyond the screen to see what Sloan Chambers was doing.

The woman Stella had earlier characterized as formidable, sophisticated, and elegant was, at that moment, peering out at the street, halfway inside the courthouse with one foot on the sidewalk. She wore dark sunglasses—not suspicious on its own, but the way she turned her head to constantly look behind her was unusual. She finally walked through the door, paced a few steps one way and then back, still glancing behind her every few seconds.

This part of town wasn't a huge pedestrian area, and the sidewalk was mostly empty in front of the courthouse, so when Stella saw movement on the opposite side of the building, she tore her eyes away from Sloan. Was the person she was waiting for coming?

Her brow furrowed, however, when she spotted Sawyer Harrington, the defendant's brother, acting similarly suspicious by a planter box. He looked from his phone to the street and back again.

At almost identical moments, two black, Lincoln Town Cars pulled up to the courthouse. One turned just in front of Stella toward Sloan and the side exit, while the other glided to a stop on the street in front of Sawyer.

Stella, heart pounding, flagged down a taxi and jumped into the backseat.

"Where to?" came the clipped voice from the front seat.

"Uh..." Her eyes flitted between the two hired cars, both idling in place. What was going on? In her head, she heard Jolene's sure, steady assertion that *Preston Harrington is innocent* and *Not all is as it seems* and Peter in New York intoning *She won't last a week.*

Sloan's car made a deft, three-point turn in the

drive, glided past Stella's taxi, and pulled even with Sawyer's ride, where it waited at a red light. The light turned green and the limos headed off down the street, moving farther away by the second. Who should she follow?

After a final second of deliberation, Stella finally pointed out the window and said, "Follow that car!"

6

"Are you kidding? Is this some kind of joke?" The cabbie smiled and looked at Stella and then out the window. "Is this a new TV show? What Would a Cabbie Do? Where's the hidden camera? Come on, you can tell me!"

"What? No, no show—I just really need to follow that car!" She pointed again at Sawyer's Town Car, which was barely visible up ahead. "I think if you go now, we can still catch up. Go!" She smiled apologetically as her last word echoed in the small space.

"Jeez, sorry!" The driver's grin faded to a frown, she pushed an unlit cigarette behind her ear and pulled away from the curb with a jerk of acceleration. She gave Stella a stern look before biting her lip in concentration. "Do you want me to keep my distance, or get right up on 'em?"

"I know it sounds crazy—I'm sorry. I just want to see where they're going."

"Are you some kind of cop?" The woman— Penny, if Stella was to believe the name plate glued to the back of the front seat—popped a piece of gum into her mouth from a pack in the middle console and eyed her passenger through the mirror.

Stella crashed into the front seat when Penny jammed on the brakes.

"Buckle up, huh?"

Stella craned her neck as she buckled up and could just make out the cars. Sloan's had disappeared out of sight, but Sawyer's had to slow for a turn at the light ahead, so it was still within reach.

"Can you turn right up there?" Stella ignored the sound of Penny attacking the gum in her mouth.

"So, not a cop, huh?" she smacked. "I always thought it would be fun to be a cop—don't have to take nothing from no one, and the job comes with a company car, doesn't it?"

"Left at the next light," Stella said, squinting against the sun to keep track of Sawyer's car. As it wove effortlessly through traffic, Stella blocked out

Penny's chatter, curious to see where he was headed and why. "Stop here," she said when the shiny, black car finally pulled up to the curb a half-block ahead.

"You gonna be long?"

"No—uh, no, I don't think..." Without taking her eyes off the limo, Stella shoved some bills toward the driver, reached for her bag, and opened the door.

"I'll wait for you, if you want," Penny offered. "You'll never get a ride *back* downtown at this hour, and to be honest, I was thinking about taking a break, anyway. I might just grab a soda from the store over there. If you're just going in for a moment, I'll keep the meter running. You come back and I'll be here, okay?"

"Hmm? Okay, sure." Stella climbed out of the car and kept her head down.

A woman's foot emerged from the limo, and for a moment, Stella was disoriented. Then *Sloan* stood tall, adjusting her skirt as she exited. The Town Cars must have switched lanes at some point without Stella realizing.

She took a step back toward her own taxi, feeling foolish, when a man in a business suit folded Drew Chambers's widow into an embrace. He had light brown skin and a wavy mass of dark hair. When he pulled back from Sloan's body, his eyes continued to drink her in. Moments later, he pulled her through the door of the closest business.

The embrace was... sensual—personal. This was someone who knew Sloan well, and he was clearly not a relative.

As the black Town Car pulled away, Stella walked forward, her feet now heavy, as if she wore ankle weights. A sudden surge of uncertainty hit her. What was she doing? Sloan wasn't on trial, so why was she following her?

Preston Harrington is innocent.

Won't last a week.

The words circled around her, pushed her forward, and forced her feet to keep moving. She didn't know why she was following Sloan, but it felt right—it felt important.

Stella finally reached the door that Sloan had gone through. It was a restaurant, and through the large front window, she saw a waiter leading Sloan and her partner to a table.

She crept in, her head on a swivel, until she spotted the pair seated at a table near the bar. She bypassed the hostess, took a tall stool at the bar, ordered an iced tea, and then bent over the menu the bartender handed her.

While pretending to get lost in the list of appetizers, she concentrated on what was happening at the table behind her.

"...long day, you look exhausted, my love." The man sighed and continued, his deep voice slightly scolding. "You don't need to be there—it's not good for you. Wait until they call you to testify."

"I feel like—like I should be there. It's important to present a united front with the prosecutor. I've already told you that."

For a moment, both were silent, and then the man's voice rumbled on. "I know your reasons, and surely you know why I'm voicing mine again. I worry."

"I know, Roo, and it's why I love you—one of the reasons, anyway."

There was silence and then the unmistakable sound of lips locking together. Stella steadied her breathing against a sudden surge of adrenaline. The supposedly devastated widow of the man murdered in cold blood had a secret boyfriend named Roo! She was in love!

The couple broke apart when the water boy approached, and Stella sipped her iced tea as they murmured their thanks. She hunched over her drink, trying to make out the timeline in the murder case. It had been more than twenty-six months since Drew Chambers died. Just because Sloan was dating someone *now* didn't necessarily mean she'd been dating him when her husband was alive. The relationship wasn't necessarily a motive for murder. Stella bit her lip. Despite the surprise of learning something new, nothing had changed, really. She didn't have enough information, yet.

She took a sip of tea and tried to remember her notes on the case. She'd read that Sloan's alibi had checked out and investigators had cleared her of the crime early on in their investigation. There was also the glaring fact that another man was currently on trial for the murder, which meant police and prosecutors had some pretty convincing evidence against him.

With a sigh, Stella pushed the iced tea forward and motioned to the barkeep that she wanted a beer. He picked up a pint glass, but instead of filling it up, he motioned back to Stella. She leaned forward and tried to keep her voice down. "What?"

"ID," he said. "I need to see your ID."

"Oh," she said, almost laughing. She pulled her wallet out of her bag then cringed when her cell phone clattered to the ground again.

She hopped down from the bar stool to retrieve the device and bumped into Sloan's chair in the process. Wine slopped out of her glass onto the table, and both Sloan and her partner leapt up —Sloan to save her outfit from the dribbling wine and Roo with a napkin to save the day.

"Dr. Ruiz, please, let me!" A waiter rushed forward with a towel.

After the immediate Cabernet threat was over, both Sloan and Roo—apparently Doctor Ruiz— turned toward Stella, who still stood in shock, staring at the table. Doctor Ruiz's startlingly clear, gorgeous, blue eyes showed a hint of humor that was missing entirely from Sloan's expression.

"I—I—I'm so sorry. I dropped my phone," Stella managed to get out at last, the words sounding lame even as she held up the shockingly pink phone as evidence. Sloan nodded stiffly, Doctor Ruiz smiled understandingly, and as if on cue, Stella's phone rang.

She tried to quiet the device. She swiped, tapped, and even shook the phone—but nothing worked. Finally, she banged it down on the bar. To her dismay, the call connected—on speaker.

"Hey, Stella, how's it goin' out there in Palm Springs? You solvin' any crimes, yet?" Lucky drawled the questions out with humor, and blood rushed to her face as she tried in vain to mute his voice.

Was every eye in the restaurant now trained on her? She refused to turn around to check, focusing, instead, on hanging up on her boyfriend.

"Bear, you there? Hello?"

Tap. Swipe. Swipe. Finally, she banged the phone on the bar again, but Lucky's voice boomed out of the speakers with absurd clarity.

"Stella Reynolds, for real, girl, what is going on over there? Sounds like you're in a war zone. I'm going to call you back."

She blew out a breath, dropped her head when the phone finally went silent, and then shoved the device into the depths of her bag, knowing she'd never be able to control it when Lucky called back.

She threw a five dollar bill onto the bar and fled. The sun was setting and the temperature had dropped five degrees in the fifteen minutes she'd been inside; the hot desert day was quickly becoming a cool desert night. She reached out her arm, hoping to flag down a taxi and make her final escape.

A horn honked in the distance and her eyes flitted toward the noise. Was Sloan coming? Did she know Stella had followed her? Now that it was all over, her detective work seemed less honorable and more sleazy—paparazzi than anything else.

This poor woman was trying to move on with her life after her husband was killed in cold blood. Who was Stella to judge the timeline?

The horn honked again, closer this time, but it wasn't until the lights on a nearby yellow car flashed that she spotted the taxi.

Relieved, she opened the rear door and said, "Tahquitz Canyon Way and El Cielo, please."

"Back to the courthouse? You gotta follow someone else?"

Stella blinked and then squinted at the driver. She looked at the name plate in the back seat to be sure before speaking. "Penny? Why are you still here?"

The cabbie turned around in her seat and squinted right back. "I told you I'd keep the meter running for you, remember? I needed a soda." She held up a can with a grin and then pointed to the dash. "Look, you're only at sixty-five dollars. Good deal, huh?"

"Sixty-fi..." Stella stared, slack-jawed, at the small red numbers flipping over to sixty-six as she watched. She hung her head. "Right. Okay, well, back to the courthouse, yes." It was closer than her hotel, but she'd need the walk between the two to get rid of her jitters.

The ride back was quiet, and Stella stared out the window, feeling lost. She didn't know this town or these people. She had no sources and no means of making any, considering she was only going to be here for a few days. She felt as out of her element as she had during her very first on-air job, and she couldn't see how anything was going to change in the next day or two.

She paid Penny an absurd amount of money, hoping she had enough in her bank account to cover the fare, and when she stepped out onto the sidewalk, her eyes lingered on the planter box where she'd seen Sawyer Harrington lurking earlier.

Where had the car taken Preston's brother that evening?

A homeless man passed, asking for change. Stella dropped a dollar bill into his cup and then put her head down against the chill of the night air. She wasn't going to stick her neck out on any more shenanigans; she was going to do her job like she'd always done. She wouldn't spend another minute thinking about who was paying to drive Sawyer Harrington around town in a limo—not one.

7

Stella couldn't keep track of the weather in this town. It was just before eight in the morning and the sky was clear, the sun like a summer dandelion hanging in the sky. Although the forecaster had assured her on the local news that morning that it would get up to eighty-four degrees, it was chilly enough that she pulled on a sweater as she and Vindi left the hotel lobby.

"I don't know why we're not driving," her friend grumbled as they set off down the sidewalk.

"Because the courthouse is only two blocks away and I'm going stir-crazy in this hotel." Stella slowed to let a car turn into the half-circle driveway of the hotel.

Instead of passing, though, the car came to a

stop right in front of them and an elderly woman opened the door. "Are you Stella Reynolds?" The woman was barely five feet tall, and she squinted up as she waited for an answer.

"Yes," Stella said, drawing out the word. She glanced at Vindi, who checked her phone, and then back to the woman, trying to force her brain to recognize the stranger. The mystery was solved, though, when the woman spoke again.

"I'm Jolene Colburne's mother, Aretha." She spoke in short, clipped words and her mouth pressed together when she was done, as if the effort of speech had cost her. She motioned behind her and the driver side door of the car opened. "This here is my husband, Ralph." He waved weakly over the roof of the car.

"Oh—hi," Stella stuttered. "I-I'm Stella Reynolds."

Vindi nudged her sharply with her elbow. "Yes, they know that," she muttered. "I'll see you in court," she said louder and took off at a brisk pace past the Colburnes and their car.

Stella watched her go with a grimace and instinctively glanced at her watch. Court was due to start in thirty minutes; unfortunately, that gave her plenty of time to chat with Jolene's parents.

"Are you headed that way, too?" Aretha asked, watching Vindi walk away.

"Oh, yes, but I have a min—"

"I'll walk with you. I know you people are always on deadline, always running late. Ralph," she turned to address her husband, "I'll be back. Move the car, you're in the way."

Ralph nodded and climbed back behind the wheel, waiting until the two women had passed in front of his bumper to put the car into gear.

She shifted her focus from the car to the woman and found Aretha already staring shrewdly back. "How is she?" Stella asked. "Jolene?"

"Not good. She's not good. She's suffered for years with anxiety and depression. I told her this job would be too much, but she didn't listen."

"Too much?"

"Yes, too much!" Aretha said. "Too much pressure, too much stress—hell, too much excitement. The pendulum of emotion swings both ways for Jolene. The highs are higher, the lows are... well."

They walked in silence for a moment.

"You're bringing her home?"

"Yes. We're making the arrangements with the hospital here for the transfer. We have a great doctor back in North Carolina—a great facility where she can rest, recover, and get back on her meds. So many of them come with side effects—

"Like what?"

"Well, weight gain is the main one, but it can affect your sexual health, too. It's more information than she'd like you to know, but there it is."

"Did you want me to... call our boss in New York and let her know, or is she—"

"Yes, that'd be great. Why don't you come by, too? She's been asking for you."

"For me? I... I don't even really know her. I mean, I know *of* her, of course—I've watched her on the news for the last couple of years—but I'm new, myself, and just met her last night."

"Well, she's been asking for you—you and our old dog, Rexie." Aretha laughed without humor. "Rex has been dead for five years, so I was delighted when the nurses told me you were alive." Stella's face must have betrayed her concern because Aretha continued, "She's all twisted up about the murder trial and she wants to talk to you about it."

"Well..."

"You've got time. We're not leaving until tomorrow or Friday at the latest."

"I..." Stella looked at her watch again, looking for any reason to not agree. They'd stopped outside a small convenience store, and Stella smelled coffee. Her phone rang, and she instinctively pushed it deeper into her bag to muffle the sound.

"Think about it. It might bring her comfort to talk to you before we leave. It would mean a lot to me, Stella." Aretha fixed her with a beady eye, and then, without saying goodbye, she turned and walked back toward the hotel.

Stella watched her for a moment before ducking into the store. She needed a drink, and at that hour, coffee would have to suffice. She looked into the depths of her bag, pushing her broken phone aside, and finally found her wallet seconds before her legs got tangled in something on the floor.

"Argh!" She started to go down, saved from a face plant on the tile floor at the very last second by a pair of strong arms.

The man set her back on her feet and then turned to say, "Careful, Tim. Not a great place, is it?"

Tim sat on the floor, leaning against a shelf of packaged sweets. An empty pant leg was tied off just above his knee, and his wooden crutch rested on a bag, levering the whole thing up a few inches and making it the perfect thing to trip over, as she'd so nicely demonstrated.

A jumble of dirty and smelly rags was piled next to him, and by the time her eyes made it up to his face, he was staring back at her.

With a flash of recognition, she said, "It's you!"

"Hold me now." The man who'd fought off the would-be computer thief the day before smiled up at Stella.

The man next to her groaned. "Tim, why don't you and Hope move over to the soda machine? That's where I put the cushion for you to sit on, if you're still not going to use the chair I set out last week."

The man on the floor stirred, using his crutch to climb up from the floor. As he moved, so did the pile of rags next to him. A frizzy dog with a patchy, grey and tan coat emerged from under a tattered blanket. The dog rose unsteadily to her feet and then ambled after Tim, her gait uneven.

"Is it—" She cut herself off, not wanting to be offensive, but she was looking at a dog missing a hind leg following a man missing a leg.

"I know, you hate to stare, but it really does make you want to look again, doesn't it?" The pair passed around a snack display and disappeared in the back of the store. "I'm Joe Jones, the owner here. So glad I caught you. I'd just told Tim to move it or lose it before you walked in."

"'Hold me now,'" Stella said, her eyebrows raised. "What does that mean?"

"First, you said you wanted coffee, right? It's on the house." He motioned that she should follow him and led her back to the coffee pot, where Tim and his dog sat nearby. "Hold me now, huh?" he asked Tim as he pulled a cup from the shelf and started to fill it. "Room for cream?"

"Yes, thanks." She turned to Tim. "Thank you, for the other day in the parking lot." Tim stared back, unblinking. "You helped me fight off that guy trying to take our computer. I never got to say thanks."

"Still pulling hero duty, huh, Tim?" Joe asked. Tim continued to stare at the pair with interest.

"What's your dog's name?" she asked.

"Learn from yesterday, live for today," the man finally said, continuing to stare.

She wrinkled her nose. "Seems like a cumbersome name for a dog. She comes to that?"

"Tim!" Joe's voice was sharp as he scolded the other man. "Right up here, miss." As they wound back through the shelves, he added, "The dog's name is Hope."

"Why didn't he just say that?" she wondered aloud.

"He did—just in his own way."

"Huh?"

"Tim is a war veteran. Iraq," he clarified. "He set up shop here a few years ago and hasn't really left."

"Well, that's very kind of you to help him out," Stella said, looking back, even though Tim was hidden among the merchandise.

"Not really. I like having him close—he reminds me of my brother. I lost him to the same war. If I can help just one vet as he battles his demons, that's what I'll happily do."

Stella nodded. "'Learn from yesterday?'" she asked. "'Hold me close?' What's that about?"

"The first must be from someone famous," he took out his phone and tapped something into the search bar. After a moment, he nodded. "Albert Einstein."

"Einstein?"

"Yup, according to this, he said, 'learn from yesterday, live for today, *hope* for tomorrow.'"

"Hope," Stella said, an incredulous smile forming. "Why in the world didn't he just say Hope?"

"What can I say? He's messed up after the war not only physically, but mentally, too. His mother lives here in town and comes to check on him often, but he can't live with her, even though she's tried to force the issue. He just can't be inside for too long." He blew out a sigh. "Anyway, he only speaks in riddles, phrases, and song titles—it's how his brain works now. It didn't used to be so bad—heck, even a couple of years ago, you'd get a moment of clarity from him. Lately, though, it's all riddles."

"Surely there's some kind of medicine that could help him?"

"He's tried them all, but most have side effects that are worse than the ailment. Well," he hesitated, "I'm not sure that's true for Tim, anymore, as he's gotten pretty bad lately. He doesn't want to take anything, though, so he doesn't."

"So, let's see... 'hold me now.'" He tipped his head to the ceiling and thought. "He'd just tripped you by mistake... Phil Collins? No, *Chicago*, that's right. The next line in the song—he was trying to say 'I'm sorry.'"

Stella bit out a laugh. "How exhausting! Do you keep Google nearby at all times?"

He smiled and then started to shake his head when she pulled out her wallet. "No, no, it's on the house. You nearly had a terrible start to your day," he said.

"Well, thanks to you, I didn't. Also, thanks to you, Tim and Hope have somewhere safe to be.

The twenty's for Tim. Is it enough to cover his coffee or breakfast this week?"

Joe tilted his head to the side, a small smile on his lips. "Thank you. That's very kind. I'll tell you what: I'll put it toward his medical bills. We're trying to raise enough for a prosthetic leg. It would sure make getting around town easier for him."

"Insurance doesn't cover that?"

"Not the kind he needs, no."

Stella's phone chirped, and she saw the time. "Well, good luck," she said with a wave. As she hurried down the sidewalk, she wondered if Luna C Engineering's new drug, Wondred, would work for Tim. They couldn't know until the murder trial ended and the company could get back to work.

She wondered how many Tims were out there, waiting for a miracle that was already in existence but stuck in the lab because someone killed Drew Chambers.

8

Stella wasn't late, technically, but she still groaned when she saw the line for the security checkpoint wrapped around the corner. She inhaled deeply through her nose and then slowly blew it out her mouth while counting to ten.

It didn't work; stress still pulsed in her gut ten seconds later.

She pushed the button on her phone to check the time: court started in twenty minutes. She heaved another sigh, realizing she had plenty of time, so long as the line didn't stop moving completely. She took a step toward a trash can, and after draining the dregs from the cup, she dropped it in. As she turned back to take her place in line, she locked eyes with a woman hurrying past: Sloan Chambers.

Recognition flickered on Sloan's face. Her eyes moved from Stella's face, to the press pass around her neck, and stopped on the garish, pink phone cover. Her expression grew dark, and she spoke in a low voice to the woman next to her. Stella held Sloan's gaze until she disappeared in the elevator. She had done nothing wrong the night before but couldn't shake the feeling that something bad was about to happen.

Thirty minutes later, as she still stood in line, a peal of noise came from her phone. She touched the screen gingerly, unsure of what would happen. "Hello?"

"Where are you?" Vindi's voice projected out of the tiny speakers and the people on either side of Stella turned to stare. She shrugged in a don't-look-at-me-my-phone-sucks kind of way. She'd find time to get to the store for a replacement later that day, but until then, there would be no secrets between Stella and anyone within earshot. "Well, I guess it doesn't matter, actually," Vindi said before Stella could answer. "They're moving us out of the courtroom. Without any explanation, the judge ruled that we can only keep a pool camera in the courtroom. The rest of us have to watch on a closed circuit screen in the empty courtroom next door."

Stella's stomach dropped. Had Sloan somehow orchestrated this move? Was she punishing her for spying on her last night? To Vindi she said, "I should be up soon; I'm stuck in security."

"No rush, anymore. See you when you get here." Thankfully, Vindi disconnected the call because Stella wasn't sure she could.

Ten minutes later, she finally walked into the elevator and pressed the button for the second floor. Just before the doors closed, though, her phone rang again. This time, it was Sher in New York.

She jumped off the elevator and walked to a corner, hoping for as much privacy as she could get with a phone that now doubled as a loudspeaker.

"I got your message about Jolene and I'm just not going to understand it until I talk to her, myself," Sher said. "Please have her call me when you can—I can't seem to get through the hospital switchboard."

"I'll try," Stella answered, "but I spoke to her

parents this morning and they were pretty certain Jolene is leaving with them soon."

"I'll be honest, Stella, when I got into work this morning, Jimmy and I talked about pulling you from the story, altogether," Sher's voice was stern and unforgiving. "Now, not five minutes ago, I get a call from the lawyer representing Dr. Sloan Chambers. She's complaining to me that you followed her client last night, made a big scene at a restaurant. She doesn't want you anywhere near her. In fact, from what I understand, she's asking the judge to kick the media out of the courtroom."

Stella grimaced at the wall. A silence stretched, and she finally said, "Not kicked out, exactly. They've decided to go with a pool camera. The rest of us will watch from the courtroom next door."

There was another pause while Sher processed that information. Her next words came as a surprise. "Any idea why?" After a few moments, Stella blew out a breath and explained her excursion from the night before. "Well, you must be doing something right. Keep at it and check in with me at lunchtime, so I know if there's anything worthwhile today for the evening news. We'll only run with it if there's something new and interesting today. Got it?"

Stella smiled, despite the rough start to her

day. Was she making headway with her new boss? "Got it," she said, then hopped into the elevator, feeling good for the first time since arriving in California.

~

DAY three of the Drew Chambers murder trial started as many days in court did: with a one hour delay while the jury was tended to, and then a half-hour break requested by the defendant's lawyers.

After the bailiff cleared the courtroom, Stella and Vindi left the media room next door and parted ways. Vindi was slated to do a live update for her station's extended morning newscast, so Stella headed to a coffee shop within walking distance.

Glass House Brewery was indeed full of light from the floor-to-ceiling windows that lined the perimeter of the store front. Stella ordered coffee and a breakfast sandwich and paid for a copy of the newspaper. The restaurant was packed, but she finally spotted an open table in the middle of a sea of strangers. She made her way to the empty chair, set her phone on the table, and dug into her meal like a starving person.

She was halfway through the sandwich when she noticed blinking lights on a TV screen on the opposite wall: a breaking news graphic zooming across the screen on CNN.

Unconcerned initially, as some networks put breaking news banners on just about anything these days, she nevertheless watched the screen with interest as the anchor in the studio in Atlanta introduced the story. She nearly choked on her mouthful of egg and bacon, though, when the anchor tossed to Maria Garcia in Palm Springs, California.

Squinting to see the screen, she lowered her sandwich and leaned forward. The graphics at the bottom pulsed with excitement.

Exclusive story.

Jailers in the case speak only to CNN.

She pushed her sandwich away, no longer hungry, as the sinking feeling of getting beat filled her stomach. She stood slowly, trying to get a better angle. With no volume, she had to read the closed captioning at the bottom of the screen to figure out what was going on.

Maria Garcia produced a sergeant from the jail to talk about Preston Harrington's frame of mind over the last few days and weeks as the beginning of the trial loomed.

"He hasn't been sleeping," the sergeant said, and Maria Garcia pounced.

"Why do you think that is?" she sent a knowing look toward the camera.

"Hard to say, but these kinds of cases really eat away at a person's soul."

Stella's jaw dropped. That was a bombshell statement, and Maria Garcia knew it. She wrapped up the interview and sent it back to the anchor.

Stella sunk back down to her seat. She still felt like she'd taken a gut-punch, but after a few minutes, her brain started to work again. Why now? Why would prosecutors allow someone from the jail to speak to the media *during* a murder trial? It just didn't make sense.

While she was pondering that question, her cell phone rang. The call was from New York City but wasn't a number she recognized. She gingerly touched the phone to connect the call, but the broken screen wouldn't register her attempt to swipe across it. After five unsuccessful swipes, she smashed her finger against the screen and the call finally connected. Relieved, she pressed the phone to her ear.

"Hello?"

"Where are you?" Sher's irritated voice echoed around Stella's head. She pulled the phone away and remembered it only worked on speaker. She tapped the button a few times to no avail—it wouldn't switch to private mode. "Hel-LO?" Sher said for the third time.

Stella fumbled with the device, finally putting the microphone to her lips and answering, "Yes, hi, this is Stella."

"Where are you?"

"I—I'm at a coffee shop," she confessed.

"Doesn't that sound nice? While you're busy enjoying a morning latte, the competition is raking us over the coals!"

"I—I know, I just saw—"

"You have let me down, Stella Reynolds! Here I am, sticking my neck out, laying it all on the line for a reporter I don't know at all, and you are failing big time." Sher Patrick didn't hold back, her voice as loud as if she shared the table.

Stella jumped up from her chair, phone in hand. She wanted to run to the bathroom or even the exit. Surely being outside and on the move while your boss reamed you out was better than a dozen strangers eyeing you from every angle. The restaurant was so crowded, however, that there was nowhere to go.

So, for five nauseatingly exhausting minutes, she listened to Sher tell her where she needed to go ("Back to court—you should never have left!") and why ("I need you to find someone who can say something about this case that's new and interesting *right now!*"). When Sher finally disconnected in a haze of swear words that made the man to Stella's immediate right snicker, she dropped the phone into her open bag, sunk into her seat, and rested her head on her folded hands. After a few minutes, the people around her started talking again, but it took Stella much longer to recover.

How was she going to find an exclusive on this story to beat a jailer talking about the accused killer's mood?

She felt a weight press down on her table and Stella lifted her head an inch to see a giant chocolate chip cookie sliding toward her on a napkin. She lifted her head a fraction more and saw a woman with sharp eyes and an understanding smile.

"Is this seat taken?"

Stella quickly wiped her eyes, irritated that any emotion was seeping out in public. She sniffed before clearing her throat. "It's all yours; I was just leaving."

"Well, if you'll give me just a minute, I'd like to have a word."

Stella's mouth twisted into a frown. "I'm sorry for the disruption—"

"Nonsense. My name is Trish McDonald," the woman interjected as she sat down across the table. "I have a feeling you're Stella Reynolds," she said with a wry smile. "I couldn't help but over-hear your boss—at least, I hope that was your boss and not your mother—on the phone just now." Stella nodded silently, not yet trusting her voice. "It's none of my business, but I wanted you to know Maria Garcia is childhood friends with Gail Abingdon."

Stella's eyes opened wider. That certainly accounted for the note passing and jailer exclusive. The hollow feeling in her stomach expanded when she realized it wouldn't be the last exclusive, either.

"They're both from Palm Springs?"

"Yes. It's a small town, and you were either in the 'in' crowd by fifth grade or you weren't. They were—been on the same team ever since."

Stella looked suspiciously at Trish McDonald. "What's your connection?"

"Well," Trish said, a small smile forming on her lips, "I also went to school with Maria and Gail."

"Oh. Great," Stella said, resisting the very

tempting urge to put her head back down on the table.

Trish chuckled. "I was never on their team, though. Gail used to pull my braids out at recess every day. They were the biggest bunch of bullies you can imagine; they made my life a living hell, especially during a particularly awkward stage from sixth through ninth grade that I'll never forget." She broke the cookie in half and held one side toward Stella. "My mom still has the pictures to prove it. Acne, braces—your typical nightmare." She sunk her teeth into her half of the cookie, raised her eyebrows, and stared at Stella until she took a bite of hers.

"When I heard your boss being... well... I just wanted to let you know what you're up against and, I guess, to tell you that you won't be alone. If you need anything, let me know." When Stella raised her eyebrows, she laughed. "Oh! I guess I haven't mentioned this, yet, but I'm the lead detective investigating the Drew Chambers homicide. I've been on the case from day one."

"Day one?" Stella repeated weakly.

"Right from the start. Maybe together, we can keep the other team from taking over the world. I mean, I doubt it. Gail Abingdon still has the most amazing skin ever, and don't get me started on

Maria's hair—you could literally put her in a commercial for Vidal Sassoon. It's ridiculous." She took another big bite of cookie and they chewed in silence for a bit. She then looked pointedly at Stella. "So, what can I do for you?"

9

*T*ick, tick, tick.

Stella looked at her watch and felt impatience bubble up. She didn't have time for this, really—not a single second to spare today.

An entire crew set up cameras, preparing for Stella's one-on-one exclusive interview for the evening news.

Beep, beep, beep.

But instead of preparing alongside them, Stella was at the hospital on the other side of town, listening to the thrum of the heart rate monitor doing its best to remind her that every second she spent here was a second she *wasn't* preparing for what was arguably the biggest interview of her life.

The thought was just as unnerving as Jolene Colburne's rapidly deteriorating condition. The other reporter, who'd uttered some coherent sentences just a couple of nights earlier, now lay prone in her hospital bed, an occasional head jerk the only thing keeping her from looking like a coma patient.

Jolene's family had rushed from the hallway into her room when the steady beat of her heart had become syncopated, staccato in rhythm. Now, some twenty minutes, four doctors, and three nurses later, her heart rate had returned to steady. Her mother kept shooting furtive looks at Stella, occasionally saying things like, "don't go anywhere," and "just one more minute."

She had to go—she was out of time—but she'd said she would stop by, and, although it sounded cold to think about in the midst of this new medical crisis, Stella needed Jolene's computer. Sher had told her in a shouty text that she'd need it to file her reports while she was in Palm Springs, and obviously Jolene didn't need it.

She squinted through the open door and past the end of the hospital bed to a chair just beyond. A stylish, tan trench coat was thrown over the back of the chair and a computer bag leaned purposefully against the arm. It might have been the last "normal" thing Jolene had done after checking into the hospital.

Stella crept into the room, hesitantly cleared her throat, and then did it again louder. "Mrs. Colburne?" The elderly woman perched at the edge of Jolene's bed continued wiping her daughter's forehead with a wet cloth. She carefully placed the cloth onto the tray table nearby and then turned to Stella, new worry lines creasing her forehead.

"I'm so sorry, Stella. It's been quite a day. It looks like Jolene switched meds on her own, and we didn't know. So, when doctors started her back on the regular dose of her usual medicine, her body didn't like it. The doctors think maybe she developed an allergy to one of them." She shook her head. "I guess that's the problem, isn't it? Nobody knows a damn thing around here."

Stella didn't say anything as her eyes were fixed on Jolene. The woman lying in a pool of sweat with a persistent tick that moved her head to the right every few seconds looked nothing like the network reporter Stella had met two nights before. Her health had deteriorated to the point that she was unrecognizable.

"What—what happened?" she asked.

"Don't I want to know?" Aretha said, unable to hide the bitterness in her voice. "Jolene has suffered from manic-depressive episodes since she was a teen, but she's been on meds to control that for ages. I think some anxiety crept in—maybe the stress from the job was too much? Jolene said her boss was very demanding, but her father and I thought she had it under control."

"When did things... change?"

"We're racking our brains, trying to figure that out. She seemed fine when she came to Palm Springs. We don't talk every day, but we do talk most. Before Palm Springs, she was up in Washington, covering those fires, and she was in good spirits." A sheepish grin stole over the older woman's face. "Well, that sounds terrible to say, but I guess you understand. The fires were exciting, and she'd met someone—wouldn't tell us who, but she sounded very happy. She seemed to be doing really well."

"And then?"

"And then she got here, and we don't know what happened."

Stella's watch beeped, and she covered it with her hand to dull the noise. "I'm sorry—my deadline," she said, and Jolene's mother smiled in understanding.

"Don't apologize. Thanks for stopping by. I wish... well, I wish lots of things, I guess."

She turned back to her daughter and Stella stood there for a moment before she remembered what she needed. "Uh, Mrs. Colburne? I'm so sorry to ask, but I need Jolene's computer. I think it's right over there? My boss wanted to make sure it doesn't get lost in the shuffle, you know?"

"What? Oh, sure. Take it, dear. We won't need it for a while, anyway." Aretha didn't look up from her daughter's face as she spoke. "I wonder if you'll be able to figure out her password? They made her change it every other week, but she forgot half the time and had to reset it," she added with a small, sad laugh.

Relieved, Stella crossed the room and took the bag from the chair. Paperwork stuck out from an outside pocket, and as she shoved it in, her hands hit something cold and plastic. She looked down and pulled out a flat, rectangular pill box, which she held out to Jolene's mother, but the other woman was focused entirely on her daughter.

"You take care of yourself, okay?" Aretha said, wiping her daughter's brow again. "This is just a job—don't let it take over your life."

She froze, a half-smile plastered on. Take over her life? She'd just signed up to fly around the country, covering news in a different city—sometimes by the day—and had no chance of seeing her boyfriend or family for weeks. She shoved the pill box back into Jolene's bag and backed stiffly out of the hospital room, her eyes locked onto the inert woman on the hospital bed.

The computer bag banged against her leg every other step as she made her way down the elevator and through the lobby.

Was she in control of her own life? Really, was anyone?

10

"What do you call that?" Stella pointed to the light stand closest to her.

Woz grunted. "An umbrella."

"That's it? It doesn't have a—I don't know—a more formal name?" It certainly did look like a small, silvery-gray umbrella connected to the light tripod just under the bulb. Its job was to diffuse the light for a softer look on video.

"Nope."

Woz moved to a table where Terry had set up a monitor and deck. His labored breathing was the only sound as Terry connected cords and adjusted the lighting levels while they waited.

Detective Trish MacDonald stood unobtrusively in the back of the hotel room, fiddling with her phone.

"She knows who's going to be interviewing her?" Stella asked, looking at Trish for confirmation.

"Yes. It took her about an hour to call me back with her answer, but she said her lawyer thought it was a good idea."

Trish went back to her phone and Stella looked around the hotel room the station had rented for the night just for this interview. The suite was significantly nicer than hers with a separate space for sleeping just beyond the heavy, French doors. They'd set up in the dining area, and Woz and Terry had completely reorganized the furniture to suit their needs. She ran her hand along the back of the chair she would be sitting in during the interview. Black duct tape covered the wires that ran from the cameras and lights to Woz's table by the back wall. He pressed a few buttons then heaved himself up.

"I'll be outside," he said before lumbering out the door. Woz would get the satellite truck fired up and beam the interview over to New York. Producers there would watch as it came, picking out soundbites to use in real time.

Tonight, with a looming exclusive with Drew

Chambers' widow, Stella's story was going to be included during the news show, *Dateline*.

Although Stella was initially terrified and thrilled by the thought of being on primetime television, Sher had quickly set her straight. "*You're not fronting the story!*" she'd said, as if the thought of a reporter telling her own exclusive story was preposterous. "No, no, no. We'll send the video over to Nancy Knight, and she'll craft the narrative for the broadcast. We might have you join the *Today Show* in the morning with the update, but that's all."

Stella had wanted to ask if Nancy Knight, a well-known fixture in the evening news magazine game, often took other reporters' work and called it her own, but she'd held her tongue. She was the new girl, after all. There was no need to ruffle feathers, yet.

Finally, there was a light tap at the door and Stella pulled it open. Sloan Chambers looked glamorous, as if she'd just stepped off the runway. Her dark hair was swept up into an effortless style that likely would have taken Stella an hour to attempt before giving up and going with a ponytail. She was one of those women who could pull off a one-piece romper with ease. The dark material set off her blood-red statement necklace and diamond earrings.

Sloan's smile didn't quite reach her eyes. "Stella, is it? This is my lawyer, Jessica Blalock. She's here to make sure we don't get too far off topic. Detective." She nodded at Trish.

Stella stepped aside to let Terry through, and while he connected Sloan to a microphone pack, she sidled up to the lawyer. "What is our topic? Do we have any restrictions?"

"My client feels, and this is off the record," Blalock said, "that, with members of the media hounding her away from the courthouse—"

"That was a total coincidence. I mean, it was my first day in town, and I had no idea—"

"Regardless, we want to make sure a respectful boundary remains. If that means sitting down to discuss a few specific things about the trial to diffuse the intense interest in her life, that's what she'll do."

Stella nodded, certain her boss would be interested in more than what Sloan did during testimony every day.

After Terry checked microphone and light levels one last time, he cleared his throat. "Ready when you are, Stella."

Stella nodded and looked down at her notebook. She'd dutifully written a list of questions about the trial, the two years since Drew died, and the fact that the defendant was a friend and business partner. As she looked across at the woman, however, only one question seemed appropriate.

"Sloan, how are you holding up now that the trial has begun?"

Sloan's eyes widened, and she glanced at her lawyer before looking back at Stella. "I—I'm surviving, I guess you'd say." Stella nodded but didn't say anything. After a moment, Sloan continued, "I mean... I used to look around at other people and feel... not sorry, but worried for them. Will they ever know the level of happiness Drew and I feel—felt—every day? It didn't seem possible."

"And now?"

"Now... it's all gone, yet somehow, I have to keep living, working, and trying to find that inner balance that lets me survive."

"Is that harder to find, now that the trial is underway, or easier, knowing the end of this stage is near?"

"Of course it's difficult, but it's a necessary step to find justice for Drew, so we'll get through it."

"We?" Stella asked, surprised by Sloan's word choice. She hadn't been sure whether she would bring up the other woman's new man, but now she didn't have to decide. "Who is 'we?'" she pressed.

"My client has an airtight alibi for the night her husband was killed!" Jessica Blalock's cutting voice was so unexpected that Stella winced. Terry's fingers moved across the top of the camera to take the shot wide. Although Blalock wasn't wearing a microphone, the shotgun mic on top of Terry's camera would capture her words. "She was emceeing a luncheon in front of two hundred people," Blalock added. "Lots of eyewitnesses."

Stella tried to digest the odd timing of Blalock's words. No one had accused Sloan of anything, so why did she feel the urge to suddenly pronounce her client's innocence?

Finally, Sloan cleared her throat. "Like I said, *I'll* get through." She shot another nervous look at her lawyer, who barely shook her head. The movement was so small and quick that, if Stella hadn't been looking right at the woman, she'd have missed it. Before she could press the issue, though, Sloan cleared her throat again and said, "I... I am finding comfort—some comfort, anyway—from a wonderful man." Stella worked hard to keep her expression neutral, and the other woman continued. "My new partner has really helped me through these dark months since Drew's death."

"New partner?"

"Yes. Manny—he understands the sorrow and stress, and he's really been a rock for me these past months."

"Dr. Ruiz?" Stella asked, remembering his surname from the restaurant.

Trish MacDonald stopped fiddling with her phone. "Dr. Manuel Ruiz," she asked from the back of the room, "the CEO of Bionic Mind Incorporated?" The name of the man and the company didn't mean anything to Stella, but she heard the underlying tone in Trish's voice that betrayed a level of scrutiny.

"Well, yes, he is the CEO of Bionic," Sloan said. "I guess that's how we first met, really. When Drew was alive, we certainly moved in the same circles, went to the same fundraisers, and asked for money from the same venture capitalists."

"How long have you two been together?" Stella asked, keeping her voice even and her expression pleasantly interested.

"A few months, now. Manny reached out after the balloon launch to commemorate the one-year anniversary of Drew's death. But it wasn't until recently that things turned romantic. He's really helping me heal, and I think Drew would be happy," she added, her face pinched, daring Stella to contradict her. "He'd be happy to know I have a chance at happiness again."

The topic turned to the trial and Sloan explained her full confidence in Prosecutor Abingdon and her team. As for the state of Luna C Engineering, she told Stella, "The company will survive and thrive. We will realize Drew's vision, and by doing so, help tens of thousands of people with this new technology." Finally, they moved on to the man accused of killing Drew: his business partner, Preston Harrington.

Sloan sat forward in her seat for the first time and looked directly at the camera when she spoke.

"I don't know why he did it, but I think Gail Abingdon is right that Preston was jealous. They say it's one of the oldest motives for murder that exists. He was jealous of Drew, he snapped, and now he has to pay the price." She sat back and focused on Stella before saying slowly, with conviction, "He just has to."

11

"Just make sure Nancy is careful with what angle she chooses," Stella repeated. Although Jimmy in New York couldn't see her, she kicked at a rock underfoot for emphasis.

"You're giving reporting advice to Nancy Knight?" Jimmy said. With a long-suffering sigh, he added, "Explain your concerns again. I got lost last time."

She already knew she disliked this producer at NBC News—this harbinger of *she won't last a week*.

"Seriously, Stella," he said before she could argue her point, "we're the only ones who know Sloan Chambers is now dating her dead husband's biggest business rival! Of course we're going with it."

"I know, I just... I mean, are police charging her with a crime? Do they suspect her of murder? Did they dismiss the case against Preston Harrington? No, the answer to all of that is no! I just worry it's going to come across... tabloid and not news."

"It's going on our news magazine program, Stella. It's perfect. How can you not see that?"

"Did you go to high school in Palm Springs?" she asked, but it was too late to find out if he was on the same team as Gail Abingdon and Maria Garcia, as Jimmy had already hung up. She swore under her breath.

"Well, that's lovely," Vindi said. "So that's what they want in a network reporter these days, huh? No wonder I'm still in San Diego."

Stella turned to find a teasing grin on her friend's face. "You're in San Diego," she grumbled, "because you love California and you'd never move anywhere else." She was still stinging from Jimmy's rebuke.

"What do you have there?" Vindi motioned to the computer perched rather precariously on the steps leading to the door of the satellite truck.

"It's Jolene's work computer—well, mine now," Stella said, hitting a few keys at random. "At least, it will be if I can crack her password. It certainly didn't help that *Jimmy*," she said his name like a swear word, "didn't connect me to IT before he hung up on me." She swore under her breath again.

"They're probably home for the night, anyway," Vindi said. "It's nearly nine out east."

Stella closed the laptop and shoved it back into the zippered bag lying at her feet. "This time change is killing me," she said, walking next to Vindi. They headed across the parking lot to her car, and Stella nodded in thanks when her friend opened the back door, where she then deposited both the computer bag and her briefcase. "It'd be one thing to *work* here, but to be here and still have to operate on Eastern Time..." Stella shook her head. "Exhausting."

Both women climbed into the car and Vindi started up the engine. "What were you working on tonight, anyway? I didn't see anything on the trial on the news tonight, but Rachel said you were buzzing around with your photographer until well after seven."

"I had this... well, *I* don't actually have anything," Stella said with a frown again, irked that Sher had given her exclusive to another reporter.

They drove in silence for several blocks, Stella

irritated, Vindi reflective. Stella took a purposeful breath of air and cracked her neck, determined to relieve the tension and enjoy what was left of her evening with a friend. With some of her foul mood lifted, she felt a thrum of energy emanating from the other side of the car.

Stella turned to her friend accusingly. "Okay, spill it, lady. Why are you so... bouncy?"

Vindi's smile turned to a scowl. "Bouncy? Ugh." Stella smothered a laugh and put her hands up in mock surrender. Vindi snorted and then said, "Okay, maybe I *am* bouncy. Don't tell anyone."

"What gives?"

"I've got a major exclusive that's going to run tomorrow." Her fingers tapped out an excited beat on the steering wheel. "I'll tell you about it if you promise not to breathe a word of it to your people before then."

"Thank heaven you work for an affiliate, or this would get really awkward. Yes!" Stella said. "I promise. Spill it!"

"I have interviews with *five*—seriously, Stella, *five*—women who all claim to have had affairs with Drew Chambers over the last two years of his life."

"What? How did you find them?"

"I am an investigative reporter, my dear. We got a call into the station, so I started digging—this was months ago—and we tracked down the first, who had a line on the second, and it just snowballed. Of course, there are more—there must be —but we decided to go with it now. It'll air tomorrow. We're promoting it all starting in the morning show, and it will lead the evening newscasts!"

They drove in silence for a few minutes before Vindi leveled her with a stare. "What?" she finally asked. "We're not going to start acting jealous of each other's successes, are we? If we are, I have a lot of issues from Montana I can start with—"

"No—no, it's not that," Stella said, shooting her friend a rueful smile. Vindi had not only gone all in with an investigation of Stella's years ago, but had also helped her break it wide open with little to no fanfare. "It's... I had an interview with Sloan Chambers earlier. That's what I was doing."

"You did? When is it going to air? I'd have thought they would have you front it for *Dateline* tonight. Are they saving it for the *Today Show*?"

"Well... no. They actually gave it to Nancy Knight—"

"I knew it!" Vindi breathed, her eyes wide. "I knew she didn't do her own reporting, anymore! I could just tell from the way she—" She cut herself off and shot an assessing look at her friend. "Wait, what did Sloan say in this exclusive interview?"

Stella looked at the clock on the dash. "It's airing right now. Sloan Chambers is dating again."

"Well... I mean, no offense, but that's not really big news, is it? It's been almost two years since her husband was killed. It's not a crime to move on, right?"

"That's exactly what I told my EP!"

Vindi narrowed her eyes. "What else?"

"Well... not that it matters who she's found love with, but her new partner is the CEO of a competing firm."

The other woman gasped. "Is that confirmed?"

"Well, yes. I mean, Sloan told me, herself."

"How long have they been together?"

"She says for just a few months... but I saw them together the other night and they didn't look like new lovers."

"Stella, holy sh—well, I'm not at network, so I won't swear, but how do we know if that's true? What's to say they weren't dating when Drew was alive?"

"I don't know," Stella said, rubbing her now throbbing forehead. "If Drew Chambers cheated on Sloan—"

"If? It happened multiple times!"

"Right, he cheated on her multiple times over the course of their marriage, and she was dating his biggest rival..."

"You know what this means," Vindi said, turning to look at Stella.

"Yes. It means Preston Harrington wasn't the only one with a motive to kill!"

12

"You're not going to believe this, and you owe me so big that I don't think you'll ever be able to repay me," Trish McDonald's voice was smug on the other end of the line.

Stella set her steaming mug of coffee on the table in her hotel room and tried again, in vain, to lower the volume of her speaker phone, worried that Vindi one floor above her might hear the scoop Trish was about to deliver.

"What's going on?" she asked.

"Preston Harrington saw Sloan's interview last night—by the way, Nancy Knight? Really? How did that happen?" Stella didn't say anything, so Trish continued, "Anyway, he wants to talk to you-- today."

"On camera? On the record?"

"Yup. The jail called me this morning. I haven't even talked to his lawyer, yet," she crowed.

"Wow." Stella sat down on the edge of her bed, shocked. "Detective, why do you sound so excited? I mean, this is big for me, and my boss might finally be happy with me, but you... you sound like a kid on Christmas morning."

Trish chuckled. "I feel that way, too. I'm going to put a subpoena in for your raw interview footage so fast, your head will spin. Preston Harrington hasn't spoken to us since the day we arrested him—won't answer a single question about where he was the day of the crime, what his company was working on, why he and Drew were on bad terms—nothing! Now he wants to do a sit-down, on the record, with the press on television? I'm elated—just tickled pink—if I'm being honest."

"I don't even know... I mean, you'll have to go through my boss in New York. I don't want to sound ungrateful, but I can't just make a copy for you. There are proper—"

"I know. Believe me, I know all the hoops I'll have to jump through. I'm sure you can give me a quick summary after, though, and you'll probably air some of it tonight?"

Stella nodded to herself. She didn't see any-thing wrong with that. "Sure," she said aloud. "When will this all go down?"

Trish gave her the details and she scribbled them down in her notebook. She needed to be in place at the county jail by eleven thirty, and it was just after eight, Pacific Time. Sher would be heading to lunch soon. She tapped the number in New York, glad she'd have just enough time before her exclusive to hit the mall for a new cell phone.

"It's great. Things are really gr—"

"Don't say great again or I'll have to get on the next plane to Palm Springs." Lucky's voice was both stern and tender. Stella was glad to hear it all in private mode on her new cell phone.

"Okay. It's not great, but it's getting better," she allowed.

"What's your biggest fear? What's making you so unsure of yourself?"

The pause while Stella considered his question was so long that she was surprised Lucky didn't hang up. Finally, she said, "When the plane was flying into Palm Springs the other day, do you know what I noticed?"

"What?"

"There were all these people—all these business travelers—and not one of them put down their books or newspapers long enough to look out the window as we made our final approach."

"And?"

"The view out the window was beautiful. You're leaving this vast desert wasteland you've been flying over for miles and miles, and all of a sudden, a ring of mountains surrounds this small, green oasis—this paradise that is Palm Springs—and they couldn't even be bothered to look out the window and appreciate it!"

"I know you're not turning into a nature nut, so what is this really about?"

"I guess I'm worried this network-level job—if I can keep it, anyway—will make me forget why I got into this business in the first place. There's such an emphasis on getting the scoop and beating the competition, the pace is breakneck. I guess I'm worried I'll lose sight of what's important."

"Stopping to enjoy the view? Smelling the flowers?"

"Not exactly, but—well, helping people! Making a difference with my work is what's important."

"Stella, nothing's changed, except the location and the length of time you have to help people in any one place. It just means you have to make each day count. It also means your stories can impact more people than ever before."

"Some of it just seems so tabloid—"

"Now, wait just a minute, darlin'. Who are you to say what's important to a story, yet? You said the company—Luna C Engineering, right?—is in lockdown until the trial is over. When the trial ends, this new drug of theirs might help tens of thousands of people. Even this murder trial isn't just about the murder, but about a company whose product might change people's lives." Stella considered Lucky's words. Terry had actually said the same thing last night. "Stella?"

She gulped. She hadn't yet mentioned the handsome photographer to her boyfriend. "You're right. I mean, anything related to what's keeping a new drug that could alter life for hundreds of thousands of people should be reported, no matter how small." After a moment, she realized silence stretched between them. "What's going on? Lucky?"

"Nothing, Stella," he answered formally. "I've got to go."

"That's right. You said you have a late lunch meeting?"

"Mmm."

Lucky's sudden brevity was confusing, and Stella rubbed a hand over her eyes. "Is everything okay?"

"Hmm? Oh, I'm sure it is, although why Star wants to meet now is beyond me."

She looked at her cell phone screen so fast her eyes nearly crossed. "Your late lunch meeting is with Star, your ex-fiancée?"

"Right."

"Why? Why are you meeting with her?" Stella pinched the bridge of her nose between her finger and thumb and took two deep breaths while she waited for Lucky's answer.

"What's wrong?" he asked, instead of answering her question.

"Nothing, Lucky," she said, tired of this game. "Have a great lunch. I'll talk to you later."

If Lucky doubted her because she worked with men, she wasn't going to give him the satisfaction of showing she didn't want him to meet with his ex-fiancée. He could have lunch with whoever he wanted—it wasn't her business. She shrugged off her hurt feelings, irritated that her boyfriend had gotten under her skin, and headed out the door. She didn't have time for boyfriend drama; she had news to break.

13

———

P reston Harrington's lawyer had been right to dress him in a warm, fuzzy sweater for opening arguments. As he sat in an interview room at the jail, Preston looked more formidable than ever in his prison scrubs. The ill-fitting, forest-green shirt and pants made him more angular and less friendly—or maybe that was the scowl.

As Stella and Terry walked in with a prison guard, Preston acknowledged them by slightly inclining his head. He didn't stand.

"Welcome to my humble abode," he said, cocking one eyebrow at Stella.

The prison guard shook his head and then looked at Terry. "You've got twenty minutes." She shifted her gaze to the inmate. "A last request from your lawyer to shut up—"

Preston waved his hand to cut off the guard before she could finish her thought. "Thank you."

The guard shrugged and then pointed to the camera in the upper corner of the room behind Preston. "We'll be watching but not listening. Twenty minutes," she repeated before backing out of the room. The door closed behind her with a click and then a deadbolt slid into place.

Stella and Terry had gone through security when they walked into the jail and all their equipment had been checked over with a fine-tooth comb. She unraveled the cord from the wireless microphone pack and walked around the table. "Run this cord up your shirt and pull it out the neck. I'll clip it on for you."

He cocked his eyebrow again. "That'll make it look nicer?" Stella nodded. "Well, we wouldn't want prison scrubs to look bad, now would we?" The snide smile didn't reach his cold eyes.

If he was trying to intimidate her, it wasn't working. Preston Harrington wasn't the first surly person accused of murder she'd interviewed, and he wouldn't be the last if she stayed in her current job.

With another frown, he ran the cord up his

shirt. Stella grabbed the end and clipped it onto the V-neck.

"I'm ready," Terry said.

Stella went back around the table to sit in the open chair. She took out her notebook and stared at the blank page for a moment before looking up and locking eyes with Preston. "So," she leaned forward. "You have something you want to get off your chest. Let's hear it."

Preston's jaw set defiantly. His eyes narrowed and he glanced at the camera lens before looking down at his folded hands. He then looked back up at Stella and said, "I saw Sloan's interview yesterday."

He fell silent, so Stella prompted him. "What she said got you thinking." It wasn't a question, but it was enough to force him to open up.

"It did." Preston nodded slowly, again looking down at his folded hands. "It got me thinking about life and how the choices we make can have unintended consequences."

Stella's brow furrowed. Was he about to confess to murder? She put her pencil down and leaned back in her seat. Suddenly, she felt like she was a spectator and Preston was about to start the show.

"What choices did you make?" she finally asked.

Preston gave a small shake of his head before his eyes met Stella's across the table. "It's not *my* choices I've been thinking about."

"Then whose?"

"Police, Sloan Chambers, and Drew. Yes, even Drew Chambers," he said when he saw Stella's surprised expression.

"Are you talking about the affairs?" she asked.

Preston's eyes opened wide. "Yes. You know about them?"

"A colleague is breaking that story today. Five women came forward."

"Who?" He leaned forward, his face animated for the first time. She flipped through her notebook and listed off the names. When she'd finished, he sat back against his seat, stunned. "The list is incomplete."

"Who's missing?" Stella asked, watching his face. He seemed to be struggling with something, but his forehead finally smoothed.

"Just know there are names missing—important names."

They stared silently at each other for several moments. Preston seemed happy to let the silence continue, but Stella knew the clock was ticking. If

Preston had requested this interview, there was something he wanted to say, but apparently she'd have to draw it out of him.

"What did Sloan say that frustrated you—made you angry—about what's going on?" She threw a bunch of words at him, unsure of which would stick.

"Everything she said pissed me off," he said, his glare back. "No one has been truthful about their relationships from the minute police were called; actually, since long before that, if we're being honest." His eyes shifted from Stella to his hands as he seemed to steel himself to say something.

"Who's not being honest?" Stella asked.

A humorless smile crossed his lips before they turned down into another sneer. "No one's been honest, least of all me—but I don't have to prove my innocence. That's not how the justice system is supposed to work. That's exactly what's happening in this case, though."

Stella pounced. "You're saying you're not innocent?"

Preston snorted in disbelief. "I'm saying the opposite. I'm saying police haven't come close to proving my guilt. Knowing a murder victim does not a murderer make." His voice had become staccato, as if each word might be his last. "There are other people who had far more reason and just as much access to Drew Chambers as I did—and they had far less to lose by his death."

"Millions at stake."

"Freedom," Preston said, his whole body tense and ready to split in half from his pent-up emotions. Terry stood tall and tensed, too, perhaps sensing the prisoner might do something foolish. The inmate blew out a breath, though, and slumped back in his seat, his anger replaced by something else—maybe sadness. "Freedom," he repeated, "is worth more than any money Luna C Engineering could possibly have earned me. What I'm saying is other people had motive and other people had access. I'm putting all the players on notice that, when I'm found innocent, I'm coming after them with a civil lawsuit that will leave them reeling."

"Not guilty," Stella corrected.

"Excuse me?"

"I said 'not guilty.' You're never found innocent —the court can only find you not guilty."

For the first time since she and Terry entered the small space, Preston's shoulders drooped. Some of the defiance seeped out of him, like a balloon with a tiny, new hole.

He nodded and said almost to himself, "You're right: it's a distinction worth noting. I'll never be innocent, no matter what, huh? No matter what."

Stella glanced at her watch to see they were almost out of time, and she looked at Preston Harrington across the table. Her initial impression of him was still accurate. He was angular and angry, yes, but there was something more—something sad—that she couldn't identify. It wasn't remorse that his business partner was dead, but remorse for *something* was simmering under the surface.

"Why were you arrested, then, Preston? Why you and not someone else?" He shook his head, but she pressed on. "Prosecutors say you were jealous of Drew. Is that true?"

"Jealous?" he exploded. "I had more than Drew would ever have—far more! There was nothing to be jealous about!"

"Where were you that morning when Drew Chambers was killed?"

Preston shook his head and a spark of some emotion crossed his face before he shut it down. Stella knew she would get no more answers from him today. He pushed back from the table, the only sound in the room the squeal of the metal chair against the cement floor.

"I'm done here." He stalked around the table to

get to the door. When Stella stood, he threw his hands up protectively and roared, "I said I'm done!"

The guard jiggled the doorknob, and then they heard the scrape of the key in the lock.

"I—I just need the microphone back," she said, pointing at his shirt.

"Oh, sorry." A sheepish expression crossed his face and, for a moment, it felt as if they could have been standing in an office building somewhere, discussing a simple misunderstanding about printer ink or something mundane. He unclipped the microphone and handed it back to Stella.

"There's a piece missing," he said as he held out his hands toward the guard. He grunted as the metal handcuffs slipped over his wrists, and without a backward glance, started to walk out the door in front of the guard. Just before he reached the hallway, though, he looked back at Stella one last time. "There's a piece missing, and I can't—I just can't—say anything else."

Preston's shoulders lowered for the second time that day, and he was soon eclipsed by the guard as she followed him down the narrow hallway.

"What piece, Preston? What piece is missing?" she called, but neither guard nor prisoner stopped and she was left staring at an empty hallway. He wouldn't—couldn't?—share his alibi for the crime with her or police, but he wanted Stella to believe he was innocent simply because he said he was.

While Terry gathered the gear, she went over the interview. Preston became agitated over two things: a sixth woman who'd had an affair with Drew Chambers and the timeline of Sloan's new relationship. He'd refused to give her any more details, however, that would help her get answers.

What was he hiding?

Who or what was he protecting that was worth going to prison for murder?

14

———

Stella stopped by the bodega for a coffee after the interview. Woz would man their camera in the media room, but she had time for a quick break before court was scheduled to begin for the day.

Her phone buzzed. When she looked down, she saw a text from Sher. *Send jailhouse interview over. Nancy Knight will use tonight.*

"What the..." Stella glared at the tiny screen. She punched in some numbers and tapped her foot while she listened to the line ring.

"Sher Patrick."

"I am not giving this interview away!" Stella fumed. "Am I or am I not the reporter you have out here to cover the trial? I refuse to pass my hard work along to someone else every day. You either want me out here or you don't, but I will not be another reporter's assistant."

"If you'd like to leave a message, please do so after the beep."

"Gah!" Stella said, slamming her phone down on the counter.

Joe Jones jumped up from where he'd been crouching behind the register with a gasp. "Wha—oh, Stella. What's going on?"

"Oh, I'm so sorry. I didn't see you there!" She picked up her phone and slammed it down again.

"I hear that's not good for a phone," Joe said, bending over to put a roll of paper towels on a low shelf. "They say, in fact, that you shouldn't throw it, either, in case that was going to be your next move."

In spite of her foul mood, Stella laughed. "You're right, I'm sorry. I just—I got a very frustrating text," she finally said. "I'd love a coffee."

"That'll be two twenty-five, and the cups are over there."

"Thanks." While she rummaged around in her bag for change, she felt a pair of eyes boring into her from behind. She turned and found Tim and his dog, Hope, standing nearby. "Hi," she said as she put her phone and wallet away and headed toward the coffee station.

Tim only stared back, but Hope wagged her tail, so Stella stopped to ask, "Is it okay if I pet her?" Tim smiled slightly and nodded. She ran her hand through the fur on the dog's back and then crouched to let her smell her hand before stroking her side. "My old dog used to love a good scratch right... here." She laughed lightly when Hope leaned into her hand and groaned.

She patted the dog once more on the head and then stood to make her coffee.

"Tim, here, has been quite interested in your court case," Joe said as he came around the counter to the back of the store. "I've never seen him so interested in anything, to be honest." Stella looked over at the two as she stirred cream and sugar into her cup. "He's been watching the recap on local news every chance he can get. I just asked him if he wanted to go into the court to watch, but... you didn't like the sound of that, did you?"

Tim shook his head. "No, thank you."

Stella looked at him in shock, until Joe said, "It's the title of a Don Henley song."

Tim looked down shyly and she smothered a laugh. "How convenient! So, you like country music," he nodded, "but you don't like courthouses?"

"Who doesn't like courthouses?"

Stella looked over and smiled as Detective Trish McDonald walked down the aisle. "Shouldn't you be in court?"

"The judge said we'll start up after lunch," Trish said with a frown. "Some days, I think we'll never get through this case."

Stella pressed a lid onto her cup and turned to introduce Trish to Joe, Tim, and Hope, but only Joe remained.

Before she could voice her surprise, the store owner introduced himself, adding, "We have the best coffee in town."

"The closest coffee shop to the courthouse is all I care about," Trish said, shaking his hand with a grin.

"We try to be both." He offered her a cup and then said with a smile, "On the house, Detective. Thanks for all your work."

While Trish fixed herself a coffee, Stella turned to Joe and asked in a low voice, "Where did Tim go?"

"He doesn't like cops," Joe answered. "They're always shuffling him off benches and doorways. He thinks they're out to get him."

"They don't mistreat him, do they?"

"Most are okay, but some are rougher than others. He steers away from them all as a rule."

She frowned, waved to both Joe and Trish, and headed out into the sunshine. As she leaned against the building, she took a few sips of her coffee, thinking. She needed to call Sher again. Although she'd calmed down since reading her last text, Stella still felt passionately that she was here for a reason. She wasn't an intern—this was her story, and she was going to be the one to tell it.

Before she could pick up her phone, though, she saw a shaggy tail crossing the street. Hope trotted faithfully next to Tim, gratefully taking a piece of donut from his fingers and swallowing it in one bite. Tim chewed his piece thoroughly as they walked away from her, the bodega, and the police detective inside.

What a stressful existence, to run from both your demons and police. She was glad Tim had a safe harbor at the bodega, but she wondered where else he felt safe enough to rest and recharge. She vowed to find out more about what Palm Springs—what the Department of Veterans Affairs—was doing for homeless vets like Tim.

First, though, she had questions for another organization: NBC News in New York. She tapped the numbers on her phone again and waited until an actual person picked up the line, this time.

"Sher, this is my story. You can't just give it away to someone else."

"Ah, I *do* have a reporter out there. I told Jimmy I'd keep giving your exclusives away as long as you allowed me to. If you can't stand up to me, I can't trust you to stand up to any authority."

"Wha—" Stella stopped, unsure of how to react to the test she'd apparently just passed.

"We'll have you live from Palm Springs tonight, leading the newscast. Make sure your IFB works this time, okay?" As usual, Sher disconnected after she'd finished her thought.

"Damn right I will." Stella dropped her phone into her bag. "It's mine, and I will lead the newscast tonight."

"Talking to yourself, now?" Trish walked out of the shop with a grin, but she quickly turned serious. "I'd rather you talk to me. What did Preston say?"

"Not much," Stella said as they walked toward the courthouse. "He wouldn't tell me where he was when Chambers died—only that he didn't do it." Trish nodded. "You're not surprised?"

"No, that's the same line he's given us since day one," she said.

"Why don't you believe it?"

"He's the one with the most to gain—and lose —from Drew's death, and he's the only one without an alibi."

"With no murder weapon, though, what evidence do you have tying him to the case?" They must have had something concrete to charge a man with murder.

"No comment," Trish said, looking down at her phone. "Ah, shoot. I've got to go."

"Is court starting early?" Stella asked, quickening her pace to keep up.

"No, something else—something that might make court start late, if I had to guess."

"What?"

"I can't, Stella. Sorry!" Trish's stride didn't falter as they walked into the courthouse; the guards let her pass around the security checkpoint without stopping.

Stella looked down at her full cup of coffee and groaned. After taking one last pull, she tossed the cup into the trash can and made it through security as fast as she could.

Bypassing a long line at the elevator, she took the stairs two at a time to get to the second floor. She wanted to know what had made Detective Trish McDonald move so fast.

15

The hallway outside the courtrooms was deserted, but Stella paced the area for some twenty minutes, wondering what had pulled detective Trish McDonald back in such a rush. As employees came back from lunch and foot traffic in the hallway picked up, though, Stella grudgingly made her way into the media room.

She spotted Woz hunkered down in a seat, staring at his phone. "Are you ready for this afternoon?"

He grunted and popped a handful of orange Tic Tacs into his mouth. "This trial is moving so slowly," he complained. When he crunched down on the candy, a burst of citrus filled the air. "At this rate, we'll be here for a year. I don't know what the judge is playing at, drawing everything out like this."

"Have you ever worked with this judge before?" After four days together, she still had no idea where Woz was from.

Woz shook his head "Never." He tucked the small box of candy into his pocket. "I'm based out of San Diego. The only time I've been here is on the way to somewhere else. It's a different kind of person who vacations in Palm Springs—and a different breed of person, entirely, who actually lives here."

The feed from the courtroom came alive. Moments later, the judge came on screen and called everyone to order. The media room settled into silence, every reporter ready to take notes—every reporter, except Maria Garcia. The CNN reporter slunk out of the room just as prosecutor Gail Abingdon called Detective Trish McDonald to the stand.

"I'll be right back," Stella said to Woz in a low voice. She rushed into the hallway, but it was empty again. She stood there for a moment, wondering what to do, when a noise at the far end of the hall made her turn.

A set of double doors opened and a police detective, along with two patrol officers, moved down the hall. What caught Stella's attention, however, was the person in the middle of their official-looking group. Dr. Manuel Ruiz, Sloan Chambers' new boyfriend, had his hands cuffed uncomfortably behind him.

She opened her mouth to ask what was going on, but as they came closer, she felt confused. The man in cuffs had brown eyes and was shorter than the man she'd seen with Sloan at the restaurant the other night. So it wasn't Dr. Manuel Ruiz—just a look-alike.

Maria Garcia was still missing, so Stella zipped around the group of men, now waiting for the elevators, and took the stairs two at a time to the ground level. She beat the elevator and managed to hustle through the lobby and out the front door, where she almost collided with Maria Garcia and her camerawoman.

The other reporter shot her a disgruntled look, but before she could say anything to Stella, her photographer said, "Here they come."

The trio of cops led the handcuffed man out the courthouse doors, past the CNN camera, and down the front steps to a waiting cruiser. The two patrol officers got in the car with their prisoner and drove away.

"What can you tell me about the arrest, Detective?" Maria asked, her microphone out and ready.

"No comment." He put his cell phone up to his ear and walked on by.

Stella's brow furrowed. What was she missing here? Did this arrest relate to the murder trial? "Detective, who was that?" she asked.

Maria Garcia smirked, and then she and her camerawoman headed down the steps. Into her cell phone, Maria said, "We got it. We'll be ready to go in five minutes."

Stella's stomach dropped. It was happening again: she was about to get beat by Maria Garcia. Even though the arrest had happened right in front of her eyes, she had no idea who the man was or why it was important.

She turned back to the detective, intending to get more information out of him, but he was staring at Maria Garcia, an odd expression on his face. "Detective?"

He jerked to attention and cleared his throat. "No comment. You can direct all questions to Detective Trish McDonald on this one." He jogged down the steps, climbed into his unmarked car, and drove down the road in the same direction as the patrol car.

Detective McDonald was on the stand, being

questioned by Gail Abingdon in the courtroom upstairs, which meant Stella wouldn't get any answers until after Maria Garcia broke this story wide open.

She gave one final, searching look at the courthouse doors, and then turned in the opposite direction. Stella crossed the street and headed to the parking lot. With most of the reporters inside, only two trucks were roaring: the one from CNN and Stella's own NBC News truck.

"Terry," Stella breathed as she raced up the steps to her truck. She wrenched open the door and burst inside the small space. Terry was leaning back on one of the wheeled chairs and jumped at her sudden appearance, dropping his sandwich onto his lap and slopping soda onto the ground.

"Jesus, Mary, and Joseph!" he grumbled, brushing lettuce off his shirt and then wiping the floor with a wad of napkins. "You startled me!"

"Can you tune into CNN?" Stella asked breathlessly.

He picked up his sandwich again and settled back into his seat. "Nope."

She glanced at the monitors, which were all tuned to ESPN. "Terry, please, this is important! I want to know what Maria Garcia has. She's just about to go live!"

He blew out a long-suffering sigh. "Stella, I'm on my lunch break. Why don't you just go outside and watch her?"

She glared at Terry, incensed at his attitude, but she headed back outside in the end and skulked around the side of her truck. She spotted Maria Garcia standing in front of a camera, lights on, earpiece in, and new blush and lipstick applied. With a sheaf of notes clutched in one hand and her cell phone in the other, she looked to be just minutes away from scooping Stella, yet again.

"Yes, I'm sure," the CNN reporter spoke into her cell phone. "I'm telling you, my source tipped me off—I'm holding the note in my hand right now! It's confirmed."

Stella's mouth went dry. Sher was never going to assign her another story after this.

A few more minutes passed before Maria spoke again—this time, to Stella. "You're missing important testimony in there." She grinned into her notebook.

Stella moved two final steps into full view. "It seems like something important happened out here," she said with a frown.

"Standby," her photographer said, and Maria's

grin faded. She was all business as the network took her live.

"That's right, Joan, shocking new developments here in Palm Springs in the Drew Chambers murder trial. Even as the lead detective takes the stand against Preston Harrington, another man is led away by police. Take a look at our exclusive video. Only CNN was recording as police detectives led Dr. Manuel Ruiz away in handcuffs."

Stella's mouth dropped open. That wasn't Dr. Ruiz who'd walked by in handcuffs—a look alike, for sure, but not the same man Stella had seen with Sloan the other night. Her stomach, already hollow, seemed to leave her body altogether. Even though it wasn't her mistake, she wanted to yell out to Maria, but the other reporter was chugging full-steam ahead.

"You'll remember Dr. Ruiz is Sloan Chambers' boyfriend. In statements to the press, she has said the two started dating well after her husband's murder. His arrest today, however, calls the timeline of their relationship into question. My sources here on the ground are telling me the relationship may not be so recent, and if they were dating before the murder, that's certainly something police will want to explore, especially as the case against Mr. Harrington moves forward."

Stella staggered back against the satellite truck and listened with only half an ear. Maria was incredibly wrong—staggeringly, shockingly, slanderously wrong!

"Clear. Good job, MG," her photographer said, and the unmistakable sounds of cleaning up a live shot rang out. The tripod legs slapped together and the generator cut off.

"In shock?" Maria Garcia came around the truck to gloat.

"Definitely." The CNN reporter's eyebrows drew together, but Stella didn't say anything else.

When she entered the working area of the satellite truck, Terry was expecting her, this time. "Did we get beat?"

"No—not even close." Stella explained the mix-up.

"She said she had a tip?" Terry wiped his mouth with a napkin and tuned in fully to her story. This was better than the highlights of the game he'd been watching just minutes ago.

"Yes, she had a note, but it was wrong—so, so wrong." Stella fell silent. Someone had set up Maria Garcia. Someone wanted her off this story, and they'd timed their tip so Maria's true source, Gail Abingdon, was unable to confirm, as she was interviewing a witness in front of a jury.

That witness was Trish McDonald, the very woman who'd been bullied mercilessly in school by Gail Abingdon and Maria Garcia. That couldn't have been a coincidence.

Her cell phone rang; when she looked down at the screen, she saw Sher's name. This time, Stella didn't give her boss the chance to speak first. "Maria Garcia is wrong—that wasn't Dr. Manuel Ruiz."

There was a long pause while Sher regrouped. She finally said, "Are you sure?"

"Yes. I saw him the other night with Sloan, and that man on the CNN video wasn't him."

"Make some calls and confirm it, then call me back."

Sher disconnected and Stella stared at the ground. She *was* going to make some calls. She was going to start making a lot of calls.

16

Tick, tock, tick, tock. Deadlines had always been omnipresent in Stella's job, hovering in the air like flies at a picnic, but now she had three hours less to tick through every day. It felt like the clock was mocking her—and doing it loudly. She could practically hear the seconds slip away as they approached the three thirty afternoon deadline.

Even Woz blotted beads of sweat from his forehead as he made the final edits on their exclusive jailhouse interview. The door to the truck was propped hopefully open, even though there wasn't a whisper of a breeze around.

Outside, Terry handed Stella the stick micro-

phone and then turned to Detective McDonald.
"After the package rolls, we'll have you step into
the shot with Stella." When she didn't move, he
gently guided her by her shoulders to the right
spot.

She blushed at the contact, and Stella's brows
ticked up a notch. That was interesting. Terry was
very attractive, and it made her smile to see it
wasn't lost on a hardened police detective.

"Stella will ask you a few questions. You just
look at her; try to ignore the camera."

"Ignore the camera, got it," Trish said. She
smoothed her hair and fiddled with her cell
phone. Terry's half-smile lingered. Soon, Detective
McDonald was smiling at him.

He held out his hand and she looked at it ques-
tioningly. "Your cell phone? We can't have it ring
on national TV."

Her cheeks turned scarlet. "Of course, here.
Thanks."

"Detective," Vindi called from the other side of
Terry, "we're all waiting for a piece of this when
you're done with Stella! Don't let us down."

Stella grinned at her tone, but Trish frowned.
"Can't you share this video with them?" she asked.

"I'm afraid not. This is a live shot, so they'll
need your interview on their own cameras. If you

do them all at once, though, you'll be done faster," she offered.

The detective harrumphed just as Terry said, "Twenty-five away from the cold open."

Stella adjusted her earpiece and gave Sher a mic check in the booth in New York. "Stella, we're five away. Woz just sent the package back. It looks good."

Stella tried not to grin. That basic, tepid remark from Sher was the nicest thing the executive producer had ever said to her.

Terry cleared his throat. When she looked up, he inclined his head slightly to the left. She glanced over and saw Maria Garcia standing off in the wings, trying to get Trish's attention, but the detective studiously ignored her old nemesis.

Music played through her earpiece, and Stella said, "Okay, guys, here we go."

Trish tensed and Terry adjusted the reflective light panel. *Hank-freaking-Smith's* voice intoned about the day's top stories, and then the camera took him live in the studio.

"We begin tonight with deception in paradise. Stella Reynolds joins us live with an exclusive interview with the man accused of murdering his business partner and friend. Stella?"

Stella calmly looked at the camera, down at

her notes, and up at the camera again. She felt the same fluttering in the pit of her stomach that had preceded her last network live shot, but before she could stress about what her line was supposed to be, she heard Vindi say nearby in a low voice, "Own it."

That was all it took for Stella to spit out the first part of her live shot and then toss confidently to her prerecorded exclusive interview with Preston Harrington.

"You had me worried there, Red," Terry said with a wink when they were safely in the package. Trish stepped into the frame, and Stella adjusted her ear piece and smiled reassuringly at the detective.

"In ten," Terry said.

"Go at me hard," Trish said, leveling a serious glare at Stella.

"What?"

"Relentless."

Stella nodded. She'd been intending to, anyway, but Trish's attitude was difficult to process, especially when they were live again.

"Joining us now for another exclusive is Detective Trish McDonald with the Palm Springs Police Department." Trish nodded tightly and Stella continued, "You've been on this case from the beginning, and today we're hearing of some late, breaking developments. Some outlets tonight are reporting that there's been another arrest in the case. Is that true?"

Trish shook her head. "Absolutely not. We brought someone in for questioning in a completely separate case, who had nothing to do with the Drew Chambers murder trial. He happened to very loosely resemble someone, but it was not—I repeat—not that person. We brought someone in for a petty theft case from a pawn shop."

In her peripheral vision, Stella saw Maria Garcia take a step back, almost like she'd suffered a physical blow.

"So you're saying no one related to the defendant, victim, or relatives of either was interviewed by your department today?"

"That's right. I suspect another media outlet, in an effort to get a scoop, didn't completely vet their information, and now a good man's name has been sullied. If I were him, I'd be contacting a lawyer."

"Detective, this is an interesting case. Even though the trial has started against Preston Harrington without a murder weapon, with new information coming to light, are you still investigating?"

Trish faltered visibly and then recovered with

a shake. "Absolutely not. I—I mean, you never stop. In this case, though, we've stopped."

"So you're confident the right man is on trial?"

"One hundred percent."

"Is anyone else in your sights? As you heard, Preston Harrington says the list of the victim's scorned ex-lovers is incomplete. Do you think you've spoken to everyone who was involved with Drew Chambers before he died?"

"I have no com—"

"Can you tell us how many women, in total, your department interviewed?"

"That's not something I can... I mean, that kind of information isn't available for me to release."

Stella would have left it at that, but the detective had told her to be relentless, so she tried one last question. "Detective, if someone out there has information that hasn't yet come to light, can they be held criminally responsible for withholding it?"

Trish paled. "Ab—absolutely. This is a criminal prosecution of murder. The public's assistance is vital to solving this crime. If someone out there knows something we don't, they must come forward."

"But are they criminally liable?" Stella pressed.

"In some cases, yes."

"All right, Detective Trish McDonald, thank you so much for your time." Stella turned back to the camera and Terry pressed a button to zoom in the shot. "The trial will continue this week with prosecutors expecting to rest their case by the weekend. Reporting live in Palm Springs, California, I'm Stella Reynolds. Hank, back to you."

After Terry gave the all clear, Stella took her earpiece out and turned to thank Trish. The other woman, however, was looking at an approaching figure. Before Stella could ask who was marching toward them with forced calm, the detective muttered, "Just follow my lead, okay?"

"Mac!" The sides of the man's suit jacket flapped behind him as he strode their way, anger etched on every feature of his face. "Mac, I told you to watch what you said! This isn't a reality show—this is an actual murder trial!"

"I told you I didn't want to talk on TV! I told you that you can't reign in reporters—especially when it's live! I had no idea what she was going to ask me. I would, however, like to ask her," she swung her attention to Maria Garcia, "who gave her the bad information earlier today! There's a leak in our office, Chief, and I want to know who it is."

The police chief spluttered to a stop, only his eyeballs moving between Stella and Maria. "I want them all out!" he roared. "I want the judge to close the trial! No more reporters and no more cameras!"

17

Stella carefully stepped off the curb and headed toward a restaurant she'd passed the day before. She was trying to clear her mind after the confusing exchange between Trish and the chief of police of Palm Springs.

"He thinks we're all one big, happy team," Trish had said after the chief left. "He has no idea Gail is trying to ruin things by feeding information to Maria Garcia."

Stella hadn't asked how Trish fit into things, but she was beginning to think her number one source in this case wasn't playing by the rules and she worried she might be the one to suffer in the end. So, she was determined to go back to the beginning of the case and start making calls, checking alibis, and talking to all the key players. Just because she didn't cover the initial crime didn't mean she shouldn't still operate as if she were gathering all the information for the first time. Frankly, she didn't want to rely on police or prosecutors for her information, anymore.

Her phone buzzed and she looked down at the screen. "Hey, Lucky."

"How's it going, Bear? You looked like your old self up there. No more nerves?"

"I don't know about that," she said, realizing she *was* nervous—just not about going live in front of millions.

"It looks to me like you're breaking news and taking names, as usual."

"Well, thanks." The street signal changed and Stella crossed at the intersection, her final destination in sight: a crappy little diner, hopefully with cheap food and good coffee.

"How's it going? You don't sound good."

Stella grimaced. "I don't know. It's—you know, it's fine," she said, determined to make it so. "Did I tell you Vindi is here covering the trial for her station in San Diego?"

There was a surprisingly long pause while Lucky processed that information. Finally, he said, "Is anyone else from San Diego covering the trial?"

"No," she said, stifling a groan. She knew he was wondering if John was nearby.

"Well, dang, sounds like a party I wish I was invited to!"

Stella chuckled. "I miss you, Lucky. I don't know how much longer I'll be in Palm Springs, but hopefully I'll be in New York soon and we can meet up."

"Wouldn't miss it, Bear—wouldn't miss it for the world."

Stella disconnected and was about to walk into the diner when she saw Sawyer Harrington, the defendant's brother, standing unusually still, scrutinizing the awning of the restaurant. Here was her chance to start her own reporting. Instead of passing him by, she reached out to tap him on the shoulder. Just before her hand made contact, though, his voice, tight and flat, cut through the air. She pulled back and ducked into the shadows just as he turned, his cell phone pressed to his face.

"It's not about the money, my dear; it's about you not being respectful of my time. That's why all of this is supposed to be laid out in paperwork, per the mediator: so things like this don't happen." His shoulder ticked up to hold his phone in place while he dug a coin out of his pocket and fed the meter. "We should all be able to budget at the beginning of the month. I don't understand how these expenses keep coming up. It can't be that unexpected." He scanned the street and muttered something else about planning ahead before he disconnected. When he turned and slipped his phone into his pocket, his eyes landed on Stella.

She waved, and he forced a smile and said, "I recognize you from the courthouse." Stella simply nodded. "Are you married?" When she shook her head, he said, "Don't do it. These days, you've got a fifty percent chance the marriage will end, and no matter how amicably things start, fully two years after the divorce was finalized, we still argue about whose turn it is to pay for the snack after the kids' soccer games. That phone call cost me more money than the bag of oranges we need to buy for the game, yet here we are, arguing about it."

He looked out over the traffic, and a line between his eyebrows pulsed while he worked out something internally. He then bit his lower lip, his forehead smoothed, and he shrugged. "We all have family issues, though, right?"

She didn't want any more misunderstandings, so she looked at the brother of the murder defendant and said, "I'm Stella Reynolds with NBC News. I was just about to duck in for a quick dinner. Care to join me? We can talk about the case—completely off the record."

She figured he'd decline the invitation. Instead, he looked up at the darkening clouds above and nodded. "Sure, why not?"

After they were seated, each placed their phones on the table in front of them, and a very disinterested waitress poured coffee for them both. Stella grimaced after her first sip. Crappy diner, crappy coffee. She added enough sugar and cream to mask the bitter taste, and when she looked back up from her cup, Sawyer was grinning indulgently at her.

He motioned to her pile of empty cream cups and sugar packets. "You can't cover bad taste."

"True, but sometimes you have to try." She stirred the contents of her cup a few more times, tapped the spoon against the mug, and set it on the coaster before taking another sip. It wasn't much better. She shrugged and then set the cup down. "So, I understand you are a silent partner in Luna C Engineering. How is all of this affecting you?"

He seemed surprised at the question and leaned back in his seat before answering. "You know, since the police, I think you're the first person who has asked about me and not my brother. Once I was crossed off the suspect list, it's like everyone forgot this trial is ruining my life just as much as Preston's."

"How is the trial ruining your life?"

His expression soured at the question. "There's a lot of money on the line, isn't there?"

"How much, exactly?" Stella asked, switching from the bad coffee to ice water. "I've heard everything from 40 million to 400 million."

"Well, that's just it, isn't it? Nobody knows, because the company hasn't gone public, yet. A week before Drew's murder, we had a valuation of three hundred million."

"Three hundred—wow," she said.

"And it was going up by millions every day."

"Now?"

"Now, nobody knows," Sawyer said. "I guess it all depends on how this ends and how long it takes. If Preston gets off, there's a fighting chance we can get right back to where we needed to be— the technology is still there and we're still the only ones who have it. It's just like anything else, though. Now that the other pharmaceutical companies know it's possible, they have a better chance of figuring out how to make it, themselves."

"What is it, exactly?" she asked.

"What's what?"

"What is so new and exciting about your company's drug? There have to be a hundred different anxiety and depression meds on the market, so what makes yours so special?"

He settled back into his seat and took a pill box out of his pocket. "We've done hundreds of clinical trials while developing the drug with no side effects in the target market reported—zero. That's, frankly, unheard of." He popped a handful of pills into his mouth and knocked them back with a swig of coffee. "Vitamins," he explained, holding out the box. "You want some?"

"No," Stella said, working hard to keep the accusation out of her voice. Why would she ever take pills from a stranger?

Before she could read too much into his strange offer, he said, "People are clamoring to get our drug. When we go public—if we go public," he amended darkly, "it's going to be huge. Bigger than Viagra—that's what all the industry insiders are saying."

"Were you guys ready, or...?" The elderly waitress popped her gum as she spoke, and her pen hovered over her notebook. They ordered and, after she walked away, Stella bit her lip. The next question on the tip of her tongue was personal, even for her, especially since there wasn't a camera nearby.

"What?" Sawyer asked, eyeing her suspiciously.

"Where were you?"

"When Drew was killed?" She raised her eyebrows and waited. He took a long sip from his mug and then pierced her with a stare before answering. "I was at the office—my office. My colleagues vouched for me."

"Well, what about your wife?"

"What about her?" Sawyer asked sharply.

"Will she get any of the money if the company goes public?"

"Sure, of course." He wrinkled his nose. "She'll get exactly half of my share—it's all laid out in the divorce decree. We were hoping it would be half of my share of four hundred million, but now we just hope there's a million to split."

At almost identical moments, the screens of their cell phones lit up.

"Court is going back in session?" Stella read her text and looked up at Sawyer.

"Mine says the same," he said, motioning across the room to the waitress for the bill.

It was four thirty in the afternoon. What could have happened to bring the judge, lawyers, and all the other key players back into the courtroom so late? As Sawyer leaned over to get his wallet out of his back pocket, she thought back to one of his earlier comments about their miracle drug having zero side effects in their target market. That must have meant there was a group no longer in their target market that *did* report side effects. She had an old college friend in the FDA who was probably worth giving a call.

By any account, the murder of Drew Chambers had cost Sawyer big—anywhere from a few million to tens of millions and maybe even his marriage. He'd said his divorce had been finalized for more than two years, which put the end of his marriage right around the time his brother was arrested for murder.

Were the arrest and his divorce connected? Had the stress of the situation driven him and his wife apart?

He seemed to be handling it all in stride, but she wondered if he blamed Preston.

18

Sawyer peeled off from Stella when they entered the courthouse, some unspoken rule keeping them apart as they made their way through the security lines and metal detectors. Stella took the stairs and met Vindi in the second floor hallway.

"Where have you been?" her friend asked. "I was looking for you and Woz said he hadn't seen you, either."

"I was having dinner—"

"Dinner? It's not even five, yet!"

"I know, but that's like almost eight my time."

"Your time *is* my time, now," Vindi insisted. "You've been here enough days that you might as well settle in."

"True. I guess it's jetla—"

"Did you hear?" Vindi interrupted.

"Hear what?"

"That Dr. Manuel Ruiz filed a civil suit against CNN."

"Whoa. What—"

"Slander." Vindi held up a sheaf of papers. "He says the reporting using unnamed sources about an arrest that never happened was irresponsible and ultimately damaging to his reputation in a reckless way."

"What is he seeking?"

"Four hundred million dollars."

The figure pulled Stella up short. "Four hundred million? That seems a lot."

"I guess they want to make a statement. Anyway, are you heading in?"

"Sure—I mean, no. I guess I'd better get a copy of this lawsuit from the clerk before they close."

"They closed at four."

"Ah, sh... why are you smiling?"

"Because I got you a copy."

Warmth bloomed inside Stella. It was nice to have a friend again. Sure, she'd had other friends since living in Montana, but there was something amazing about having a reporter friend. Sometimes Stella worked with friendly people, but ultimately they were all hoping for the same exclusive, so things were never quite as chummy or trusting as they were with Vindi.

"Thank you," she said, taking the stack of papers.

"No problem. Let's go." Vindi led the way into the media room and they parted ways, each sitting next to their own camera person.

Woz grunted hello, and they only sat in silence for a few minutes before the judge entered the courtroom next door and called everyone to order.

"I will start," she said, turning away from the camera, "by addressing you, the ladies and gentlemen of the jury. It has come to my attention that some false reports are circulating in the media about various people's guilt or innocence. First, I should say many of the recent reports, specifically on CNN, were erroneous in nature. Second, I worry what this constant and unending barrage of coverage is doing to my jury.

"With that in mind, and after painstaking deliberation with both prosecutors and defense council, I have made the decision to sequester the jury for the remainder of the trial."

A buzzing broke out in the courtroom, and the lone pool cameraman hurried to zoom out his shot to include as much of the courtroom as he could without the members of the jury.

The judge allowed the din to die down on its own, which led Stella to believe much of the grumbling came from the jury, itself—she doubted she would show such restraint in quieting the gallery.

"Ladies and gentlemen, I do not make such a decision lightly. I know this will put a strain on your lives." She looked at her watch. "It is five fifteen. I'll expect you back here at the court house at seven with all of your things. A bus will take you to the hotel tonight. Thank you. Court is in recess until tomorrow morning at nine."

The camera panned to the right, making sure the jury stayed out of frame as they stood and filed out of the room. With the new shot, Stella saw Preston Harrington turn around in his seat to smile victoriously at someone in the back.

Squinting at the small screen that folded out from Woz's camera, she leaned in for a closer view. What was Preston celebrating, and with whom?

She leapt up from her seat and hurried to the door. When she pushed it open, she scanned the hall, hoping she could spot Preston's friend. Did she even know who she was looking for, though?

The first out were the curious—old retirees

who lived in Palm Springs and waited in line every day for the tickets to the trial like some kind of free matinee of entertainment. The lawyers would exit last. In between those two groups, a young woman walked out of the courtroom, oddly out of place.

She moved down the hall alone, toward the elevators. Stella crept forward, keeping her in her sights. She was gorgeous. Tall and slim, she was dressed very precisely with heels, a long, flowy skirt, and a fitted, button-down shirt topped by a feathery cardigan to soften the outfit. A mane of meticulously curled and pinned chestnut-brown hair fell halfway down her back.

"I wonder what kind of product she uses?" Vindi had crept out of the media room and stood by Stella's side, now, watching the girl walk away with similar interest. "Hair doesn't bounce like that on its own—at least, not for me, anyway."

"Who is that?" Stella asked.

"I've never seen her before. She must be a daily," Vindi said, referring to the matinee-watchers.

Stella didn't move until the elevator doors closed on the woman. She then turned, and they walked back into the media room.

Maria Garcia was pacing a short circuit in the corner, talking low and fast on her phone.

"Uh-oh," Stella said, motioning to Vindi. "What's happening there?"

The other reporter shook her head. "Did you hear the judge? It's like he was specifically talking about CNN's bad report—*her* bad report—and then this civil suit? It's safe to say it's been a bad day for Maria Garcia."

"Do you think she's getting... reassigned?"

"Or fired?"

They watched her pace for another minute before Vindi said, "I've got live shots coming up. Are you staying?"

"Nah, I'm going to head back to the hotel. I'll see you there."

"Okay."

Stella lingered by her bag, however, while Woz packed up his gear, her eyes trained on Maria. As the room emptied, the CNN reporter seemed to pay less attention to her volume—or maybe she was just so upset that she didn't notice herself getting louder with each pass in the corner.

"I'm telling you, I did have two sources for the story. I don't—I don't know why they're saying that. They definitely told me it happened. I mean, I saw the handcuffs with my own eyes. Why else would she... Yes, I know it looks bad, but all I can say is my source told me he was under arrest, and then I saw a homicide detective walking him down the hallway in handcuffs. Why would a homicide detective make the arrest, though, if it was just for petty theft? It seemed to make—"

"Ready?" Woz asked, pulling his camera back strap over his shoulder and heaving the tripod off the ground.

Stella nodded, a hollow feeling in her stomach. Had Maria Garcia made a mistake, or was the bad information in her recent report something more sinister?

She nearly ran into Detective McDonald in the hallway outside the media room. The other woman leaned against the wall with a small, satisfied smile. "Can we talk?" Trish asked.

Stella waved to Woz and took out her notebook. "What's going on?" she asked, wondering whether Trish was there to wait for her or to gloat about Maria's fall from grace.

"I hear you're checking alibis."

Stella felt her heartbeat quicken. "Where did you hear that?"

"Sawyer felt you were out of line, so he asked me about it."

Stella shrugged. "Sometimes you've gotta start at the beginning."

"I thought I'd save you some time," Trish said.

She held out a small cassette tape, and Stella took it from her carefully. It looked fragile.

"What is it?"

"It's the full recording of the police interview with Rita Perlman." At Stella's blank look, she elaborated, "The chair of the Rotary Club? She's the one—well, one of many—who confirmed Sloan's alibi."

"Oh."

Trish leaned forward. "I don't want you questioning all these people again. We did our job, you know, after the crime? We checked alibis and cleared people from the pool of suspects. You don't have to redo our work."

Stella heard the defensiveness in the detective's voice. She didn't want to rely on McDonald for information, but she also didn't want to alienate her number one source. "Who was that man—the one who was arrested today?"

The quick change of subject seemed to startle the detective. "He wasn't Manuel Ruiz."

"I know—I saw him—but why did homicide make the arrest if it was just a petty theft case?" She'd understood at least part of what Maria Garcia said on the phone and had to agree that something about the arrest was off.

"I'd have to check." Stella looked pointedly at

the phone in McDonald's hand. "Not now—it's late. I'll get back to you, okay?"

Something stopped her from pressing the issue, but she'd bet that after Maria Garcia's bad report on CNN, everyone in the police department knew the guy's name and why homicide had made the arrest.

Trish pushed away from the wall and headed for a door across from the courtroom. "You didn't get that from me, okay?" She motioned to the small tape.

"Sure," Stella said, watching the detective swipe a badge over a card reader and then push open the newly unlocked door. She disappeared, and Stella looked down at the tape in her hand. What was going on? What game was Trish Mc-Donald playing, and why was Stella part of it?

19

The next morning, Stella's alarm blared at half past five. She groaned and hit snooze. Vindi was right: she was getting used to California time and could no longer convince herself that it felt like half past eight. When the alarm went off again exactly nine minutes later, she remembered why she'd set it in the first place: she had someone to see, and she was running out of time.

She climbed out of bed, threw her hair up in a ponytail, took a quick shower, and then pulled on sweats. She knew it would get up into the seventies that day, but when the sun wasn't up, the desert air turned cold. She grabbed her coat and headed down to the hotel lobby.

"Need a cab?" the doorman asked.

"Sure. I'm headed to the airport."

"No bag?" he asked, checking behind her.

"Nope. I'm not leaving, just visiting."

Minutes later, her cab pulled up to the airport. She probably should have walked—it was that close—but it was early and dark.

"Thanks." She slipped some bills over the seat and climbed out. She'd just caught sight of the Colburne family. Ralph and Aretha were making quite the entrance as they walked in front of the orderlies who pushed Jolene's stretcher.

"Mrs. Colburne! Over here," Stella called, hurrying through the space; she had to catch them before they went through security. The line was short, but they bypassed it entirely, heading to a special entrance where a TSA agent seemed to be waiting for them.

If she'd hit snooze one more time, she would have missed them.

"Such a beautiful airport, isn't it?" Mrs. Colburne said. She looked past the security checkpoint. "Imagine not even needing a roof over the hallways! The weather is that nice here!" Mr. Colburne walked ahead with the stretcher and medical personnel, and they handed paperwork over to the TSA agents.

Past them, Stella saw the open air areas of the airport with tall fences surrounding them. Palm trees swayed and a fresh breeze blew into the enclosed screening checkpoint. It was much different from your typical, institutionalized space.

"I guess the nice weather is the only good thing I'll remember from this whole trip." Aretha shook herself slightly and then turned to Stella. "Thanks for coming out to see us off. I hated to ask, but... well, these are unusual times for us. I found some papers on a corner table in Jolene's room. She won't need them, but I didn't want to just throw them away." Mrs. Colburne handed a stack of papers to Stella. "On top is a page from her planner.

"I'm sorry. Everything seems meaningful to me nowadays, you know? I have especially enjoyed going through her planner, though. She's kept one since middle school. She used to color-code things with different pens. As you can see, those days are long gone, but she was a very meticulous planner. I gave you that page because it seemed to have something to do with the murder case you both— well, you're covering. I hope it helps."

"Thank you, Mrs. Colburne. Good luck."

"You, too, Stella. Remember, take care of yourself."

She watched them walk away and waited until

they disappeared through the double doors before turning around and scanning the area for a coffee shop.

"Room for cream?" asked the smartly-dressed barista in an emerald-green apron.

"Please."

"That'll be six dollars and forty-two cents," the barista said.

Stella had half-forgotten she was in an airport. "Uh, never mind. Sorry." Ignoring the barista's irritated expression, she pivoted and left the airport without the wildly expensive drink. Instead, she walked past the taxi stand and took the long way around the airport parking lot toward her hotel. The sun was so blindingly bright that she stared at the ground as she walked, only able to get three sidewalk squares ahead before it forced her eyes shut. She hoped she might pass a regular, non-airport coffee shop on the way.

Twenty minutes later, settled back in her hotel room with a full cup of perfectly brewed coffee lightened nicely with plenty of cream and sugar, Stella tapped the edge of Jolene's laptop with her pen. She hadn't been able to crack the password and, despite three separate calls to the IT department in New York, she was getting no help. She didn't mind using Woz's computer or writing out scripts out by hand, but the web department had started leaving her angry voicemails about it. Without her script typed into the news program, they had to transcribe all of her live shots and interviews for the network's web and social media stories.

She flipped through the pages Jolene's mother had given her, reading a sentence here and a line there, but not making sense of much.

Eventually, she packed everything up and headed to the bodega, or as she liked to think of it, her home away from home. There were only a few tables set up, and after paying for another cup of coffee from Joe Jones, she found the free Wi-Fi and settled in, determined to crack Jolene's password.

Most people used familiar numbers or names in their passwords, but since Stella didn't know anything about Jolene, she took out her phone and searched the internet for information about the other reporter.

After trying passwords that included her birthday, her mother's maiden name, and the long-dead dog Mrs. Colburne had mentioned days earlier, she was about to give up. She set her phone aside, reassembled the papers strewn about the table, and searched for more that might still be hiding in Jolene's bag. A scrap from her planner fell out, along with the other woman's pillbox.

Stella gave the flat, smooth box a shake and a half-dozen pills rattled inside. She'd just seen an identical container at dinner with Sawyer, but she shrugged and pushed it back into Jolene's bag—she supposed thousands of people had that exact same box. She slipped it back into the bag and noticed a name scribbled in the upper corner of one of Jolene's planner pages. It had nothing to do with the trial, but was written over several times and circled, a little heart squiggled into the lines: Cory+Jolene. Could this be the firefighter her mother had mentioned?

Not expecting much, Stella typed it into the password slot.

She was in!

She looked around victoriously, but the bodega was quiet at that hour—not yet seven in the morning. Grumbling about a lack of fist-bumping options, Stella turned back to her new project and immediately started poking around the news production program. Within just a few clicks, she found some of Jolene's recent stories on the trial and read through them with interest. She was surprised to learn a few things that hadn't come up in her research, yet, like the fact that

Sloan and Drew had looked into adoption before he was killed.

The last script Jolene had written, however, left Stella scratching her head. The sentences didn't make any sense and some of the facts were plain wrong. Overall, it was very sloppy, as if someone who'd never had any schooling in proper grammar had written the story.

She wondered if that final script had anything to do with Jolene checking herself into the hospital. Was it a decision she'd made on her own, or had the managers at the station made the suggestion?

As she pondered that question, Tim ambled into the bodega followed closely by his loyal companion. While he fussed about making a cup of coffee, Hope hopped over to Stella. She scratched her neck and crooned hello to the animal, then felt Tim walk up behind her. He leaned over her shoulder and, for several minutes, read Jolene's last story on the computer screen.

When he stood, he said, "Never going to give you up." Stella's expression must have belied her confusion, because he said it again and then whistled for Hope. The dog jerked to attention and the two walked out into the bright day ahead.

She grabbed her phone off the table and

quickly typed out Tim's words. "That's new," she muttered. "Hey, Joe!"

Joe Jones poked his head around a shelf he was restocking. "What's up, Stella?"

"Have you ever heard of 'rick rolling?'"

He sat back on his heels and looked up at the ceiling. "Why does that sound familiar? Wait," he turned back to her, "it's when people sneak the first letter of that song into their term papers, right?"

"Yeah, it says here that you make the first word of each sentence spell out *Never Gonna Give You Up*."

"Did someone rick roll you?" Joe chuckled as he started refilling the candy on the bottom shelf. "People are nuts. Like, who really has that kind of time? I'll tell you what, if I had that kind of time, I'd be..."

Stella tuned him out and frowned at Jolene's computer. Had Jolene rick rolled a script? She moved the cursor around, adding line breaks between every sentence. Sure enough, hidden in the midst of Jolene's poorly written story, a message began to take shape. When the first letters of the sentences in the script were lined up along the left hand side of the screen, Stella read the new words: *beware the false doctor.*

20

"What does that even mean?" Vindi asked twenty minutes later.

Stella had walked from the bodega back to the hotel and called Vindi to come straight to her room. It was half-past seven in the morning and her friend was still wearing pajamas.

"Well, I don't know. I mean, there are more doctors in this murder trial than lawyers—didn't you say that?"

"Hmm. Are you sure she wasn't talking about the doctors treating *her*?" Vindi said, crossing her arms over her chest and leaning against the wall with a yawn. "I mean, you said yourself that, according to her mother, she'd been messing with her meds. It makes more sense to me that she was talking about one of her own doctors. Maybe she was feeling a little paranoid or something?"

"Why would she have hidden it in a *news* script?"

Vindi stared at her for a beat, her eyes open wide, as if Stella was missing something obvious. "Uh, because she's a total mental case who just had to be flown home by her parents for full-time treatment?"

"That doesn't mean she's incapable of seeing what's going on around her," Stella said, thinking specifically of Tim. He only spoke in song titles, lyrics, or famous quotes, yet he'd spotted the secret message in seconds.

"Who's to say it's actually a warning?" Vindi said, unwrapping one of the plastic-covered cups from the service tray on the desk. "I mean," she walked over to the sink, "maybe it was just a coincidence."

Stella shot a look at her. "A coincidence? I looked over the last ten scripts on her computer and then pulled up the last fifteen from our newscast last night. The only other phrase I found using the first letters of adjacent sentences was *I Jobs McGee,* and I'm not sure that counts."

Vindi raised her eyebrows and Stella smiled.

"It was a story about Ian McKellen coming to the Jesuit school in Ohio," she said. "I'll spare you the script, but the sentences actually spelled out words —if you count 'McGee' as a word..."

Vindi set the cup down and started to open one of the coffee pods from the same service tray when her hand stopped halfway through tearing the packet open. "What's that?" She pointed to the small cassette tape McDonald had handed her the afternoon before.

"Oh, I kind of forgot about it." Vindi continued to stare at her, so she added, "I actually don't really know what it is. I can't find a machine to play it back on."

"Who's it from?"

"Detective McDonald."

Vindi's face flushed red and she groaned. "What's on it?"

Stella bit her lip. Her friend's body was suddenly tense, with waves of anger emanating from her very core. "Uh... she told me it would confirm Sloan's alibi. Like I said, though, I can't find anything to play it back on."

Vindi turned on her heel. "I'm going back to my room to get ready. Good luck with that doctor beware business."

"Wait, Vindi, don't be like that. It's only—"

"Don't! Just don't try to justify the fact that, somehow, you come to town and, three days later, have managed to make better sources than I've made in three *years* here! Do you know how many times I've put in interview requests at the jail and knocked on Sloan Chambers' door? It's just so infuriating. There, I said it. You are infuriating." She pulled the door open roughly and it rebounded off the doorstop and nearly slammed shut again before Vindi caught it, opened it more carefully, and stalked through.

Stella watched the door swing closed with a sinking feeling. She didn't blame Vindi for being upset, but she wished her friend had given her a chance to explain.

She didn't think Detective McDonald was doing her any favors. In fact, she was convinced that Trish had set Maria Garcia up with that look-alike perp-walk. She didn't know what game the detective was playing, but she was certain that she, herself, would come out the loser if she wasn't careful.

She sighed again and finally pushed herself off the bed. Woz didn't have anything that could play the small tape—the kind you'd expect to find in an old analog dictation recorder—so she'd made an appointment with a business in town that might have a playback deck that would work. She wanted to know what Detective McDonald had given her, and then she could try to figure out why.

She picked up Vindi's cup and set it back on the tray, and then moved the coffee pod still halfway inside its wrapper into the trash can.

After she'd searched the floor and behind the desk, however, she finally realized the tape from Detective McDonald was gone.

Vindi had taken it.

~

"I don't know, would you call that theft?" Lucky asked.

Stella glowered at her phone and said, "She took something that wasn't hers without asking. I think that's kind of the textbook definition."

"But why?"

"It's cut-throat here, to be honest." She stepped off the curb to cross a deserted street. The light was green, but there wasn't a car in sight, so she thought she could risk it. "I guess I just didn't expect it from her."

"What did you expect?"

"Sunshine and rainbows, of course."

Lucky chuckled. "I wish I could come out. I've got a thing tomorrow. Maybe after?"

Her heart leapt at the offer, but she bit her lip, not wanting to sound desperate. "I mean, if you're sure you have time."

There was a long pause on the other end. Lucky finally said, "That wasn't exactly the answer I was hoping for."

"Oh, Lucky, you know what I mean. I just—" she cut herself off. She'd only been in one other relationship in her adult life, and it had ended after a rather short, disastrous attempt at long-distance dating. Was this relationship doomed, as well? "I would love that, Lucky. I just don't want you to feel—"

"To feel like what, Stella? Like I want to see my girlfriend?"

"I just—I'm not sure how I see this working sometimes, you know?"

"Where is this coming from?" Lucky asked, exasperated. "I call to say good morning and suddenly we're discussing our future? Is there something you're not telling me—*someone* you're not telling me about?"

"No! God, no, Lucky, of course not. I—I'm sorry. I'm just out of sorts."

"Then save any future discussions or thoughts about our relationship until I'm there and we can talk them out in person, okay?"

"Okay," she said.

"I love you. No matter where you are or where I am, I love you."

"Me, too, Lucky. Me, too."

They disconnected and Stella rested the phone against her chin, waiting for her blood to stop rushing through her ears. She didn't doubt Lucky, but the distance between them was challenging. The farther apart they were physically, the farther apart emotionally she felt from her boyfriend.

Even after a few calming breaths, though, the low, thrumming sound continued. She looked to her right and saw a pickup truck. The sound she'd thought was blood rushing in her ears was actually the hum of an engine. With a startled gasp, she saw that she was standing in the middle of the street while a very tolerant driver sat in his truck, stopped in the middle of the intersection several feet away, waiting for her to finish her call.

She dropped her phone into her bag and stammered out an apology. "I—I'm so sorry!" she called, hustling off the street and up onto the sidewalk, looking back with a last, apologetic wave.

"There's only one person I'd wait for so patiently," the driver said. She shielded her eyes against the sun and looked back toward the incredibly familiar voice. The driver leaned out the window and smiled, his blue-gray eyes twinkling in the sunlight. "And it's you."

21

A horn blared behind them and John Stevenson waved in apology to the other driver as he pulled over to the side of the road.

As he unfolded himself from behind the wheel, Stella forced herself not to sigh. He was tall, like Lucky, but where Lucky was lean and rangy, John was all muscle and brawn. He walked forward, they hugged, and she breathed in his familiar aftershave. It was something woodsy, like cedarwood, with light lavender thrown in at the end.

"Must have been bad." He pulled back to look Stella over from head to toe.

"Hmm?" He hadn't changed a bit in the last

few years, except that his dark hair might have been a bit longer now. One wavy lock escaped the rest and she tamped down the urge to fix it.

"That phone call," he said. "I've never seen someone stop in their tracks before. Is everything okay? Your family's all right?"

"Oh," Stella said, feeling her cheeks heat up. "Yes—no, yes," she finally said with a self-conscious laugh. "Everyone's just fine.

"Did Blanche ever go back to work? I was just thinking about her the other day for some reason."

Stella smiled, more pleased than she should have been that her family had been in his thoughts. "No, my sister is still home. She's half-convinced she's going to start home-schooling the kids. What are you doing here?" she asked, changing the subject. "Don't you anchor the news in San Diego in..." she looked at her watch, "about eight hours?"

"Not tonight. I'm taking a few days off up here at my cabin."

"You have a vacation home?" she asked. "In Palm Springs?"

He nodded. "My sister and I bought it after I signed my last contract. It seemed like I was going to be here for a while and thought it'd be nice to get away from time to time, and she wanted somewhere to take the kids. So, here I am."

"Here you are."

They stared at each other for a few long moments before John spoke again. "How's the trial going?"

"Oh, it's... meh," she said, looking at her watch again.

"You're late for something?"

"No, it's just... well, yeah, I have an appointment."

"What are you doing for dinner?" He stepped close again.

"Vindi and I have plans," she said automatically, not trusting herself to be alone with John. At his disappointed look, though, she blurted out, "You should join us!"

"I don't want to impose."

"No, it'll be fun to all catch up."

"No one will mind?"

She thought he might be asking about Lucky, but she purposefully misunderstood him. "I know Vindi will be glad to see you."

She gave him the details and then they stood awkwardly, staring at each other for a moment.

"I'll see you tonight, Stella."

"Yes. Tonight."

He didn't move, so she finally turned and walked into the shop. As soon as she was inside, though, she hurried to the window. He continued to stare at the door though which she'd disappeared, and his small smile grew bigger before he shook his head slowly and climbed back into his truck.

"Can I help you?" The wheezy voice came from behind her, and she turned to find an older, greying, portly man standing behind a long counter.

She gave John's departing pick-up one last look and then said, "Yes, I have an appointment with Dale Baker?"

"That's me," he said, retying the string of a faded, maroon apron around his middle and walking out from behind the register. "You must be Stella Reynolds." She smiled and explained what she was looking for. "We have just what you need. Probably something like this?" He waddled over to a wall of boxes on the far side of the shop and pulled down a small recorder. His breathing was labored, like the short walk across the room had been a marathon.

She inspected the device, popped open the tape door, and tried to picture if the cassette McDonald had given her would fit.

"Where's the tape?" Dale asked, obviously thinking along the same lines as Stella. He held out a hand. "Let's make sure it'll fit."

"I don't have it... here," she finished with a frown.

"Well, that wasn't very smart, now was it?"

She grinned at his honest assessment of the situation. "No, it wasn't," she agreed. "How much?"

He pressed a few buttons on the register, and five minutes later, she was the proud owner of a small tape recorder.

Stella wanted nothing more than to head back to Vindi's hotel room and demand she return the tape so she could find out what exactly McDonald had given her, but if she didn't hurry, she was going to be late for court—again.

At a main intersection downtown, she flagged down a taxi and managed to make up some time. She walked into the media room with five minutes to spare and made a beeline for Vindi, but her friend spoke first.

"Where have you been? I brought your tape upstairs with me because I had a playback machine I thought would work. Perfect fit!" she said, holding out the device.

Stella's emotions were at war. She wasn't sure

she trusted the sunshiny smile on Vindi's face—
that girl didn't grin like that about anything.

"What?" Vindi asked a little too innocently.

"Did you listen to it?"

"No! It's yours. I mean, I'd like to know what it
says, but you get first crack."

"So you don't know what's on it?"

Vindi had the grace to blush. "Okay, fine. I listened to it. It's just that old woman from the Rotary Club confirming Sloan's alibi. That's it. I don't
know why McDonald felt you should have it—it's
not even worth mentioning." Stella frowned.
"Okay, I'm sorry! Gah," Vindi was at a loss for
words. "I was wrong. I'm sorry I snapped... and
took your tape. That was a crappy thing to do."

Stella tucked the tape and playback device into
her bag before looking back at her friend. "It's
okay. I'm sorry I signed you up to run interference
between me and John at dinner tonight."

"What?" Vindi's voice was so loud that several
photographers in the room glanced over.

She grinned. "He was driving by and stopped
when he saw me." She decided to leave out the
part about stopping in the middle of the street
during a quasi-argument on the phone with
Lucky.

"Stella, he lives more than two hours away and

knew you were here. He wasn't just driving by—he went out of his way to find you."

"No, it's not like that. He owns a home here."

"That doesn't matter—it just makes his story more believable. What does Lucky think about all of us getting together?" Vindi asked.

"What does he think about a group of friends getting together to reminisce?" Stella said, inspecting her fingernails.

"Sure. You keep telling yourself that, Reynolds."

The speakers in the room creaked to life. "All rise. The Honorable Catherine Jenkins presides."

Vindi and Stella parted ways, each heading to their own photographer to watch the day's proceedings and take notes.

The judge called in the jury and then spent several minutes asking them about their hotel accommodations. It was tedious.

Off-camera, they heard one of the jurists complain about the TV options in the hotel. Another wondered why there were waffles in the breakfast buffet but not hard-boiled eggs.

Stella couldn't believe it when she saw Preston Harrington turn to his attorney and roll his eyes at the fuss. Was he completely unaware of how he was coming across to everyone, or did he just not care? It was curious, but his behavior almost confirmed his claim of innocence. It stood to reason that someone trying to get away with a crime would put more effort into not looking so guilty. The more she watched him, the more she realized that Preston wasn't a jerk—well, maybe he was, but that wasn't all. He was angry for being put on trial for a crime he didn't commit.

"Why is the jury leaving?" she whispered to Woz when the camera zoomed out. What had she missed while she'd been studying Preston Harrington's behavior?

"She said she wants to talk to council."

After the jury filed out, the judge said, "As per the defendant's motion filed late yesterday afternoon as to whether the information about Sloan Chambers' relationship with Dr. Manuel Ruiz can be shared with the jury, I have made a decision."

Preston leaned forward, looking interested in the proceedings for the first time in days.

"Mr. Yarley," the judge addressed Harrington's lawyer, "your brief does not conclusively show that the relationship began before Mr. Chambers' death, therefore it does not meet the criteria set forth before the start of the trial. Because of that, I will not allow it to be introduced to the jury during this trial."

"That is bullshit!" Preston said. He didn't shout, but he certainly didn't whisper, either. The words rang across the room as if he were wearing a microphone.

Bang, bang, bang. Judge Jenkins' gavel slammed against the sound block on the bench. "You are out of order, Mr. Harrington. I will not allow that kind of language in my courtroom."

"That's bullshit," Preston repeated, "and I'm so tired of all of the bullshit in this courtroom, I just can't take it, anymore. Big. Bull. Shit." He punctuated his final words by pointing first at the judge, next at Gail Abingdon, and finally at his own lawyer, who had his head cradled in his hands.

"You are in contempt, Mr. Harrington. Bailiff, get him out of here."

22

As the courtroom erupted, the local reporters around Stella did, too. She looked at the clock hanging over the door: it was still early enough that some of the marathon four-hour-long morning newscasts were still going strong on air. Several reporters grabbed the tapes from their cameras and left the room, headed for their live trucks, while their respective photographers clambered to put new discs into the cameras.

Maria Garcia, Stella only then noticed, was nowhere to be found. The CNN photographer sat alone in the corner.

Stella opened her laptop and sent a message to Sher about the new developments, and then sat back and waited, curious to see what would happen next.

The judge, her face scarlet, banged her gavel again after Preston was led out of the courtroom in handcuffs. "Order, order. Council, please approach the bench."

Yarley and Gail Abingdon walked to the judge. She held a hand over the microphone and the court stenographer sat back, flexing his fingers during the break.

The trio muttered for a few minutes before they broke apart. Judge Jenkins said, "Bailiff, please call the jury back in." When they were seated several minutes later, she said, "Ladies and gentleman, I'm sorry to say we will need to take a brief recess—"

General groaning broke out in the courtroom, and the judge started to pick up her gavel again before she realized it was the jury making the noise. She held up a calming hand and said, "I know how frustrating it can be to feel like your time is being wasted, but I assure you the wheels of justice are still moving. Sometimes those wheels have to move outside of this courtroom. We will adjourn until after lunch." She then picked up her gavel and banged it once.

"Where did they take Harrington?" Stella

asked. A roomful of photographers shrugged at almost the exact same moment. She bit back a smile and then headed out to the hallway, hoping to find someone who could answer her questions.

Harrington's lawyer was just leaving the courtroom as she passed. "Mr. Yarley, can you tell me what's happening to your client right now?"

"He's cooling off in an office space one floor down," he said, wiping his brow with a handkerchief. The woman Stella had noticed the day before—the meticulously dressed one with gorgeous hair—walked out of the courtroom and waved at Yarley. He grimaced and muttered, "Off the record, he needs to spend a little more time worrying about his own future and less time about someone else's."

Stella frowned. "If Sloan or her new love interest had something to do with the murder, though, he should be worried."

The lawyer closed his eyes and then nodded slowly. "Yes, you're right, of course." He wadded the handkerchief back into his breast pocket and spent a moment tucking the corners in. Others leaving the courtroom streamed past, flooding the elevators and stairwell. Finally, when they were mostly alone, he looked up. "My client will take a moment to cool down, and then we'll have a hearing after lunch, when I'll encourage him to apologize to the judge. After that, hopefully we'll be ready to move on with the case. Good day."

He strode past Stella, but his face remained pinched and closed off until the elevator doors closed.

His reaction when she'd mentioned Sloan had confused her: he'd looked surprised. If that's not whose future Harrington was concerned with, though, then whose was it? She was missing something and it felt like she wasn't the only one. What was Harrington hiding?

~

"So, Stella, it sounds like a rocky start to the court proceedings today, but they got back on track?"

She fought the urge to shield her eyes from the intense light that Terry was beaming at her face, and instead answered *Hank-freaking-Smith's* question. "That's right, Hank, after an extended morning recess during which Preston Harrington was held in contempt of court and told by the judge that she would add ninety days onto any potential sentence handed down by the jury for every future outburst he has in the courtroom."

"Now that the prosecution has rested their case, what's next?"

"Because the jury is sequestered, there won't be a weekend off. Defense will be presenting their side of the case first thing tomorrow morning."

"On a Saturday?"

"That's right, Hank."

"Stella Reynolds, live for us in Palm Springs, California, tonight. Thank you."

"Clear." She nodded to Woz through the camera, disconnected her ear piece, and turned the microphone switch to the "off" position.

"I hear there's a party tonight?" Terry nonchalantly took the camera off the tripod and carefully placed it on the ground.

"A party?" Stella asked. "Where?"

"I overheard your pretty friend, Vindi, talking to her photographer. Mind if I join in?"

Stella's eyebrows nearly lifted off her forehead. Did Terry like Vindi? "Oh—uh..." She wanted Vindi's full attention that night, which wouldn't happen if there was an attractive, available man at their table. "You know, we're just meeting with an old friend we both used to work with. It'll probably be kind of boring. You know how it is—so many inside stories..."

Terry looked up hopefully. "Sounds fun! I'm

getting tired of hanging out with the retirees at the hotel bar. What time?"

"Uhhhh," she said, feeling trapped. "I'm not sure. I'll let you know, okay?"

He gave her his number and she tucked it into her purse. She had three hours to wait until Vindi was done for the day, so she headed back to the hotel and showered, telling herself the whole time that she wasn't "getting ready" for anything—just cleaning up after a long day at work.

She took extra care to pick out a flattering out-fit, though, and dried her hair until it was shiny and straight. She then added lipstick, blush, and earrings.

To assuage her guilty conscious, she dialed Lucky's number. The call went straight to his voicemail, so she left an upbeat message about how she couldn't wait to see him in just a couple of days.

Afterward, feeling unaccountably nervous, she headed to the hotel bar and ordered a glass of wine.

"It's happy hour, you know. If you're going to drink more than one glass, it makes sense to just order the whole bottle. Cheaper that way, ya know?" The bartender was in her fifties, with short, grey hair, and by the way a half-dozen older men were staring at her, she had her work cut out for her that night.

"Oh, okay, sure. Trudy, is it?" she asked, reading the woman's name tag. "Let's do a bottle of the house Sauvignon Blanc."

The bartender left to fill her order just as her cell phone buzzed on the table: it was Lucky. She reached out but her fingers froze a few inches from the device. It rang again, and then a third time, and she finally hit the "dismiss" icon on the screen. She was too amped up to talk, but she refused to think about why.

The bartender went through an extended process of opening the bottle and presenting the cork to Stella. Just as she waved it off, a shadow fell over her.

"I wondered if you'd be here early." John sat down in the open seat to Stella's right. "Mind if I join you?"

23

The wine flowed freely, and Stella had fun for the first time since boarding the plane for Palm Springs a week earlier.

"Worst on-screen flub?" she asked, setting her wine glass down so roughly that some liquid sloshed over the side. Had the table moved? She eyed it accusingly and then refocused on John as he swooped in with a napkin and dabbed it up.

"Let's see... first job or after?"

"After, of course. How could we ever order the Montana mess-ups? That's all we'd be talking about."

"Hmm. Okay, then, I'd have to go with Knoxville. I was anchoring after that explosion—"

"When the microphone kept cutting on and off?" Stella giggled at the memory.

"I swear someone in the control room was mad at me," John said with a grin, "because the microphone clipped on and off with such precision, people at home heard me say—"

"'The sex explosion injured two firefighters and a dog,'" Stella said robotically with long, pregnant pauses mixed in.

John burst out laughing. "That's awful. Those key words about the sex *shop* explosion, *three employees were* injured, and two firefighters *rescued a cat* and *a bird inside but not* a dog. I still get emails from a woman whose grandmother was so shocked that she passed out from the imagery!"

Stella snickered. "Yeah, I'll bet that's why she still emails." John's gaze rested on the tears of laughter pooling in the corners of her eyes. His half-smile made her bite her lip at the surfacing memories.

"I'm proud of you, Stella. You're tearing it up. I knew you would, but it's great to see."

She smiled at the praise. "You're no slouch, yourself! Main anchor in San Diego? That's a great market. You could stay there forever and be happy, John. No more moving around, no more uncertainty."

"I could," he said, a wistful look on his face, "but—"

"You couldn't wait for me?" Vindi said, plopping down on Stella's left. "Is it still happy hour? I could use a drink or three. Hey, hey, hey," she said, grabbing the bottle of wine and motioning to the bartender for a glass. "No lovey-dovey stuff, okay? At least, not until I down half of this baby."

Seeing Vindi reminded Stella about the fourth person joining their party that night. "Oh, I forgot. Terry was asking about you."

"Terry?" Vindi said a little too innocently. "Who's that?"

"My photographer? Not the old one, but the young, um, kind of fitter one?"

"A fit photographer?" John said. "This I've gotta see."

"Well, that's what I'm trying to say: you're gonna. He wanted to hang out with you tonight, Vindi."

"That's okay, right?" Terry said, appearing between the two women. "Hi," he looked down at Vindi with the greeting, and she covered the blush that quickly spread across her cheeks by downing half a glass of wine in one sip.

Things only got worse from there.

Two hours and three bottles of wine later, the

group was laughing louder than anyone else in the bar.

John looked at his watch. "It's late. Don't you two have to work tomorrow?"

"You mean us three?" Terry said, but John ignored him.

"Ack, don't remind me," Vindi groaned, finishing the last swallow of wine in her glass. "Should we get one more, guys?"

Stella reached for the menu, but her hand knocked into her empty glass, which tumbled over the edge of the table to the ground, mercifully not breaking when it hit the carpet. When she leaned over to retrieve the glass, however, she knocked her purse off the bar, spilling its contents.

"Crap," she muttered, hopping off the chair to collect her things. When she picked up her phone, she saw two more missed calls from Lucky, and suddenly her giddy enjoyment of the evening started to dissipate. She stood and swayed at the suddenness of the movement. "No! No more wine. I think it's time to go."

"I'll walk you to your room," John offered, standing just as quickly.

"You're not driving home tonight, are you?" Stella leaned against the bar for support. "Can you take a taxi?"

"How would I get my truck tomorrow?" he asked.

"Another taxi?" she suggested, rubbing her hand over her forehead. "Or you could just stay here." She was surprised when John nodded.

"Yeah, sounds good," he said, his smile oddly wistful as they headed toward the elevators.

"Stella!" Vindi called. She turned back to find her friend sitting on Terry's lap. "Be good!"

A snicker rose into her nose and she snorted. "Vindi is so bad," she said, leading John into the lobby. She pressed the call button, and they leaned against the wall while they waited for their ride.

"What happened, do you think?" John asked.

She sobered a bit as they stood under the bright lights of the lobby. "To us?" she asked, instinctively knowing what he was asking about.

"Yes. I think about it a lot, actually—what went wrong and what I should have done differently. I'm not sure what would have made the difference. Have you thought about it—about us?"

Stella gulped and was glad for a moment to collect her thoughts when the elevator doors opened and a crowd got off.

"Well... Katie, obviously," she said, looking reproachfully at her ex as they stepped into the small, intimate space.

"Katie only happened because you left Montana."

"I left Montana because I lost my job. I was there for the job, and then the job... wasn't there."

They were standing so close that she had to work to keep John in focus. His expression was tender but also open. She knew right then that she could hurt him badly if she wasn't careful.

"When you left Montana, you also left me. It hurt. I shouldn't have let it, but I did."

"I'm not sure... I'm not sure what I could have done differently. You were locked into a contract and I was unemployed. I—I—"

"I guess I just wish that we'd tried harder."

She nodded, and when the elevator doors opened, she stepped off the car first.

As they walked down the hall toward her room, she realized what she'd said to John was true: long distance is hard, but it can work out if both people really try to make it work. They got to her door and she took out the key card and handed it over. "Let me just get a few things."

John's eyebrows shot up. "You're going to... get your things?"

"Well, yeah. I'll just get what I need and sleep in Vindi's room. I don't want you driving, tonight John. Right?"

He leaned against the wall with his arms crossed and slowly nodded. "Right. You're right." She grabbed her nightgown and toothbrush and then saw the cassette tape and the playback device she'd bought earlier that day. She shoved all of it in her briefcase and slung the bag over her shoulder.

"I do miss you, John—too much, if I'm being honest."

"I miss you, too, Stella. Too much."

He opened his arms and she walked into them, breathing in the embrace like it was their final goodbye. It felt right and wrong at the same time, and after a moment, she stepped away.

"Goodbye, John. I'll see you..." Later would likely be a long time, but tomorrow was too soon. "I guess I'll see you," she said.

They stood on opposite sides of the threshold, staring at each other, and although they were only a foot apart, it felt like miles.

With a final, emotional sigh, Stella turned and went back the way she'd come. As she stepped onto the elevator, she felt as if she'd traveled years in the span of several minutes.

She'd done the right thing—of course she had —but she felt an undeniable sadness at the finality of saying goodbye to John when that evening had just proven how great they could be together.

When the elevator doors opened again, she stepped into the lobby just in time to see Vindi and Terry walk into the elevator across the aisle. As she watched them holding hands and kissing, she didn't think *they* were going to say goodbye at the door.

"Well, crap," Stella said, realizing she was homeless for the night. "Now what?"

24

Nothing had a sobering effect at half past midnight after sharing four bottles of wine amongst three friends quite like having nowhere to go at a hotel.

The person working the front desk assured her there were no extra rooms at the hotel that night, and although she briefly considered heading out in search of a room at another hotel, she ultimately decided against wandering the streets of Palm Springs alone after dark.

She called Lucky back, but he didn't answer, and she didn't leave a message.

With nothing else to do, she headed back to the bar to order some food before they closed for the night. After she finished the extra-large order of French fries, two Tylenol, and two large glasses of water, she decided to sort out her options.

She used the bathroom off the lobby to brush her teeth and wash her face, and then headed back into the main entrance of the hotel.

She found the most comfortable-looking seat and, with a screech of metal against wood, she pulled a large, heavy coffee table closer. She then walked to the self-serve hot beverage station by the concierge's desk and made a cup of tea. Back at the couch, she put her feet up and took out Jolene's laptop—*her* laptop. Still feeling slightly fuzzy with the beginnings of what was sure to be a raging headache by morning, she powered up the device and stared at the message Jolene had left behind.

Beware the false doctor.

She opened a new document and typed out all the doctors involved in the Drew Chambers murder trial.

Drew Chambers.

Sloan Chambers.

Preston Harrington.

Sawyer Harrington.

Were there others? To be thorough, she wrote "Jolene's doctor" on one line. With a flash of insight, she remembered Sloan's new boyfriend, Manuel Ruiz, also fit the bill.

Beware the false doctor.

Was Jolene saying one of the doctors wasn't really a doctor, or that one of the doctors involved in the murder trial was lying? The latter seemed more reasonable, but she figured it would be easy enough to check off the first potential claim as well. Using the free Wi-Fi in the hotel, she researched each of the five doctors. She'd have to call Jolene's mother in the morning to get the names of the doctors treating the reporter.

After she got past current news articles about the murder trial, she easily confirmed that Sloan Chambers had been back to speak to her alma mater several times. Articles from university publications called her Dr. Sloan Chambers, used her maiden name, and even included her graduation years.

The same was true for Drew Chambers, and in this new slate of articles, she saw the Chambers family had donated large quantities of money to their respective universities. Good alum, Stella thought, copying the information over to her research document.

Dr. Manuel Ruiz also had a long and illustrious speaking circuit dating back many years. Several articles about his company listed his medical school, but she couldn't find anything online from that university extolling the virtues of their famous graduate. She diligently wrote down the registrar's phone number and made a note to call in the morning to confirm the year of his graduation.

Researching the Harrington brothers proved to be more difficult. She couldn't find any information about where they went to medical school referenced in any of the online articles, and they weren't listed as major donors to any universities. In fact, until this murder trial, they didn't seem to exist—at least, online.

She wrote down phone numbers for the Medical Board of California and the state licensing agency, both of which she'd call in the morning. She rubbed her eyes, exhausted and unsure of what to do. She finally wrote a quick email to her friend at the FDA and then closed down her computer.

The longer she sat on the couch, the more uncomfortable it became. The lobby was deserted now, the bar long-closed, and even the overnight hotel check-in clerk was nowhere to be seen.

She must have dozed off for a bit, because the next thing she knew, she was jerking awake with the ding of an arriving elevator car. She looked over and locked eyes with Terry as he stepped confidently into the lobby.

"Goodnight, Stella," he said with a grin. He swaggered out of the hotel and disappeared into the night, making Stella wonder where NBC was putting him up, if not at this hotel. She started to call after him to ask but stopped—she didn't want to have to talk about what had likely just happened up in Vindi's hotel room.

She picked up her cell phone and dialed Vindi. "You dog," she said when her old roommate picked up.

"*You* dog," Vindi said back with palpable exuberance. "May I remind you that I am perfectly unattached, unlike *some* people who just got lucky? Oh," Stella could almost see her wince. "Bad word choice, sorry." After a pause, she recovered some of her earlier glee. "I knew it was going to happen, and I'll be honest, I was hoping it would. You and John are *right* together, Stella, you always have been. Don't tell me you're getting cold feet now! It's too late."

"It's not too late," she said with an attempt at a chuckle. It sounded sad, even in her own ears, and she cleared her throat. "I said goodnight to John at my door and let him sleep in my room."

"Well, where are you sleeping, then?"

"I was planning to sleep in your room... but it became clear that wasn't going to work. I've been in the lobby since quarter to one."

"Where is John?"

"Upstairs, in my room."

"You've been in the lobby?"

"All night."

"You have not!"

"I have!" Stella's voice echoed creepily through the empty lobby. She lowered it to add, "I'm still sitting in the lobby with nowhere to sleep, but I just happen to know you have a recent opening in your bed. I mean, room." She grinned.

There was a long pause while Vindi took in that information. "Come on up. I'll leave the door unlocked."

"Yes!" Stella quickly gathered her things. It was three-fifteen in the morning—only six hours until court would be back in session and probably five hours until she could start making calls about the various doctors in the case and get some answers.

25

The clock said 7:03 when Stella pried one eye open and saw a blurry image of Vindi sitting up in the other bed. She had wild hair and a ripple across her cheek where the sheet had pressed against her face. She reached for a glass of water on the nightstand as Stella successfully opened her other eye.

"You look like hell," she said, eyeing Stella over her drink.

"Back at ya." Stella pushed herself up. It was the latest she'd managed to sleep since arriving in California. Unsurprisingly, she felt less than rested.

She stood unsteadily, downed the glass of

water she'd filled and left on the nightstand the night before, and said, "I should stick with beer."

"Why's that?" Vindi asked. She walked to the dresser where two bottles of water sat on a tray and moaned, "Five dollars each?" She unscrewed the cap, took a sip, and sighed. "Totally worth it." She continued sipping the water like it was fine wine and waited for Stella to answer.

"Beer fills you up—you can only drink so much before you're done. Wine is like water. You just... keep going."

"Huh." Vindi said, looking at herself in the mirror. "I don't know about that, but I do know I need a shower... and a toothbrush... and maybe like, a cheeseburger?"

Stella laughed and then grabbed her head. "Aack." With a slight rattle, something landed on the bed next to her. She forced her eyes back open and saw a bottle of Tylenol lying next to her. "Thanks," she said, popping two in and drowning them with half a glass of water.

"I guess I'll go kick John out. I need to get ready, too." Stella pulled on her clothes from the night before, stuffed everything else back into her bag, and gently closed the door behind her. She trudged to the elevators and pressed the down button.

She winced at the ding announcing the elevator car's arrival and rode down to her floor, but when she rounded the corner, she froze.

Lucky stood by her door, his fist raised high, about to knock. She opened her mouth to call out a warning, but before she could land on anything to say that would make sense, his fist made contact.

She stood rooted to the floor, her mouth open. *Oh, God.*

The door—her door—slowly opened, and John's deep voice said, "Oh. Hello, Lucky."

Lucky froze for several long moments and then stepped back to look at the door number. "I—I thought... I thought this was Stella's room."

"It is."

Just then, the door to the stairwell on the far side of the hallway opened and Terry walked out. He looked no worse for wear after a late night of wine and Vindi, and his muscles rippled in a tight, white T-shirt. "Hey, man," he said to Lucky, before he looked to John. "Is she in there? I have a question for her."

"Who are you?" Lucky asked, looking critically at the new arrival.

"I work with Stella. Who are you?" His tone turned aggressive.

"Are you... are you Woz?" Lucky's face had gone from pale to a rapidly reddening hue as he looked at the two men in front of him.

"No, man, I'm her photographer, Terry. Nice to meet you." He held out a hand, but Lucky stared at it like it was alien and Terry finally dropped it to his side.

"I'm apparently gravely mistaken in coming out here this morning," Lucky finally said. He backed away from the door, turned, and headed directly for Stella. It took a moment for her presence to register, but when it did, his expression darkened considerably.

"You," he said, coming to a stop several feet away. He looked at the hotel doors on either side of them and lowered his voice. "I'd ask you to explain, but I'm not even sure where you'd start. Old, sweaty photographer? That lie now seems to be the least of my concerns when I fly out to surprise you and find an ex-boyfriend in your room. Maybe he's not so ex, or are you going to tell me that's not your room?" He stopped, waiting for her to answer.

"Lucky, it's not what it looks like." It was all she could think to say when almost anything else about her night, she knew, would be both hard to believe and upsetting.

"I guess I'm glad to hear that, because it *looks* like I've been an idiot. It *looks* like you're not the person I thought you were. It *looks* like things are over—and have been for a while."

Stella's mind wasn't up to the challenge of refuting Lucky's claims. Her brain was still foggy from the wine and she felt like he was on fast forward while she was stuck on pause. "I..."

"I thought we agreed: no fading away and no moving on without telling the other person. After less than a week—not even five full days—you just totally give up on—"

"Thanks, Stella," John interrupted as he walked by wearing his rumpled clothes from the day before and a grin. "It was great to see you. Let's do this again."

Stella's entire body went cold. How could he do this to her? "John!" she snapped, the fog finally lifting. "Don't make it look—"

"I've always loved the beds at hotels," he added while smirking at Lucky. "You never know what it's going to be like. Springy? Bouncy? It adds to the excitement."

"Now that's just completely out of line," Stella said, ignoring the pounding in her head. "John Stevenson, you tell Lucky right now that you slept in my room alone after we had too much to drink last night and that I slept in Vindi's room."

John's step faltered. She'd hurt his ego, but dammit, he was trying to end her relationship with Lucky over something that hadn't even happened!

When he turned back around, she expected him to look hurt or maybe even angry. Instead, he looked victorious. "Terry," he called past them to the photographer, "where did you sleep last night?"

The photographer looked between all three, confused. He glanced at Stella, his expression torn.

Lucky cleared his throat. "Do you have anything that would shed some light on this situation? If you do, by all means, don't hold back now."

"Well, I *was* with Vindi last night," Terry finally said.

Lucky sucked in a breath and cut his eyes to Stella. His entire countenance had been angry until a moment ago—he'd been practically vibrating with barely-suppressed rage—but with Terry's few words, his whole body fell and he stepped away from Stella, as if he'd been knocked back by a bullet.

"Oh, Stella," he said, taking another few steps away from her. He clapped a hand to his chest,

"My heart." He turned, walked past Terry, and then disappeared into the stairwell.

Stella's knees felt weak. She'd been struck mute by Lucky's expression, but when John cleared his throat, her mind started working over-time. She whirled on her ex, who was grinning at the stairwell door, and pushed against his chest with both hands. He stumbled back, and the grin seemed to freeze on his lips.

"You are unbelievable, John! How could I have had even the tiniest of doubts about you—about *us*—last night?" Her voice had risen, and she glanced warily at the hotel doors surrounding them and then lowered her voice, jabbing her finger into his chest. "You are an awful, vile human being, and I hope I never see you again."

She turned and ran down the hall after Lucky.

26

The fluorescent lights in the stairwell felt like daggers in her eyes. She ran in, anyway, and called for her boyfriend. "Lucky!" her voice echoed in the concrete box. "Lucky!"

Head pounding, she flew down two levels before she heard a door farther down slam shut. She took off toward the noise, and when she burst into the lobby, she had to pause to get her bearings.

Lucky's long stride was taking him quickly to the exit.

"Wait!"

He stopped and turned, and what Stella saw almost made her retreat. His usually open, joking expression was stony. His face had lost all color and his lips were pressed into a thin, stark line, as if he was worried about what might slip out.

"Lucky—you can't believe that I would—that I'd ever do that to you. With him!"

He continued to stare at her without emotion.

"Yes, we hung out—me, Vindi, Terry—" At the mention of Terry's name, the vein running along Lucky's temple pulsed, and she realized she had more explaining to do than just about John. "Yes, Terry is a photographer I work with, but not the only one. Woz is the old sweaty one. I hadn't met Terry, yet, when we spoke the first time—"

"And the other times?" Lucky asked, his words clipped. "The other times we spoke, you never mentioned him."

"It was—it seemed easier not to—"

"Was it easier to cheat on me with John than tell me you don't—don't—" He had difficulty maintaining his anger as another emotion seeped in.

Stella looked wildly around the lobby, wondering how she could convince Lucky that her version of events was true. Her eyes landed on the couch she'd spent the better part of the night on.

"Look! This is where I sat until Terry left Vindi's room at nearly three in the morning. My tea is still here!" She nearly cried with relief. "See—yes, you can see my lipstick on the mug!"

Lucky looked critically at the cup, but Stella was heartened to see his temple was no longer throbbing. When he turned to look at Stella, though, his eyes were still sad and broken.

"Why were you with John at all? Why didn't you answer any of my calls last night? Because you were too busy with John? I don't know what to do with that. I just don't know what I'm supposed to do."

"Stella?"

She ignored the voice as she desperately tried to come up with something to say to Lucky—something to make him understand what he meant to her. He started to walk away, but she reached out.

"Stella?"

She shook her head, trying to swat away the distraction. She needed to focus. "Lu—"

"Are you going to run with that audio recording? If not, I'm going to give it to another reporter."

Confused, she turned toward the voice. "Detective McDonald? What are you doing here?" She resisted the urge to look at her watch; she knew it was early, but she didn't need to know how early. Instead, she turned back to her boyfriend, but he was gone. She hung her head, disappointed, angry, confused, and painfully hungover. It was the worst combination of emotions she'd ever experienced.

"The audio, Stella? I'll give you until your deadline tonight and then I'm going to release it officially. Just wanted to give you a head's up."

Detective McDonald walked away, and although Stella didn't want to talk to her, she'd never felt more alone in her life.

She tried Lucky three, four, and five times on his cell phone, and each time the call went straight to voicemail, a knife burrowed deeper into her heart.

She stood in the lobby in a state of shock for some time, and finally, after a bellboy asked for the second time if he could get her anything, she trudged back up to her room.

It wasn't empty. She looked coldly at John. "I don't want to see you. I want you to leave."

"Stella, wait. I know that wasn't fair, but I've known for a while now—years, really—that I didn't fight hard enough for you last time. I should have fought with everything I had to keep you, and that's what I did this morning: I fought for you."

"That wasn't fighting, John. That was lying." She refused to enter her room until he was out of it.

"Sometimes you have to play dirty to win."

"Well, you didn't win."

"You and Lucky didn't break up?"

"I don't know what's going to happen with Lucky, but I do know what's going to happen with you." Suddenly, anger at her ex overwhelmed her. "*You lied!* You lied and ruined everything. I want you to leave. Now!" she shouted when he reached out to her. "Get out!" She crossed her arms and refused to look at him as he gathered his belongings.

He walked past, a wounded expression on his face, but she ignored him, stalked into the room, and slammed the door. She heard someone make a tsking noise and whirled around in surprise.

"Vindi?"

"Stella, was that really necessary?" Vindi said from the bed. "John feels terrible. He knows he overstepped, but he loves you. *He loves you,*" she repeated.

"That doesn't give him the right to lie," she said, breathing hard both from the shock of finding another person in her room and because she felt defensive about her reaction. She was right to be angry—surely Vindi could see that.

"What happened?" her friend asked gently. It was her soft voice that almost pushed Stella over the edge from shock to utter, inescapable despair.

"He left—Lucky. I might have convinced him that nothing happened, but in the end, it doesn't matter. He feels like I cheated on him just by having drinks with John last night. I guess I can't really blame him." She dropped her bag to the floor and then sat heavily on the opposite side of the bed, not caring that her bag fell over and the tape, recorder, and nightgown spilled onto the floor. "I mean, how would I feel if he had drinks with his ex? Not great," she answered her own question.

"He's never met up with Star since they broke up?"

"I don't know," Stella said, not wanting to give Vindi the satisfaction of being right. Lucky had just told her on the phone that he and his ex were having lunch. She gulped. He'd *told* her about the meeting—no secrets.

"Humph," Vindi said, standing. "Well, we'll have to figure this out later. Court starts in forty minutes. I'll meet you in the lobby?"

"Okay," Stella replied, her voice dull and emotionless.

After her friend left, she flopped back on the bed and stared at the ceiling. What a disaster! No one had cajoled her into having drinks with John. In fact, she'd suggested it and then invited him to sleep in her hotel room! It didn't matter that she hadn't slept here with him; she was guilty in Lucky's eyes, and she deserved to be.

She went through the motions of getting ready for work but felt sick to her stomach—and it had nothing to do with how much wine she'd drunk the night before.

She saw the tape and recorder lying on the floor and dispassionately put the cassette into the device and hit play, wondering what sort of scoop Trish was giving her about the case and why.

After a few confusing sentences, Stella got used to the tinny voices coming out of the small speakers and soon identified Detective McDonald's voice, along with Rita Perlman, the chair of the Rotary Club.

In the dead silence of her room, the audio came out sounding clipped, almost as if someone had edited the original version.

Click.

"Sloan Chambers was the guest speaker?" McDonald asked.

Click.

"Right, and she gave a really marvelous speech about the public health crisis facing this country," the other woman said.

Click.

"How did she appear? Nervous? Worried?"

Click.

"Just as you'd expect. I mean, she was talking to over 300 people, so maybe nervous, but nothing unusual. She did try the cheesecake, though—I remember that."

Click.

"Thank you so much, Mrs. Perlman. We'll be in touch."

Stella rewound the tape to the beginning and listened to it again. The clicking sound was still there. Why would Trish give her an edited version of an interview to prove Sloan's alibi? She thought back to when Trish had handed it over. The detective had just learned Stella had asked Sawyer about his alibi. She'd said she was saving Stella time by giving her the interview. So, why did she show up at the hotel this morning, trying to pressure her into running the interview?

She frowned, tucked the cassette tape between the mattress and box spring, and put the playback device into a drawer of the dresser. When she left the room, already five minutes late to meet Vindi, she hung the Do Not Disturb tag on her doorknob.

Stella didn't really know Detective McDonald, and suddenly, she didn't trust her.

27

In the media room next to Preston Harrington's trial, Woz was already set up and ready to record when Stella and Vindi walked in.

"Where have you been?" he grunted before taking a massive bite of a donut. Powdered sugar sprinkled down over him and his camera, which he brushed off. "Bailiff said they'll be starting in five minutes."

Stella plopped down into the open seat and took a sip of the energy drink she'd picked up at the bodega on the way in. Tim and Hope had been there, along with Joe Jones. She'd said "hello" to all of them, but Tim had only said something about the highway or traveling. She'd been too exhausted to riddle out, so she'd only nodded and said something about how exhausting the road could be before taking off for court.

"All rise." The familiar words rang across the small media room, echoing from several recording devices and speakers.

After the judge and jury filed in, Preston's lawyer stood. Today was the beginning of Preston's case—his lawyer's chance to show the state hadn't proven his client's guilt. The talk in all the papers that morning had been about whether Preston would take the stand or they'd rely on other people to tell their story.

Stella tried to focus on what his lawyer said, but her mind kept wandering. She snuck her phone out of her bag and dialed Lucky's number. The call went straight to voicemail.

Because her mind couldn't handle her uncertain love life, she turned to the tape from Detective McDonald, instead. She just didn't trust the detective or the tape. How could she be certain it was a true account of what had happened?

She tried to tune in to the lawyer.

"The fact is that my client has just as much to lose—maybe more—than anyone with Drew Chambers dead. My client didn't submit to a fit of rage. Mr. Harrington is hardly prone to fits of anything..."

The answer dawned as if someone had turned on a light switch in her brain. Was she a reporter or not? She had the tape and the name of the women being interviewed.

She jumped up. "I'll be back, Woz. Write down anything good, okay?" she called as she made her way out of the room.

She bypassed the stairs and took the elevator to the main level, where she sat on a bench and entered Perlman's name in her phone.

"I knew it!" Stella crowed quietly when the woman's phone number came up in the white pages. It was infinitely harder to track down younger people, as none of them had landlines, anymore. She tapped in the phone number and held her breath. Rita answered on the first ring.

"Sure, I'm home. Watching the news right now, as a matter of fact."

Stella slowly stood, took a breath to steady her queasy stomach, and headed outside to hail a cab.

RITA PERLMAN WAS nothing like Stella had expected. The curvy woman who answered the door wore head-to-toe leopard print with bright red lipstick drawn far outside her actual lip lines. She'd used a heavy hand with dark brown pencil on her eyebrows, as well, leaving her with a permanently interested expression.

Her jet-black hair couldn't be natural, and when she held out her hand to shake Stella's, she saw the only thing that Perlman couldn't hide about her age: the wrinkles covering her gnarled, knotted hands.

"Stella Reynolds? Well, I don't recognize you at all. Who did you say you worked for?"

"NBC, but I'm new."

"Well, come in, come in. Do you want coffee or tea? I'm out of coffee cake, but I do have some prunes, if you'd like."

"Ah, no. I'm all set, thanks." Stella walked into a peculiar, plastic-covered homage to the nineteen-seventies. Black wallpaper with a fuzzy, raised print lined the entryway, except for one section by the light switch (also black) that had rubbed away, revealing teal paint underneath. Everything about the room was high drama, from a fabulous, silver and glass chandelier in the foyer to the teal, velvet couch that seemed a focal point. "Wow," was all she managed.

"I know; everybody just loves this room. Joni

Scarano decorated it, you know." At Stella's blank expression, she elaborated, "The Italian designer? Well, anyway, we haven't changed it since he was here in the seventies. It's a priceless masterpiece—at least, that's what Stanley used to say."

"Stanley?"

"My husband. He's been dead eleven years, God rest his soul. Chocolate?" she asked, holding out a box of small squares.

"No, thank you. Mrs. Perlman, I wanted to ask you some questions about the day of the Rotary Club meeting—the one Sloan Chambers emceed?"

"I already told the detective all I could about it and then some," she said, traipsing over to the couch and sitting with a flourish. "Everything from the appetizer to the main course and all the boring things in between."

"I guess I was more interested in the timing of everything. When did the luncheon start?"

Rita popped a chocolate into her mouth and chewed noisily before answering. "We meet at eleven thirty on the second Wednesday of the month, always at the Nurabu Hotel. They have the best cherry cheesecake, and at my age, I'm over skipping dessert. If I want it, I get it, okay?"

"Where is the Nurabu? Downtown?"

"Sure. It's not far from that coffee shop place—the one with the snacks? Oh, yeah, the bodega."

Stella blinked. "That means it's also just a block or so away from—"

"I know! So close to where Drew Chambers was killed that our hotel was in lockdown for about an hour after the body was discovered. That's why I told the detective that Sloan was late. I mean, she was kind of flustered. At the time, I chalked it up to her being late and almost missing the start of the program, but when we found out about Drew, I don't know... it seemed important. She'd only been inside the hotel for a minute or two when police closed the entire building off."

Stella sat gingerly on the edge of the plastic-covered cushion. "How late was she?"

"Oh, maybe thirty minutes or forty-five? Like I told the lady cop, I was in the bathroom. I tested a piece of the cheesecake before the luncheon started and it did not agree with me."

"How long were you in there, do you think?"

"Oh, I don't know, maybe five minutes."

"Five?"

"Okay, maybe twenty-five. It was a slow burn."

Stella hid her grimace. "How do you know Sloan was late, then, if you were in the bathroom?"

"Well, I almost missed it, didn't I? When I

came out of the bathroom, I was in a rush because the luncheon had started by then. I happened to look out the window in the hallway, though, and saw her outside, practically running down the street our way. Right after she walked into the banquet room, we got the announcement about the lockdown. It was good for us, actually, that everyone had to stay for the entire program. Some people like to leave after lunch," she added darkly.

"Do you remember anything else about that day?"

"I don't remember anything new, honey, if that's what you're asking. Sloan was late, in a rush, and a bit flustered. I don't know—maybe that's a bit revisionist of me. I wonder sometimes if she just seemed flustered to me after I found out her husband was dead, you know? Maybe she was just rushing because she was late. It's hard to remember, dear—it was two years ago now."

"Hmm," Stella murmured, now thoroughly confused. Detective McDonald had made a point of giving her the tape with Perlman's interview, supposedly to prove Sloan's alibi. In person, however, Rita had just done the opposite! According to her, Sloan had been rushing away from the scene of the murder moments after it happened!

"What was the weather like?" she asked, grasping at straws.

"The weather was gorgeous. What do you mean? We're in Palm Springs—it's always gorgeous. It was clear enough that I could see that poor homeless man with his dog. You know the one? Have you seen him? His mother, Jane Price, used to be in Rotary but had to drop out. Of course, she's focused now only on poor Tim. She's hoping to find a cure for his particular type of depression and anxiety. Regular meds won't work—they put him right back in Iraq, I guess, and give him terrible nightmares. Poor thing."

"Wait, you saw Tim that day? Where?" Stella leaned forward, wondering if the elderly woman was getting her days mixed up.

"I only noticed him because he seemed to be staring at Sloan, too. I thought, here we both are, staring at the same woman, but we're worlds away. He was leaning against the bodega door, just like always."

The more Stella pressed, the more it felt like Detective McDonald had given her the taped interview with Rita to ensure she didn't interview the woman on her own—like Rita had information McDonald didn't want made public. She had to be sure, though, so she directed one final question at the other woman. "Did you tell all of this to Detective McDonald—about Sloan, about Tim?"

"Sure. We had a whole conversation about Sloan *and* Tim, just like you and I are now. Everybody likes to talk about Tim, but nobody likes to help him."

28

Stella left Rita Perlman's house thinking about motivation. What had motivated Mc-Donald to give her a heavily edited copy of the interview between her and Perlman? Had she purposefully cut out the information about Sloan being late and Tim seeing Sloan? If so, why?

She looked at the clock on the dash of the Taxi. She'd probably already missed the first witness for the defense. She had to get back to court, but the only thing she wanted to do was find Tim.

She fought through a crowd of people as she ran up the courtroom steps. Minutes later, she burst into the media room only to skid to a stop. The room was empty.

She went back down the steps twice as fast, dialing her phone the whole way, and hit the main level at the same time Woz picked up.

"Where are you?" she panted, weaving through people in the lobby to get to the main doors.

"Defense rested. I'm sending video back to New York."

"Defense rested? Who took the stand?" She made it outside and walk-ran to the crosswalk to get to the parking lot that held all the live trucks.

"No one," Woz answered.

"No one?"

He sighed. "Is this some kind of new game? Pete and repeat?"

The satellite truck was finally in sight, so she dropped her phone into her bag and ran over, wrenching the door open. "What are we doing?"

"Network wants a live hit for CNBC in five."

Stella swore. "What did Yarley say?"

"Your best sound bite is cued up to feed back if you want to sit and listen."

She nodded, grateful she would at least know something before her live shot. "And then they broke for a recess?"

"Nope. Both sides did closing and then the judge gave jury instructions."

Stella's jaw dropped. She'd missed a lot by going to find Rita Perlman. "Wow."

"Yup. We're done until the jury reaches a verdict. Could be today, could be tomorrow. You never know with a sequestered jury—they might make us wait until Monday," Woz said with a frown. They'd have to keep vigil at the courthouse all weekend. "Where did you go, anyway?"

"I was checking something."

He picked up the phone in the truck and dialed New York. "I have a soundbite for engineering," he said before turning to Stella. "Was it worth your time?"

"Well... I totally debunked Sloan Chambers' supposedly airtight alibi for her husband's murder, so I guess it was worth it. Now we know someone besides Preston Harrington had opportunity—and motive, with all those affairs..."

Woz wasn't listening to her, though; instead, he grinned at something someone on the other end of the phone said, hit play on the computer, and said, "Here it comes."

On screen, Harrington's lawyer addressed the jury. "You might want to hear from Preston —have him tell you he wasn't there and didn't kill Drew. Well, he didn't, but he doesn't need to say it, because the prosecution didn't do their job. They didn't prove Preston did anything other than care about his growing business and how Wondred will help friends and strangers alike.

"Did he feel overshadowed? Hardly. The prosecution has said Preston snapped, but their supposition that the company was losing money, forcing Preston to kill is simply ridiculous. Luna C Engineering was exactly where they wanted to be, capital-wise, on the cusp of a huge investment from a well-known VC in Silicon Valley, and waiting on FDA approval that would have launched their drug into the stratosphere of successful companies. The prosecutor over there spewed a bunch of conjecture and they were wrong, and that, ladies and gentlemen, is important. You can't find my client guilty just because *someone* should pay for Drew's death. You can't find my client guilty because you think he looks mean. You can only find him guilty if you think the prosecution proved it beyond a reasonable doubt, and they didn't."

"Hmm," Stella said, squinting at the screen. "I guess it's compelling...."

"Not as compelling as Preston saying it, though?" Woz asked.

"Exactly. Why wouldn't he take the stand?"

"Okay, thanks. We'll be ready," Woz said into his phone. "They'll take you as soon as you're plugged in."

Stella hopped up and dialed in her IFB, plugged in her ear piece, and hustled down the steps to the parking lot.

Terry handed her the microphone and she had all of ten seconds to gather her thoughts before a new voice entered her ear.

"Stella? This is Robert Wright. I'm producing this hour for Shawna Gibbons, who's going to intro the story and toss to you. After the sound bite runs, you'll have about forty seconds of back and forth. Sound good?"

"Sure," Stella said, wondering what kind of questions Shawna Gibbons might ask her.

"Okay, we'll take you right after this story on the economy wraps, about twenty away."

She walked in front of the camera, ready.

Soon, Woz piped the programming into her ear and she heard Shawna say, "Now, breaking news in Palm Springs, California, where a murder trial we've been closely following had some major developments today. Stella Reynolds is covering the trial. She joins us live with the latest."

Out of the corner of her eye, Stella saw Detective Trish McDonald cross the street and head toward the media area. She shifted her focus back to the camera and started talking.

"After calling no witnesses and offering little

insight into where Preston Harrington was the day his business partner and friend was killed, the defense rested their case, telling the jury they didn't have anything to disprove after listening to prosecutors for the last week."

As soon as the sound bite started playing, McDonald came to a stop next to Terry. "Tick, tock," she said, pointing to her watch.

Terry gave her a puzzled look, but before Stella could say anything, she was live on TV again.

"Now the fate of Preston Harrington is in the jury's hands."

"Stella, did Harrington's lawyer make any suggestions as to who killed Drew Chambers if it wasn't Preston Harrington?"

She wanted to swear. She had no idea—she hadn't been there.

Woz piped into her ear piece, "No."

Stella nearly laughed with relief. "No, Shawna, the defense said his job isn't to solve the case but to protect the rights of his client."

"What are *his* rights?" Shawna asked. "He's accused of killing someone in a fit of jealousy," she added, a tone of superiority coloring her voice.

Stella paused for a moment, assuming it was a rhetorical question, but when Shawna also remained silent, she said, "Ah, well, Preston Harrington has the same rights as all of us: innocent until proven guilty. His lawyer today was saying simply and clearly to the jury that he did not believe prosecutors had met their responsibility to prove his client's guilt."

Someone laughed in her earpiece, but she wasn't sure who.

"Stella Reynolds, live for us in Palm Springs, California. Thank you."

Was it her imagination or had Shawna sounded put out by her answer? Before she could unplug her earpiece from her cellphone, it rang. Lucky's name lit up her screen.

At the same time, McDonald cleared her throat. "Stella?"

She had put others before Lucky last night and it had been a disaster, so she held up a finger and said, "I'm sorry, Detective, this is important." She then turned away from everyone and said, "Lucky! I'm so glad you called."

"I want to see you before I fly home. I'm at the Flamingo Royale hotel. I'll be waiting." He disconnected.

The natural high that always followed a breaking news live shot ended with the call. Lucky didn't sound friendly or even like Lucky. He sounded like he was talking to a stranger—like she was the enemy.

"Stella?" McDonald asked more insistently this time. When she turned, Trish was pointing to her watch. "You're on the clock. I spoke to your Executive Producer, Sher. She's expecting a call from you."

"You called my boss? Why?"

"I wanted to make sure she knew about your exclusive. I didn't want you to miss out." The detective turned and walked away, a satisfied smile on her face.

What was she up to?

29

Stella wanted to go find Tim and Hope and needed to go talk to Lucky, but she had to get ready for her live shot for the news.

She tapped a number into her phone and waited until Sher Patrick answered.

"Go."

"Did you speak to a homicide detective out here?"

"Yes, and I'd love to know why you're hiding an exclusive, Stella. We're paying you to break news, not follow it."

She explained the weird clicking noises she'd heard in the recording, along with the fact that some key information calling Sloan's alibi into question appeared to have been removed altogether.

"Thanks for your diligence. We can't put lies out there, only truths. Have Woz send it over and I'll take a listen."

Satisfied she'd bought herself some time but surprised it was so easy, Stella scanned the street, hoping a taxi was nearby to get her back to the hotel for that tape.

"Hey, uh..." Terry pawed at the ground with his toe. "I don't suppose you have Vindi's number? I must not be reading her handwriting correctly. I mean, it's a bit chicken-scratchy. Anyway, I'm getting a number wrong."

When he held out a piece of hotel stationary, Stella grimaced. Vindi had scrawled a number on the paper, all right, but it wasn't hers.

"Oh... umm..." She cursed her friend silently for putting her in this position. "Isn't she right over there at her live truck? I'm sure you have a few minutes to go say hello."

When Terry looked over, Stella made her escape, but not before seeing his disappointed expression when he looked back down at the paper.

She grabbed a taxi back to her hotel, unearthed the small cassette tape from under the mattress, grabbed the playback deck from the dresser drawer, and asked for maid service on her way back outside.

Fifteen minutes later, back inside the satellite truck, she sat in front of the monitor to watch closing arguments before her next live shot. "Hey, thanks, Woz. You really saved me out there."

"All part of the job, kid," he said, popping a tiny mint into his mouth. "What'd the cop want?"

"I think she was giving me... I don't know, a warning?" She told Woz about the tape and what Sher had told her she'd do.

"Sher Patrick wants me to send it over?"

"Mmm-hmm." Stella was trying to listen to the courtroom speech.

"She said you're not using it tonight, though?"

"Right."

"So who's she going to have front the audio?"

"What?" Woz finally had her attention. "No, she said they would make sure it checked out and then decide what to do." Woz didn't answer, and Stella's stomach dropped. "You don't think that's what's going to happen?"

He shrugged and she pushed away from the console. "Where are you going?"

"I'm going to get my own damn exclusive, and it's going to be one hundred percent legitimate," she said, leaving the truck.

She picked up her cell phone. "Lucky, I need you."

~

FIFTEEN MINUTES LATER, Lucky stared up at the bodega sign with reserved curiosity. He kept Stella an arm's length away and refused to look at her, keeping his eyes trained straight ahead.

"Let's go in," she said, walking ahead of him. He was angry, but her step felt a bit lighter. Surely he wasn't too mad at her if he'd shown up. She glanced back and caught him scowling at her. She bit her lip.

"Hi, Joe," she said when she caught sight of the owner. "Is Tim here?"

"Great, more men," Lucky grumbled. "Is there something you need to tell me about you and Tim?"

"In the alley, Stella. Said he needed the air." Joe pointed toward one side of the store, and she led Lucky back outside. Before they rounded the corner, Sloan Chambers came out of a store across the street. If she recognized Stella, she didn't show it.

Hope's tail pounded a steady beat against a wooden crate when she recognized Stella, and

Tim started to push himself up from his spot on the ground.

"No, no—don't get up!" she said, hurrying over to pat Hope and help Tim back down onto his cushion. "Tim, I wanted you to meet my boyfriend, Lucky Haskins."

Lucky winced at the introduction, and her stomach plunged to her knees. Were they that far gone? Was there no hope for them, already? She tamped down her feelings of despair; her deadline was looming, as usual.

"Hey, man. Nice dog." Lucky crouched down and Hope tottered over, her uneven gait made even less steady by the thwacking of her tail as it met obstacles on every side.

Tim smiled slightly, pointed at Lucky, and said, "I can drive 55."

She nodded, recognizing the Sammy Hagar song. "Yes—do you recognize Lucky?" He nodded and she said, "Tim, I thought Lucky might be able to help me figure out what you were trying to tell me this morning."

Tim looked blankly back at her and she gritted her teeth as grim determination overtook her. By the end of this day, she might have lost Lucky, any semblance of success at her job, and maybe even her chance at happiness, but not without a fight.

"Tim was injured in Iraq and now communicates mostly using song titles and quotes," she said, turning toward Lucky. He raised his eyebrows and she continued. "He seems to have a particular taste for country music, which you know much better than I do. I thought you might be able to help... translate for me."

"Stella, what's going on?" Lucky asked, standing up from Hope and taking a step backward. The dog followed. "I don't have time for this, and frankly, I don't want to be here. No offense to you, Tim," he said, looking down at the wounded vet. Although Stella was vexed by his attitude, she had to hand it to him: he'd taken the odd information about Tim's way of communicating in stride.

Tim looked between Stella and Lucky with a gentle shake of his head and then called Hope over with a series of clicking sounds. He laid a hand on her back when the dog leaned into him. "It must have been love," he said sagely, staring at Lucky.

"But it's over now," Lucky agreed, crossing his arms over his chest.

Stella threw her hands on her hips and glared. "It's not over now, no matter what Roxette said in the nineties. You and I have a lot to discuss, Lucky Haskins, but first, I have to not get fired from my job today, and that means I need your help!" She looked guiltily at the pavement when her last words echoed in the alleyway. She was shouting angrily at the very person she hoped would not only help her *now* but also forgive her later.

When she looked back up, she saw a ghost of a grin cross Lucky's face before he forced another frown and said, "What do you want?"

She blew out a cleansing breath and knelt near Tim. "This morning, you told me something, but I wasn't in the right frame of mind to hear it," she said apologetically. Tim took a bite of the muffin he was holding and then tore off a piece to share with Hope.

He finally nodded at Stella. "Highway Patrolman."

"Okay, you remember." She nodded encouragingly and looked to Lucky for support to see him staring back, obviously confused. She looked back at Tim. "Does that have anything to do with the murder case I'm covering here?"

He cocked his head to the side and studied Stella.

Encouraged, she said, "I spoke to Rita Perlman today. Do you remember her? She said she's friends with your mom. She said the day Drew Chambers was killed, she saw Sloan running down the street, away from the crime scene. She saw you, too. You were watching Sloan from this store."

He shook his head, but his eyes never left Stella's.

"Did you see something important that day, Tim—something you haven't told anyone?"

He looked down at his muffin and then offered the last quarter of it to Hope. She licked it up in one bite and he smiled and patted her on the head before leaning forward. When he looked back up at Stella, his face was earnest and his tone serious. "Highway Patrolman," he said, enunciating each word carefully.

With that, he pulled himself up using the handle of the cooler behind him and clicked for Hope to follow. Instead of passing Lucky, though, he stopped and looked him over from head to toe. "Glass," he said. When something flickered in Lucky's eyes, Tim nodded and walked toward the sidewalk, his crutches tapping against the ground rhythmically as he left.

"Glass? What does that mean?" Stella asked.

Just past Lucky, Tim rounded the corner and disappeared. A man sitting at a table on the opposite side of the street raised a hand in greeting. It was Sawyer Harrington. Stella shifted her attention back to her boyfriend when he cleared his throat.

"Why am I here again?" Lucky asked.

"I need help. I don't know what he meant by that. Was he talking about cops? Did he see the cops do something weird that day?"

Lucky snickered. "'Highway Patrolman' isn't about cops—it's an old Bruce Springsteen hit about brothers."

"Brothers?" Instinctively, her eyes flicked to Sawyer Harrington, but he was gone.

30

After Stella wrapped up her live shot, she didn't unclip her IFB or turn off her microphone. Instead, she stared critically at the monitor in front of her, waiting to see if the dodgy audio from McDonald would make a surprise appearance on the evening news.

Her mind wandered through the next story on an upcoming royal wedding. If Tim was trying to tell her, in his own, odd way, that *brothers* was a key part of the murder case that no one knew about, she needed to start digging around on the only *brother* she knew about: Preston's.

The night before, while stuck in the lobby, attempting a little drunk computer research, she'd been unable to confirm anything about his doctorate or where he practiced medicine. She would have to start there, although, judging by the clock, she'd be lucky to get anyone on the phone at this hour—especially on a Saturday afternoon.

As she shifted her focus back to the monitor, she felt secure that the audio tape from police would stay under wraps—at least for another night.

When Woz finally lumbered down the stairs, she handed the microphone to Terry.

"Woz," she called, motioning for Lucky to join them, "I'd like you to meet my boyfriend. Lucky, this is Woz, the sat-truck operator."

Lucky bit back a grin when he saw the underarm sweat seeping out from Woz's gray shirt, but he stuck a hand out gamely. "Woz, nice to meet you, man."

"Lu..." Woz stared and, for a moment, his eyes glazed over. "Lucky Haskins?" When Lucky nodded, the man's awe-shucks smile warmed Stella's heart. "Man, I just watched you at Eldora! That race was awesome."

Before she realized what was happening, Lucky had reached out and pulled her close while he and Woz continued their conversation—now on Tony Stewart and why he chose the middle of nowhere, Ohio, to run a dirt racetrack.

She leaned into him and he rubbed a hand across her back. When Woz paused to take a breath, Lucky jumped in and said they had to get going. Stella walked next to him, unsure of what he was going to say when they finally got away from prying eyes.

He led them to a bench at the far end of the parking lot. It was in the shade, under a large palm tree, and Stella worried with a pang that he was going to end things. She was suddenly glad for the seat, as her legs didn't feel like they could support her much longer.

"Tell me," he commanded as he sat next to her. Where she was weak and worried, he was wound as tight as a spring. He could hardly sit still as he stared at her.

"Lucky, I've been thinking a lot lately about what motivates people, and I guess I want you to think about what motivated John this morning—"

He held up a hand, silencing her. "Save it, Stella. This ain't my first race, okay? I know exactly what John was doing this morning—I don't need you to spell it out for me. What I need to hear from you is what you want." She opened her mouth, relieved that he hadn't bought John's outrageous lie, but he held her off. "If you can't last more than a week without doubting us, we need to make a change. It's that simple."

"I wasn't doubting us," she said, her breath catching in her throat. "I would never doubt you, and I'm sorry I gave you reason to doubt me. I love you, Lucky. I don't know how this is going to work, with your racing schedule and me flying all over the country, but I know I want to try. I know I *want* it to work, and I'm willing to work for it—work for us."

He cleared his throat and continued to stare at her.

"It was—I know it sounds unbelievable, but I literally ran into John yesterday morning. He suggested dinner, but I thought it would be better as a group. With Vindi there, it really did seem like a reunion of old friends. We all drank too much, and I didn't want him driving home. That's all."

"I don't think it was a coincidence that John was here," Lucky said slowly, again bemoaning her expression with a groan of his own. "Think about it, Stella. He knew you were here covering a story, and Palm Springs is small—he knew just where to find you. I trust you, but I don't trust him. It was certainly a shock to find him in your room this morning."

She gritted her teeth—she would never forgive John—but she felt lighter than she had all day at Lucky's words. She scooted closer to him on the bench and, when he opened his arms, she slid in.

"I love you," she mumbled into his shirt.

He chuckled and moved some stray locks of hair away from her face when she pulled back. "I love you, too."

"How long are you staying?"

"I don't have anywhere to be until Monday."

She grinned. "I happen to have some free time, myself."

"Are you done with work?"

"Not done, but I can take a break," she said innocently, looking up at Lucky. "We can head to my room?"

His face took on a pained expression. "Bear, I never want to go to that room again." She ducked her head. "I have a room, though, and it's all ready for us."

"It is?"

"Mmm-hmm," he murmured, his eyes roaming over her body. She reached up and ran her hand over his shoulder.

"Is there anything I can do to make up for the last few hours?"

He caught her hand and pulled her up. Heat flooded her stomach as she pressed herself against her boyfriend, tilted her head up, and planted a soft kiss on his lips. He groaned and deepened the kiss before breaking it off, their breathing ragged.

"I'm sure we can come up with something."

STELLA HURRIED down the hall and unlocked her door. True to his word, Lucky didn't want to see her hotel room again, so while he waited for her in the lobby, she went to grab a few things for the night. The room, which at first had seemed so luxuriously quiet and private, now felt intrusive and uncomfortable.

She flicked on the light and reached for her suitcase, but her hand froze halfway to the chair.

"What...?"

Clothes and makeup littered the ground, the mattress was partially off the bed, the shower curtain had been ripped off its hooks, and Stella noted with surprise that her toothbrush was floating in the toilet.

The room had been thoroughly ransacked.

Her only thought as she stared at the wreckage around her was to echo Sher from her first full day on the job: she must have been doing *something* right. Something she'd done in the last day had made someone angry, but whom?

31

L ucky stormed up the stairs, the elevator either too slow or too enclosed for his liking.

"What the hell, Stella? What's going on?" he asked, striding down the hall to where she stood in the open doorway of her room.

"I don't know—"

"I'm calling the cops!"

"No—no, don't." At Lucky's outraged expression, she added, "I can't be sure one of them isn't involved!"

"What do you..." Lucky took a deep breath and then steered her into the room to the nearest chair. He swept her possessions to the ground, made her sit, and then knelt in front of her. "What in God's name is going on?"

Haltingly, with several pauses to remind herself of the timeline, Stella filled Lucky in on her side-investigations since arriving in Palm Springs, and how she now wondered whether Preston's brother, Sawyer, might be somehow involved in the murder.

"What about police? Where do they come in?"

"I'm just guessing here, but Detective Trish McDonald's motivations are confusing. I think she's on a mission to get back at some old tormentors."

Lucky snorted. "She'd put her job on the line —a man's future on the line—for that? No way."

"Ah," Stella said, reaching up to caress his jaw. "Spoken like someone who's never been targeted by the school bully."

"What does that mean?" he asked, grabbing her hand. He twined their fingers together on her lap and said, "Just because I wasn't bullied doesn't mean—"

"Yes," she interrupted, "it does. There's a whole depth of emotional damage that you and I can't even imagine. Someone made her life a living hell when she was a teenager. Isn't it possible that all those emotions and feelings of anger come roaring back thirty years later?"

Lucky looked unconvinced. "What do you think happened here? Was someone sending you a message?"

Stella looked over at the mattress, where she'd hidden the tape the other day, and had another idea. "Maybe they were looking for something, like evidence."

Lucky stood. "I'm sorry, but I think it's more likely that John was angry at how things played out today."

"What? No..."

He raised his eyebrows. "What? You can't imagine *John* doing something like this?"

"Well," Stella looked around the room and shook her head. "No, I guess I can't!"

Lucky blew out a frustrated sigh. "Look what he did this morning. Did you ever think he'd lie like that?"

"No," she drew the word out, thinking. That *had* been a surprise, but John wasn't the destructive type, just the win-at-all-costs type. When she looked over, Lucky was frowning at her. "What?"

"I just don't—I don't know why, no matter what he does... why is he always the good guy to you?"

"What? That's not true!" Stella said, although she realized with a pang that's just what she'd been thinking. "Lucky, let's not fight again. Let's just..."

"What? Let's pretend this," he gestured around the messy space, "never happened?"

"For now. Let me just get some things and we'll—"

"No," he said mulishly. "I want you to call police and file a report."

"Against whom? Lucky, I—I don't want anyone to know this happened!" she shouted. "The last thing I need, as I *mistake* my way through this first network assignment, is news of a break-in complaint to get out! Good God, I can barely even make it through a live shot! If I file a police report about this, I become the overly dramatic reporter who can't keep her act together at a hotel!"

Lucky's expression softened. "It's been a rough first week, hasn't it?"

She flicked an unexpected tear away and turned from Lucky to pick up a shirt off the floor. Instead, though, she crouched down and pressed her fingertips between her eyes. Once she was in command of her emotions again, she stood to face her boyfriend. "I feel like an amateur and I don't like it. Just let me take care of this my way, please."

Lucky took another slow look around the room. "Pack your things. You'll stay with me until this is all cleared up."

"But you leave on Monday."

"Then you'll be safe with me until Monday."

THEY DIDN'T HEAD STRAIGHT to Lucky's hotel after Stella packed her bag—the spell from earlier had been broken by an intruder with unknown intentions.

They shared an appetizer at the hotel bar when Lucky looked over Stella's head and nodded at someone. She looked over her shoulder and found a familiar woman hanging back, staring at them intently.

Stella turned back to Lucky, but she was puzzled by his expression. "What?" she asked.

"I think that person wants to talk to you."

"Who? That woman by the bar?" Stella turned back, and it was all the woman needed to step forward.

"Are you," she started, hesitantly. "Are you Stella Reynolds?" Her voice was raspy, like a classic radio DJ or someone who's smoked cigarettes for years.

As the woman walked forward a few steps, a flash of recognition hit. Stella had seen her before, leaving the courtroom. "Yes. Can I help you?"

"I—I'm not sure."

"Just give me five minutes," she murmured. Lucky frowned but didn't object as Stella led the woman to the bar and sat down. When she got the bartender's attention, she looked at the woman next to her. "Can I get you a drink?"

"Just water," she said primly.

Stella ordered two waters and they waited in silence until the bartender set two shimmering glasses down and left.

The woman took a sip and then cleared her throat. "So... I, uh, I guess I wanted to talk to you— off the record."

Stella nodded. "About what?"

"Do I... do I have your promise that this is off the record?"

"Sure," Stella said, her eyes never leaving the woman's face. Through a heavy cover of makeup— more than she would ever wear on air, she noted dispassionately—the woman was pale and nervous. What could be so worrisome? "What's your name?"

"I am Tanya Harrington."

"Harrington?" Stella asked, stirring her water

with a little black straw. She knew *Sawyer* had kids —he'd mentioned it at the diner the other night— but she'd assumed they were younger. She hadn't come across a sister or aunt in her research, but maybe she'd missed someone on the family tree. "Are you related to Preston, somehow?"

She laughed. "You could say that."

Stella tilted her head to the side. She was missing something. "Well, how would you say it?"

"Preston is my father."

"Your—are you sure?" Stella asked, even though she knew the question was ridiculous. How could the fact that Preston had a kid have gone unreported for more than two years? "You're his daughter?"

"Well... not exactly."

32

The bartender slammed two vodka-sodas down in front of the women. "Are you sure you don't want one?" Stella asked, moving both drinks in front of her.

"I'm sure," Tanya answered, looking at the glasses distastefully. "I stopped drinking about six years ago. I was never my best self with alcohol involved."

"Well, I guess that makes me lucky. I just get better and better," Stella said with a derisive chuckle. "So, you're 'not exactly' his daughter? What does that mean?"

"Um, I guess I need to start at the beginning."

"Please," Stella said, picking up the glass closest to her and taking a small sip. She had a feeling things were going to get complicated, and she needed to keep her head. She glanced over at Lucky and found him already looking at her, his brow furrowed, his drink untouched.

"My parents divorced when I was just five," she said, swirling the ice cubes around in her glass. "Dad moved a few blocks away, but Mom got custody. She's had a series of boyfriends ever since," Tanya laughed humorlessly, "none of them anything to write home about. When I was ten, she picked a particularly bad one. I—we just didn't get along. There were other problems... there were many reasons..." she stared into her glass, having trouble finding the words.

"Tanya, it's nothing to be ashamed about. Lots of kids really struggle through a divorce and everything that follows. God, it's a lot of pressure to put on kids. You look like you came out of it all right," Stella said kindly.

"Well, anyway, back then, I went by... Tony." She looked up quickly at Stella, who couldn't help but stare back with wide eyes.

Several small things about Tanya suddenly clicked into place. The fashionable, tall heels were covering unusually wide feet. Tanya's hair was styled beautifully, as if by someone who'd always wanted long, gorgeous hair and not by someone who'd debated a ponytail that morning.

Heartened, perhaps, that Stella hadn't been rude or demeaning, Tanya hurried on. "When I started the transition to Tanya, it just didn't go well. Mom tried to understand, but she was struggling, and her *boyfriend* at the time," she said the word like a curse word, "thought I was a freak. I get it—I mean, a lot of people felt that way. The kids at my school were particularly awful about it. Anyway," she set her water down and finally looked up at Stella, "by then, Dad was living part of the year in San Diego for work. I thought I could use a fresh start—a clean break, so to speak. Dad said he was planning on moving to California full-time, anyway, but I think he did it just for me." She smiled at the memory. "We moved out here together when I was seventeen. I came here as Tanya and have never looked back."

"Tanya?" Stella asked.

She grinned, almost relieved at the question. "I know, isn't it awful? A ten-year-old should never be allowed to pick their name." Her smile lingered for a moment and then waned. "Dad bought a condo here in Palm Springs and it's been a charmed life ever since, living in paradise. He's never once judged me—he just wants me to be happy. That's why I had to come find you, to tell you."

"Of course you love your dad, Tanya!" Stella said, finally understanding why the woman had come. She couldn't imagine how difficult it would be to see a loved one go through such a public ordeal.

"No, you don't understand. I—I was with Dad... when Drew Chambers was killed. He was with me."

"He was with you during the murder? *You* are his alibi? Why didn't you tell police?" Stella looked suspiciously at the other woman. It felt like a reverse confession. Why now? Why her?

"Well... he was with me at the doctor. It was my first appointment about gender reassignment surgery."

The words hung heavily in the air as Stella processed things. "You're going to let him go to jail so no one knows you used to be Tony?"

"It's what he wants!" she said defensively. "He said I shouldn't tell anyone."

"Tanya, I mean, things have changed since you were ten. Sure, it'll still be tough-but this is a murder conviction! This could be life in prison for your father."

"Or it could be life in prison for me—if every-body knows the truth about me!"

Silence settled between them.

"No one else knows? What about Sawyer?"

"Uncle Sawyer has been great. Of course he and his wife know. I met their kids as Tanya, so that's how they've always known me and that's how it's going to stay."

"What do police know?"

"Only that I exist as Tanya. They don't know—"

"That you lied to them?"

"No, that Dad was with me. They didn't even ask where I was during the murder—I'm not a suspect!"

Stella took a slow sip of her drink and stared at the woman, thinking. "Could your doctor confirm he was with you?"

"N-no... I won't allow it. Dad won't allow it."

"He's a surgeon, though, right? No one would have to know—"

"He's a plastic surgeon who specializes in gender issues. Everyone would know."

Stella bit her tongue. It wasn't her job to press Tanya—especially when everything she said was off the record. "So... why are you telling me any of this? What do you want me to do?"

"I just thought, if you knew he really was innocent, maybe you could do something."

Stella barked out a laugh. "Well, it's a bit late in the game now, isn't it? The jury has the case. This could all be decided by tomorrow! It's also the weekend—what can I possibly do now?"

"I—I don't know." Tanya hung her head and pushed the water away. "I just wanted someone to try."

Stella finished her first drink and picked up the second.

"I've been happy here—happy for the first time in years. I can't go back to my old life—that prison —with demons chasing me at every turn. I know I'm a terrible person for it, but I just have to hope justice will win. I just have to believe someone will find the lead that finally breaks the case wide open."

"Tanya, with you lying about where your father was, no one's even looking! Police think they have their guy, prosecutors think they have their guy, and I'm sorry to say that, after the way your father has behaved in court, even the jury probably thinks they have their guy."

Tanya's lips flattened at the end of Stella's speech. She squared her shoulders and stood, putting her purse primly over her shoulder and leaning close so she and Stella were eye to eye. In her peripheral vision, she saw Lucky get up from the table and walk toward them.

"Well, now you know he's *not* the guy. Make a difference in this case. What are you going to do with your knowledge?" Just as Lucky's hand rested possessively on Stella's shoulder, Tanya straightened, adjusted her shirt, and nodded. "Goodnight."

After they watched her walk away, Lucky picked up Stella's second drink and took a sip. "What was that about?"

"Deception, lies—you know, typical family drama," she said darkly, still staring at the exit.

As Lucky led her back to their table, a new and unsettling thought crept into Stella's mind. If Tanya was telling the truth and her father was innocent, the break-in and ransacking of her hotel room took on a whole new, darker meaning. There was a killer walking the streets of Palm Springs. Was that person worried enough about what Stella knew to brazenly break into her hotel room without trying to cover their tracks?

She gulped, her mouth suddenly dry, and looked across the table at Lucky. Was she putting him in danger right now? She looked nervously

around the room and said, "Let's go to your hotel. I
—I want to get out of here."

Lucky looked up sharply at her tone, stood,
threw some bills on the table, and grabbed her
suitcase. "You look like you've seen a ghost, Bear."

She laughed weakly and walked quickly out of
the hotel, glancing over her shoulder every few
minutes. When they were safe in the cab, she re-
laxed a fraction but jumped when Lucky put his
hand on her knee.

"Are you okay?" he asked, squeezing her leg in
concern.

She didn't answer. She felt exposed and un-
safe, like she was being hunted.

33

The next morning, after a restless night of tossing and turning in an unfamiliar room with strange sounds, Stella awoke alone in bed. She propped herself up on one elbow and saw, through a crack in the French doors that led to the sitting area of Lucky's suite, that the lights were on in the other room, the TV flickering highlights from some sporting event.

She went to the bathroom and then padded out to the bedroom in search of Lucky. "What are you doing? It's not even six! Come back to bed."

"You forget it feels like nine to me. Not all of us have been in California for a week."

"What is that?" Stella asked, pointing to his open suitcase. "I thought you were staying until

Monday?" While she spoke, he shoved a folded shirt between the side of the suitcase and a shoe.

"I have to head back now—Brenda told me there's a charity thing she forgot to put on my calendar. I guess I've been down for it for months, and it somehow got missed."

She wanted to say, "What about me?" but didn't want to sound so pathetic, so she plastered on a smile and nodded.

"Bear? You don't think I'm just abandoning you, do you?"

"No—of course not. I'll be fine. I will," she protested when he gave her a look that said he didn't believe her.

"Bear." He tilted his head down and raised his eyebrows.

"Lucky, of course it's okay. I'll just get a new room back at my hotel and keep the chain on. I'll be just fine," she repeated, trying to convince herself as much as Lucky. While she slept, a small dose of reality had managed to sneak into her subconscious, and she was suddenly terrified that someone involved in a murder—a case she now knew was one hundred percent *unsolved*—might have broken into her room, looking for evidence of their own guilt. She swallowed before forcing a smile back onto her face.

"It didn't keep you up at night like it did me, but I can see you're there now," Lucky said, and she noticed an edge to his voice she hadn't before. His temple was pulsing, and she realized he was as stressed out about leaving as she felt. "After you told me you think Preston is innocent, I realized it wasn't John who broke into your room. It probably wasn't a cop, like you initially thought, either. It might have been a killer, and Jesus, now I have to leave! I don't know why you're always on the edge of danger, Stella. I hate it." He slammed his suitcase closed, but it made a very unsatisfying *thwack* as it caught on a pair of socks. Lucky kicked at a nearby chair in frustration. "Why can't you just be a regular, ole NASCAR wife?"

Stella was so startled by the question that she started stuttering. "I-I-I-can't." She shook her head. "What does that even mean?"

In spite of his anger, her boyfriend chuckled at her reaction. "That wasn't a proposal, if that's what you're worried about. I just mean all of my buddy's girls, they just—I don't know—get their nails done or want to have babies."

"Is that what you want?" she asked, momentarily distracted.

"No," he said, drawing out the syllable, "not yet." His smile was lopsided as he moved toward her. "I definitely want the option with you, though, which won't happen if you're killed by some lunatic murderer here in California."

Despite the gravity of the situation, Stella smiled. "You don't have to worry, Lucky. I was up half the night, too, and I don't think anyone's going to kill me. Whoever broke into my room was worried, but hopefully, when they didn't find anything, they realized there's nothing to find! If the jury comes down with a guilty verdict, then whoever they are will have nothing to worry about again," she added darkly.

"I'm not taking any chances."

"What does that mean?"

"It means you're not going back to that hotel and you're not staying here alone."

"I'm not?" Stella asked, assuming that's exactly what he'd been planning.

"If they could break into one hotel room unnoticed, they could break into this hotel unnoticed, too."

"Listen, I know you're worried, but I can take care of—"

"No, you can't, and yes," he said, seeing her nostrils flare, "it is my business. I'm going to make sure you're safe when I'm not here."

"Oh, please. I don't need—"

"Yes, you do."

At an impasse, they stared at each other with identical angry expressions and crossed arms. After a momentary standoff, they grinned.

"All right, Lucky. What's this great plan?"

"I already sent your bag over. Now I just have to deliver you."

"W<small>HAT DID</small> T<small>IM MEAN</small>?" Stella asked.

Lucky's mouth ticked down a fraction before he flicked his eyes at Stella. "What?"

She cocked her head to the side and stared. "You know what I mean. When he left the bodega yesterday, he said, 'Glass,' and you... I don't know, you kind of shared a look. What was he talking about?"

"It's a country song about treating each other carefully, because we're fragile and break easily."

"Oh." Stella looked at Lucky's jawline and saw it was pulsing. Wherever he was taking her, he wasn't happy about it. "Is it... a breakup song or a get-back-together song?"

"It's a love song, Bear." He gently took her hand in his and raised it to his lips before twining their fingers together. She leaned back against the headrest but kept her eyes on her boyfriend.

He slowed the car and she tore her eyes away from him to see where, exactly, they were.

"This looks like the setting from *Last House on the Left,*" Stella said. In front of them sat a lonely house at the edge of the woods. "It feels like the beginning of a horror movie, too. 'Send the girl into the deserted woods—she'll be safe there. Until the killer finds her hideout *and there's nowhere to hide!*'"

"That's not funny."

She stared at Lucky, unable to read his expression. He should have been victorious or at least happy to win the where-should-Stella-stay argument. Instead, he looked at the house with trepidation bordering on dread.

"Where are we?" He refused to answer, but when his expression turned dark, she followed his gaze in time to see John walk out of the house. "You've got to be kidding me!" she snarled, rebuckling her seatbelt and crossing her arms. "No way."

"Stella, I don't like it either, but you'll be safe here."

"Safe from the killer, maybe, but not *safe.*"

"Don't say that."

She turned her body to face Lucky. "You saw how he was! What are you thinking?"

"I'm thinking only of you, obviously." He grimaced as John approached the car.

"Lucky. Stella." John barely moved his lips as he spoke. He clearly wasn't happy, either.

She leaned across her boyfriend to talk out his window. "I'm sorry, John, but I don't think this is necessary—at all," she glared at Lucky. "It was so nice of you to offer, though." When he blew out a sigh, she corrected herself. "Well, it was so nice of you to at least agree to it. I-I just don't think it's a good idea, though."

"It's also probably not a good idea to go back to the hotel, right?"

"Well..." she gritted her teeth. What was it with everyone suddenly being the voice of reason? "I don't really think—"

"But you don't know, and I guess that's the problem," Lucky said, turning his deep, brown eyes to her and taking her hands in his. "I can't take that chance. Besides, you said yourself the trial will be over soon, so it's only for a few days."

She could feel Lucky's consternation in the way he was looking at her, and she knew he must have been more worried than he was letting on to have decided staying with John was the least risky option. So, despite her frown, she nodded a fraction, and he blew out a relieved breath.

She unbuckled her seatbelt, but before she could open the door, he pulled her across the center console onto his lap, lowered his face, and planted a soft kiss on her lips. She knew his motivation was to show John she was his, but before she could admonish him, he nipped her bottom lip and, in a low voice, said, "Take care of yourself, Stella. That's the most important thing. You take care of you." He pushed open his door and climbed out of the car before carefully setting her on her feet. His hands ran down her sides before releasing her, leaving streaks of hot desire behind, and he climbed back behind the wheel, started the car up, and drove away without another word.

34

"So," John said, finally tearing his gaze away from Lucky's taillights. "Dare I ask what's going on?"

"It's nothing—" She cut off at his expression and cleared her throat before starting again. "I think Lucky is overreacting," Stella continued nonchalantly. No matter their history or their recent fight, she reminded herself that John was also the competition. If she let anything slip about what she knew, it would be like giving the story away to another news outlet.

"I'm on vacation, remember?" John said, sensing her hesitation.

"You're never on vacation and neither am I."

He blew out pent-up breath and turned to the

house. "Come on. I'll show you where you'll be sleeping."

"Gosh, that sounds familiar, doesn't it?" Stella said with a light laugh. She and John had had a very brief stint as roommates back in Montana, and although it felt like lightyears had passed since then, his words managed to bring her back to her first months at her first job, like she was watching a TV show.

He paused for a moment, but then, with a little shake of his head, he led Stella up the front steps into a quaint entryway. She counted five pairs of Wellies from small to large in all different colors from black to green, and one pair even had little, pink ladybugs. They all lined the heat register that ran along the bottom of the wall.

"Kate's kids?" she asked, pointing to the boots.

"What? Oh, yes. They come here a few times a year. Those are Claire's," he said with an indulgent smile as he pointed at the pink boots. "They haven't fit properly for about six months, but she refuses to try a new pair.

"Come on back." He walked through a small but tidy kitchen and then pointed to a set of stairs. "Your room is the last on the right. I put clean sheets out but didn't have time to make the bed, yet."

He left her alone and she reached for her phone. She had a dozen new emails, but only one caught her eye. It was from the personal email account of Caleb Crone, her old college friend, who now worked for the FDA. She tapped the email and raced through the first few lines about his wife and Stella's job. Things got interesting in the second paragraph.

Luna C Engineering is waiting on final approval from the FDA. The only hitch in their application came when testers reported adverse effects if they started at higher level doses. The fix was simple: doctors are required to prescribe small doses initially or risk serious harm to the patient. Labeled usage includes regular appointments with the doctor to monitor increases until the right dosage is found.

"Serious harm?" Stella said, re-reading the paragraph. "What does that mean?" Caleb didn't elaborate, although he did include a link to a research paper on the drug. Her eyes glazed over halfway through the first line.

She tucked her phone into her pocket and walked downstairs, her bag still slung over her shoulder. John sat at the table in the kitchen, staring outside, a contemplative look on his face.

"Thank you, John. I'm sorry to inconvenience you," she said somewhat stiffly.

"It is what you do best, Stella."

"Well, hold onto your socks, because I have another favor." He raised his eyebrows, waiting for the punch line. "I need to borrow your truck."

"Why?" he asked when he realized she was serious.

"I just have some... things to check out," she said evasively.

"Is this for a story?" When she didn't answer, he groaned. "This is almost as bad as getting beat by you on a near daily basis in Montana," he crossed his arms and added with disbelief. "And Knoxville. Now you want me to help *you*, a reporter from another station, run off to get some kind of exclusive?" He stood and paced a tight circle in the kitchen, nearly knocking over a small vase of flowers before catching it and righting it. He finally looked up at her with a piercing stare. "Can you go alone? How does your handler feel about that?"

"Lucky trusts me, obviously," she said, looking pointedly at John.

He snorted. "You're unbelievable." After another pause, he said, "Keys are on the hall table." When she pivoted on the spot, he called, "I need to leave here at three thirty!"

She was already halfway down the hall. "I'll be back by three!"

Stella threw her purse into the vehicle and then climbed behind the wheel. John was back to driving a Ford pickup truck, and unfamiliar with the sensitivity of the pedals, she accidentally spun the wheels in the mulched driveway as she pressed the gas pedal. "Sorry!" she called to John's astonished face in the doorway of the house, before waving out the open window as she drove down the winding, two-lane, gravel road that led back to town.

At a stop light, she looked up Sawyer Harrington's wife's address and entered it into her phone's GPS. "Twenty-eight minutes away," she said aloud as the directions populated her screen. Before she could decide which way to turn to get on the correct route, however, a phone call came in, covering the directions on her screen completely.

The number wasn't one she recognized, but she pulled over to the side of the road and answered the call.

"This is June Montgomery with Halpern University returning a call from Stella Reynolds."

Stella nearly forgot she'd put some calls in two nights ago, trying to check everyone's backgrounds.

"Yes, hi," she said to the registrar. "I wanted to confirm that Sawyer Harrington graduated from your medical school." She gave the woman the range of years and then suffered through a pause so long that she finally said, "Hello? Are you still there?"

"Yes, I'm so sorry. The board decided it wasn't important enough to issue a press release, but if anyone called specifically asking about it, we felt it was important to set the record straight."

"On what?" she asked, searching her bag frantically for her notebook and pen.

"On Sawyer Harrington's school record. I am authorized to say he did not graduate from our facilities."

Stella used her teeth to take the pen cap off and spoke around the plastic. "What do you mean? Did he transfer to another school?"

There was another pause. "Well, that's just it. He never graduated from any medical school, from what we can tell."

"But..." Stella looked down at her notes with a frown. "I guess I don't know exactly how it works. The usual path is you get into medical school, graduate, and then go on—either to residency or to... what?"

"There's only one way to become a practicing

physician: get matched to a hospital for residency after graduation and then pass a medical licensing exam."

"And Sawyer Harrington did everything but graduate from your college?"

"No, you misunderstand me. He hasn't done any of that."

"He doesn't have his medical license?" Stella spluttered. "But he's a practicing physician!"

"Not anywhere we could find. He might say he's a doctor, but he doesn't have offices or a practice anywhere in the state of California."

After they disconnected, Stella stared at a nearby street sign several minutes, lost in thought. If Sawyer wasn't a doctor, what was he? How did a non-doctor get involved in Luna C Engineering? She pulled out of the lot and drove toward Sawyer's ex-wife's home, hoping she could shed some light on what, exactly, her ex-husband did and how he did it.

35

Stella slowed the car as she approached Heidi's house. This was one of the most awkward parts of being a reporter: showing up unannounced, uninvited, and often undesired. Feeling especially obnoxious in John's huge, black pickup truck, she idled in park on the curb for several minutes before she turned off the engine and climbed down to the pavement.

A series of ride-on toys and bikes littered the front yard. The garage was open, revealing a small SUV in the middle of the space, tipping her off that Heidi likely lived here alone with the kids—no boyfriend or new husband around to need the other half of the garage.

She knocked on the front door over a cacophony of noise from inside. Children screamed and yelled with laughter, and just as her fist made contact with the wooden door for the second time, a crash from inside made her jump.

A woman's raised voice screeched all the way through the door, and then Stella leapt out of the way as four children suddenly filed out past her with serious faces. A fifth child—the oldest and tallest by several inches—came marching out with a mischievous smirk and then let out a celebratory whoop before leading the charge down into the grass. All five boys grabbed bicycles, scooters, and skateboards from the ground and took off down the street at top speed—and top volume.

Wide-eyed and staring after the kids, she only turned back to the house when a woman yelled, "And don't come back until dinnertime!" The door started to close when the woman noticed Stella leaning against the house for support. "Oh, sorry. I didn't see you there. I hope Lincoln and the other kids didn't run you over!"

"Not quite," Stella said with a weak smile.

After she introduced herself, Heidi's eyebrows drew together for a moment. She then shrugged and said, "Well, come on in. I don't know what I can tell you, but I've got a few minutes." She led Stella into what looked like a barely-used sitting room. "I need a few minutes before I face the mess they left behind," she said, shaking her head. "The boys are ten and twelve—just old enough to be trouble and just young enough to know they can still get away with it."

"Heidi," Stella said, biting her lip. "I don't know how to ask this without sounding rude, so I'm just going to say it. Is Sawyer a doctor? Does he have a medical license and practice somewhere?"

Heidi was already shaking her head. "God no, he hated clinic when he was in med school. Touching all those sick people all the time gave him the heebie-jeebies. That's why he transferred and finished his degree at another school."

"So he has a PhD but not a medical license?" Stella asked, trying to make sense of the process.

"A PhD? No, no, he switched over to DDS," Heidi said, "but he didn't like mouths, much, either. He does love *learning*, though, and ended up staying on at the university to teach."

"To teach *dentistry*?" Stella asked, her pen poised over her notebook. No wonder she hadn't found him in the PhD registrar for the state! She'd been looking in the wrong database.

"Well, to do research, really. He doesn't like the students."

The couch on which Stella sat faced an open

doorway into the dining room. Papers and art supplies covered the entire table with some additional scraps and glue sticks underneath. Heidi saw what Stella was staring at, and with a small sigh, she resolutely turned her back on the mess and said, "Don't sweat the small stuff. I learned that from Sawyer, believe it or not. One of the only things..." She cut herself off and looked up apologetically. "He's a good father. That's what's important, in the end."

"What happened between you two? I sense some tension, still, although Sawyer said the divorce has been finalized for a while."

Heidi's brow furrowed. "What did he tell you?"

"Nothing," Stella said. "I just got the impression that things aren't easy."

The other woman bit her lip. "I cheated on him," she blurted out, glancing at the front door when the screen banged from the wind. Satisfied that it wasn't her children coming in, she looked back at Stella with a nervous, breathy laugh. "What is it about you?" she asked. "I feel like I'm in a mini-confessional and I just want to tell you things. It's so strange."

"That must've been a difficult time," Stella pressed on, her gaze never wavering from the other woman.

"You don't know the half of it." She laughed again, but there was no joy in the sound. "It was very difficult. I'm just so thankful that Sawyer didn't—" Again, she shook herself as she remembered she was sitting in front of a stranger. When Stella leaned forward, though, Heidi's words came tumbling out. "I had an affair with Drew Chambers." She blew out a sigh and leaned against the back cushion of the couch.

"It was a tough time for me and Sawyer—the kids were younger. You just never understand how exhausted you are all the time when you have kids. It's like you'll never sleep again—like there's no hope." She crossed her arms and hunched over, almost like she was bracing for what was coming next.

"So, there I was, knowing it wouldn't last with Drew. Sawyer was working long hours, though—I think he didn't *want* to come home because it was so chaotic here. He preferred to be in his quiet office doing his quiet research. Drew was so... Well, now that I've heard about his serial cheating ways, it all makes sense. He was flattering, complimentary—he knew just what to say, and in the end, I guess I'm not sorry. I needed it and Sawyer couldn't give it to me." She looked up at Stella and shrunk a bit under her steady gaze.

"When did this happen?" Stella asked.

Heidi blanched. "It was a while ago—I guess maybe two... two and a half years ago?"

"It started two and a half years ago or it ended two and a half years ago?" The distinction seemed important. Had the affair ended because Drew died?

Heidi's face paled and she shook her head repeatedly. "Sawyer had nothing to do with it," she said. "It was just a coincidence, the timing of it all. He told me he was at his office that day at the university, nowhere near the building where Drew was murdered."

"Do you believe him?" Heidi had the grace to blush slightly as she attempted to nod, but she didn't—couldn't—speak. Stella continued, "Days? Weeks? How much time elapsed between when your affair with Drew Chambers ended and when he was murdered?"

The woman rocked back and forth on the couch, then finally got up, opened the front door, and peered out onto the street. Apparently satisfied that they were alone, she closed it again but left her hand lying flat against the wood. She continued to face the door and finally answered Stella without looking at her, as if she couldn't face her.

"The affair ended when Drew died."

36

It was clear, as Stella drove back to John's cabin in the woods, that she was in over her head. Preston Harrington was innocent with a secret, airtight alibi, and meanwhile, Sloan Chambers' alibi had fallen apart. Now Sawyer Harrington's ex-wife had told her Sawyer had motive and had been lying to investigators about both his resume and his feelings about the victim. Would his alibi stand up to increased scrutiny?

Preston must not have called attention to his inconsistencies because Sawyer knew the truth about Tanya and didn't want to risk his daughter's happiness.

Did Preston suspect his brother was the killer?

Did Sawyer know he'd left a trail of clues behind?

Did Heidi know she was the only one who could now connect her ex-husband with a motive for murder?

Most interestingly, what did Detective McDonald know? According to Rita Perlman, Trish knew about Sloan's shaky alibi, but did she know about Tanya or Heidi Harrington's affair? If she did, why was she hiding it?

Before she slowed to make the turn onto John's long drive, her phone rang. The reception was poor, so she pulled over to answer.

"Stella? This is Jolene Colburne."

"Jolene! Wow, how are you?"

"I—I'm better, thank you for asking. I know you're busy—I saw... I saw that the jury has the case now."

Stella looked away from her own gaze in the rear view mirror. She hated feeling guilty for doing her job. "I'm really sorry that I took over—well, I mean, had to jump in when you... when it..." She blew out a loud breath and fell quiet.

After a moment of silence, Jolene spoke to someone in the background and then Aretha came on the line. "Stella, you have a place at our table whenever you're in North Carolina.

Don't you feel bad about doing your job, you hear?"

There was more muffled conversation and then Jolene came back on the line. "Sorry about that—my mother." Heightened breathing made it sound like Jolene was walking somewhere. "Let me just get outside. I know you're busy; I don't want to take up too much of your time."

"It's no trouble," Stella said, opening the windows and then turning off the engine. "You're... well? You're feeling well?"

"Yes, so much better. I actually felt much better at the airport, but I was... well, I was too embarrassed to talk to you. It's been a rollercoaster these last days, and I just hate feeling weak, you know?"

"I'm so glad—"

"The reason I called is because I think someone tried to poison me."

Stella's eyes whipped back to her own reflection in the narrow mirror. "Umm... do you want to put your mom back on the—"

"I know it sounds crazy, but I am not crazy or paranoid. I just got a clean bill of health from my doctor."

"But—"

"I know I felt great when I got to Palm Springs, and I would never stop taking my medication—

not even for a cute boy, like my mom is convinced happened. I was on my meds when things got hazy. Something happened to me that changed my body chemistry, and someone did it. I'm sure." Stella didn't know what to do with Jolene's story, so she didn't say anything. Finally, Jolene spoke again. "I was getting close to... something. I can't say what, because I promised the information would be off the record, but there was evidence..."

Stella had to tread lightly. "Information about Preston's family?"

Jolene was just as cagey. "What do you know?"

"I know he has a good alibi that's not public."

She breathed out a sigh. "Yes, you've met Tanya. I was hoping she'd connect."

"Do you think Tanya poisoned you?"

"No, but I think the killer is close to the case, and I think they knew I was digging and they didn't like it. Mom—Mom, just give me a minute, okay?" She laughed without humor. "My mom isn't happy to have me thinking about work, but I just wanted to warn you to be careful. Someone in Palm Springs is nervous, and I think they're willing to kill again." With those ominous words, she hung up.

Stella started John's truck and turned onto the gravel drive that led to his house. As she navigated the deep potholes and uneven grading, she realized she was going to need help. She picked up her cell phone and dialed a familiar number.

"Are you busy tomorrow?"

"No," came the bored reply. "I have a nail appointment at ten, but other than that, I'm free." After a pause, Vindi added, "Why?"

"I'll explain tomorrow." They set a time and then Stella turned into John's driveway. It was 3:46.

"Crap," she muttered, hopping down from the cab and hurrying up the front steps. "Sorry!" she called after wrenching open the door. "I... hit some traffic on the way back," she lied. "I hope you won't be too late. You said you had to leave at three thirty, right?" She was drawn toward the kitchen as warm, delicious, spicy air wafted her way. "What are you—oh!"

John stood in the exact center of the kitchen, wearing a white apron over his T-shirt and jeans. He should have looked goofy with the words, "World's Best Chef" embroidered on his chest, but when he picked up a glass of deep-burgundy wine and took a sip, Stella's heart beat unevenly in her chest.

"Dammit," she muttered under her breath.

He grinned. "Stella, I hear you and Trish have gotten to know each other over the last week."

Her face scrunched until she followed John's gaze to a tiny alcove in the corner. As Detective Trish McDonald raised her own glass of wine in greeting, Stella's heart trembled in her chest and she braced herself against the nearest counter.

The shock of finding the cop here, in the middle of nowhere, when she was essentially trying to hide from the world was almost enough to send her panting to the floor. She wondered at the fact that she didn't scream and run from the room, her hands over her head like a character from a cartoon.

"Where did you park?"

"Here by the back door," McDonald said, pointing to the kitchen door.

Stella smiled, hoping it didn't come out looking forced, and said, "Wow, what a nice surprise." She looked at the wine in front of McDonald. "Are you two... celebrating something?"

"Just the end of this case—or, at least, almost the end," Trish clarified before tilting her glass back for a sip. "John covered Drew's murder; he's been on the case just about as long as I have."

"Kate and I were closing on the house when the newsroom called," he explained, holding out the bottle of wine. "Care for a glass?" She shook her head and he set the bottle back on the countertop. "Trish has been a great source throughout it all."

Had Trish followed her here? Was there a chance she had rummaged through her room yesterday? Could she trust John? Even more importantly, did John know Trish wasn't to be trusted?

Stella's smile froze on her face. "Maybe I will have some wine," she said weakly. She turned toward the cabinets under the guise of getting a glass and took a moment to compose herself as she pulled one down from the top shelf. With a shaky hand, she reached out for the wine bottle.

"Here, let me," John offered, stepping closer. He rested a steadying hand on her arm, and she felt her tremors quiet. She could trust him—of course she could.

"What have you been up to?" Trish asked. Stella nearly spit out her wine.

"Oh, you know," she mumbled when she'd finally stopped coughing. "Just a drive around town. It's been a busy week—exhausting, really."

"John was telling me you two used to be together?"

"Ages ago," John clarified, looking at Stella with a lopsided smile. "Sometimes it feels like another lifetime."

"Sometimes it feels like just yesterday," Stella added. John guffawed.

"Well, I'm impressed you two can still be friends. Most exes hate each other or don't care about each other at all. Friendly exes, though? Now that's something new." Trish finished her glass of wine and stood. "It was nice to touch base, John. Stella, I'll see you soon." When she didn't answer, the detective cocked her head to the side. "In court? Won't you be there when this all ends?"

"Oh—right, of course. See you in court," she stammered.

John left the kitchen after Trish to walk her out, and when they were gone, Stella slumped into a seat at the small table by the back window.

"What was that about?" John asked when he walked into the kitchen alone a few minutes later.

"You don't want to know."

"Try me." He moved the chair opposite her around the table so that, when he sat, they were knee to knee. "You were frightened when you saw her. What's going on?"

"I wasn't *frightened*, I was—I..." Stella shook her head. She didn't even know where to begin.

John leaned over and tucked a stray strand of hair behind her ear. "I know I was out of line yesterday morning, and I'm not exactly sorry," he continued to talk over her outraged snort, "because I promised myself I'd never miss a chance to fight for you again. It was a Hail Mary, though, I see that now, and I'm done. I wanted you to know I'm not waiting, anymore. I—I'm going to move on."

She looked up. "You are?"

He nodded. "That doesn't mean I don't care about you, though, and despite what happened yesterday, you can trust me, Stella—you know you can. If I can help you..." he reached a hand out but stopped just before he touched her cheek. He dropped it back to his side and said, "Let me. Okay? Let me help you."

She blew out a breath. "I'm fine. Thank you, John, but I can take care of myself."

"I know," he said, standing.

Before she could blink, she was staring at his naked chest. "What are you doing?" she asked as he tossed his apron and T-shirt up the stairwell behind him. His arms rippled with the motion and she dragged her eyes away from his body to the clock above the door.

"I'm on vacation. I'd just gotten the hot tub ready when Trish showed up, so I'm going in. Care to join me?"

"I didn't..." Again, she had to tear her eyes away from his sculpted chest. She cleared her throat, but her voice still came out raspier than she liked. "I didn't bring a suit."

"Doesn't matter to me," John said, stalking past her to the door. Before the screen slammed closed, his jeans landed at her feet. The splash of water when he climbed in was quickly followed by another invitation. "The water feels great, Stella!"

"I thought you had somewhere to go?"

"Nah," he called. "Just didn't want you running around town with my truck all night.

She poured herself another glass of wine and took it straight to her room. She didn't trust herself, and despite what John had said about moving on, she didn't trust him, either.

37

Monday dawned cool and bright, although the morning meteorologist assured Stella that temperatures would soar to a very comfortable seventy-eight degrees by midday. Clattering in the kitchen told her she wasn't the only one awake.

She dressed carefully, wearing layers and comfortable shoes. She and Vindi would likely walk several miles before the day ended, and she didn't want sore feet to be the reason she didn't get to the bottom of things.

Before she headed downstairs, she put in a phone call to Sawyer's office at the university. She'd gotten the information the day before from

Heidi, and she wanted to check on his alibi. No one answered, so she left a message.

She knew John knew something was up in the Chambers murder case, but she couldn't say anything and neither could he. The secret pushed them apart even further than his lie from Saturday morning; frankly, the job always would, as long as they were both in TV news. It was a strange place to be for two people who knew and even liked each other.

When she turned the narrow corner of the stairwell into the kitchen, John took a moment to look at her with a lopsided grin. "I won't even ask. I guess I'll just tune in tonight."

"Tomorrow, if we're lucky," she said with a sad smile.

"We?"

Just then, a horn blared from the driveway. Curious, he headed down the hall and then chuckled when he recognized Vindi's voice as she yelled out the driver's side window, "Reynolds, let's go!"

He turned toward her, his eyes soulful, as he braced himself against the banister. "I'm going to give you space—no more pressure and no more tricks or games. Just know that I'm going to move on. I need to move on from you."

"Yes, you—you need to, John. I'm sorry," she said when he winced at her words. "I wish..."

"Me, too," he said with a slight frown. "Are you coming back tonight?"

"No," she said, pointing at the suitcase she'd brought down earlier. "I'll probably stay with Vindi tonight. It's going to be a long day and maybe a long night, so..."

He nodded and backed away. "Goodbye, Stella."

"Goodbye, John."

He gave her a sad smile and turned away. Stella bit her lip, turned, and clambered down the steps with her bags.

"Jesus, you two could make a Lifetime movie look happy," Vindi said, but her eyes were warm and her smile kind as she popped the latch for the trunk.

Stella hefted her suitcase into the back and then walked around the car to sit next to Vindi. After she buckled her seatbelt, she closed her eyes and leaned back against the headrest. "Just drive."

"Yes, ma'am." The engine roared to life, and they didn't talk until they got to the edge of downtown. Stella was lost in thought, and Vindi shot quick glances at her between navigating other cars and lights.

It was late morning on Monday and the streets were crowded.

"When everyone's retired, weekdays, weekends —they're all the same," Vindi grumbled, easing her car around a Buick Regal that couldn't decide which lane to drive in. As they passed the car, the older driver, wearing a driving cap and sunglasses, smiled and waved. "Also, I'm just going to say it: old people shouldn't drive. There should be a new test starting at fifty that you have to pass annually—"

"Fifty?" Stella exclaimed. "Fifty's not *old*. My mom's nearly sixty and she could take you down on the tennis court. Game, set, match!"

"Fine," Vindi said with a grin, "sixty—sixty-five at the latest. Maybe as soon as you file for social security, bam! You start the annual driver's test."

"Argh!" Stella shouted, and Vindi slammed on the brakes.

While she'd been busy telling Stella about terrible drivers, she hadn't noticed the car in front of them had stopped for a pedestrian crosswalk. They screeched to a halt, leaving wavy skid marks behind.

After a moment of shocked silence during which they both watched a man walk his bicycle to the other side of the street, Stella said, "I don't know, maybe twenty-seven is the right age to start that test."

They looked at each other and then burst out laughing.

Once traffic started moving again, Vindi, her eyes locked onto the road ahead, said, "Fill me in. What's going on?"

"First, what do you know about Luna C's new drug?"

Her friend scowled at the windshield. "Wondred? Just that it's going to be worth millions and maybe billions, if it ever gets off the ground."

Stella rummaged around in her bag and pulled out her phone. "I got an email that mentioned a problem with the drug during trials."

"Nope," Vindi shook her head, "no side effects. That's what everyone keeps saying."

"Right, no side effects if dosed properly, but do you know anything about a higher dose?"

Vindi hummed out a sound while she thought. At a light, she turned to Stella. "There was something—you're right—but I only read it in the paper. It was far too detailed for TV news. It was something about everyone having to start at dose zero, so to speak. No one has built up an immunity, and there was one person in a clinical trial who almost died just by starting with the same dose as her other medication."

"Unusual?"

"Well, sure. I think nearly dying in a clinical trial is pretty bad for the drug. Where are you going with this?"

"I don't know. It's just something Jolene said."

"You talked to Jolene? What did that crazy lady want?"

"Vindi," Stella looked reproachfully at her friend. "She's doing better. Did you ever see her talking to anyone involved in the case?" If Jolene thought someone had tried to poison her, was it so unreasonable to think it might have been done with a large dose of Wondred? Lots of people close to the case had access to the drug.

"Not really—well, no, that's not true," Vindi said. "I guess I saw her talking to Sloan Chambers during jury selection."

"Sloan? Are you sure?"

Vindi shrugged. "I mean, we weren't friends or anything, so it was just something I noted in the back of my mind. Like, okay, what's she going to scoop me on, you know?"

Stella nodded, and her friend turned up the radio. Did Sloan have an opportunity to poison

Jolene? How, though, and why? They drove the rest of the way in silence.

～

"WHERE ARE WE STARTING THIS MANHUNT?" Vindi asked after she'd parked the car in a spot downtown.

"Do you have the pictures?"

"Yup, in my bag," Vindi answered, motioning to her briefcase on the floor between them.

"Let's go to the Nurabu Hotel, where that Rotary Club meeting was held the day Drew died. We can start there."

Vindi pointed her car in that direction and, within minutes, they stood on the sidewalk outside the hotel, each with a picture of Sawyer that Vindi's photographer had grabbed from a still-frame of video from court.

"Let's split up," Stella said. "What we're looking for is anyone who remembers seeing Sawyer the day Drew was killed."

"Two years ago?" Vindi asked doubtfully.

"I know," Stella answered with a sigh. "It's a place to start, at least. Maybe ask about old surveillance video, too."

"Didn't police already canvas this strip?"

"Yes, but you know people—sometimes they don't want to talk to cops," Stella said, thinking specifically of Tim, dodging police as a matter of daily life.

Vindi looked at the row of stores distastefully and then squared her shoulders. "I'll take this side. Meet you at the other end of the block?"

Stella nodded and they parted ways. For the next twenty-five minutes, she asked persistent, friendly questions of store owners, employees, and even customers, but no one remembered seeing Sawyer.

"Nope, don't recognize him," a Somali man with a heavy accent said after looking at the picture critically. "Two years ago?" He tsked. "We have dozens of customers come in every day for milk and cheese. That was a long time ago, miss."

"Hard to say, sweetie," a woman wearing sunglasses—both over her eyes and on top of her head—said, scrunching her whole face up when she looked at the picture. "Middle-aged, slightly overweight white guy? They're everywhere." With a subtle jerk of her head, she motioned to a man in the back of her sunglass shop perusing a spinning display. He had lighter hair and a bigger paunch than Sawyer, but Stella understood what the woman was saying: there wasn't anything unusual or memorable about Sawyer that would make anyone remember him two years later.

She walked to the next shop but froze at the door. If she was going with the thought that Tim's reference to "Highway Patrolman" was about Preston's brother, Sawyer, she was still missing a major piece of information: why did *Tim* remember Sawyer Harrington two years later? What had made the brother stick out to the war vet?

She scanned the other side of the street, looking for her partner in crime. Vindi came out of a coffee shop holding both Sawyer's picture and a twenty-ounce hot drink.

"Vindi!" She waved to catch the other woman's attention and then hurried across the street. "I think we're missing something."

"Yeah, no kidding," she agreed. "No one here remembers anything."

"We need to go find my friend, Tim. He can be difficult to understand, but I think he might be able to—to tell us what we're missing—to help us solve this case."

38

Stella figured they'd start at the bodega, Tim's home away from home. Joe Jones might know where he went when he wasn't munching on pastries or coffee. "At least we can get a drink," she muttered to herself.

"I'm good to go," Vindi said, holding up her cup. "Triple vanilla latte."

"You know there's more sugar in that than caffeine?"

Her friend took a pull from the cup and then let out a long, satisfied sigh. "Don't care—the combination is sublime."

By now, it was long past noon. Downtown was busy with meandering pedestrians, and they were heading in the wrong direction, so it was slow going.

"Excuse *me*," Vindi said through gritted teeth when a woman rolled over her foot with a baby stroller.

"You're fine," the woman answered with a breezy smile. Stella suppressed a laugh at her friend's outraged expression.

"Come on," Stella said, pulling her into the bodega behind her. The store appeared empty. "Joe?" she called. She pressed a desktop bell twice and they waited. "That's so strange. He's usually right here..."

They turned at a clattering toward the back of the store and Joe hurried out. "Sorry, can I help you?" He rounded the corner and smiled when he recognized Stella. "Oh, hey, Stella. What can I do you for?"

She grinned at the wording and introduced Vindi. "We're looking for Tim. Have you seen him today?"

Joe frowned lightly. "No, and that's odd. He's usually waiting for me outside when I get here in the morning to open, but not today." Stella frowned. She didn't know where else to find him. "I'm actually a bit worried about him," Joe added.

"Not just because I haven't seen him—that's not terribly uncommon. Sometimes he finds a shelter for a night or someone offers to buy him a hot breakfast." He wadded up a paper towel and tossed it in a nearby garbage can. "He's been off his game lately."

"Off his game?"

Joe's mouth slanted at an angle. "Yes, more than usual."

"Did something happen recently?"

He leaned against the counter and eyed Stella critically. "Well, I'd say it started when he met you."

"Me?" Wide-eyed, she tried to make out if Joe was joking. "But—"

"I'm not saying it's you," Joe clarified, "but when he found out you worked on TV, he was interested. He said, 'Let's watch,' which I looked up, and it is not a song title—that I could find, anyway. So, I cued up the news at night and we watched a few of your live shots. Maybe I'm imagining things, but... darn if he didn't go downhill fast."

"We're talking about a homeless guy who only speaks in song titles?" Vindi said, scrunching up her face. "I'm sorry—not to be rude—but... how could you tell?"

Joe frowned. "It's hard to explain. He used to

have moments of clarity, but they're fewer and farther between."

"Since when?" Stella asked.

"It's been a couple of years, I guess. Sometimes we could have a conversation. It was stilted and often confusing, but he could get a sentence or two out, just normal-like." A man walked up to the register with an apple and a hot dog. "'Scuse me; I'll be right back." Joe left to ring up the customer. After the transaction was complete and they were alone in the store again, he walked back over to Stella and Vindi, with a tortured, almost guilty expression. "There was... an incident here, at the store."

"What happened?"

"Well, I never would have pressed charges, but two patrol officers happened to be here getting coffee. Tim came in, very upset about something, and when I was trying to calm him down to—to figure out how I could help, he knocked over a display shelf. It caused a huge ruckus—Hostess and Little Debbies flew in every direction." He shook his head. "Like I said, it was just Tim, but the patrol officers didn't know that. I don't blame them, either, I just wish... I just wish they'd tried to calm the situation first."

"What did they do?" Stella asked.

"Now, listen, I'm not one to disrespect police. I'm glad they're here, and I appreciate how difficult their jobs are on a near daily basis. They slapped handcuffs on him without asking a single word, though—without listening to me at all! For a war vet who's been locked in his own mind since coming home, being in cuffs was like the straw that broke the camel's back."

Stella's hand flew to her chest as she pictured the terrible scene.

Vindi's practical voice broke in. "So, what happened?"

"Police took him away. I refused to press charges, of course, but the damage had been done. Prosecutors tried to charge him, anyway, so we had to get a little creative on the strip."

"How so?" Stella asked. She liked the way he'd started to grin.

"I called a quick business district meeting, and everyone agreed to keep mum on any complaints against Tim. Prosecutors hit a wall of silence and had to drop the case."

"Did you ever find out why he was upset to begin with?"

"He would never speak of it again after the arrest, but before the incident, he kept saying something about a man with a stroller—and the stroller didn't have a baby." Silence descended while they all chewed on that. Finally, Joe added, "I got to thinking after the fact that maybe he saw a dad and realized he'd lost his chance for a family—for a child? I don't know. It never made much sense to me, and like I said, he didn't want to talk about it."

"It was about two years ago?" Stella asked, the first tingles of excitement forming at the base of her stomach.

"I have the date, actually, if you hold on a moment," Joe said. He rang up another customer and then headed to the back of the store, motioning for the women to follow. "Prosecutors requested the surveillance video, and I saved a copy, too. It shows how distressed he was and how knocking over the shelf was just an accident. I'm keeping it in case they try to use it against him in the future. I want everyone to know he just needs help, not jail time."

He walked into a tiny, cluttered office space and opened a file cabinet. After a moment of rummaging, he pulled a file folder out. A thumb drive fell to the floor, and he groaned as he bent down to retrieve it.

Flipping through the pages in the folder he said, "Here it is. August twenty-fourth, just after one."

Vindi's eyes opened wide at the date.

"That's the same day Drew Chambers was killed," Stella said, knowing in the pit of her stomach that his murder and Tim's freak-out couldn't be mere coincidence.

According to Rita Perlman, Tim had seen Sloan Chambers hurrying down the street just before noon. Perlman had said he was calm and observant, so what happened during that next hour that had made him so upset?

"Vindi, let's go. Joe, thanks so much. You've been very helpful."

"He sometime hangs out in the town square by the fountain," Joe called after them.

"Where are we going?" Vindi asked.

"Back to the Nurabu Hotel. We were asking all those store owners and employees the wrong question."

39

The streets were even more crowded than when they'd walked into Joe's store, and they left the car wedged into the spot by the curb, opting to walk back to the strip of stores to save time.

"What are we doing?" Vindi asked, looking down at the picture of Sawyer still gripped tightly in her hand.

"One of the shop owners I spoke with said she would never remember a middle-aged white guy passing by two years ago. A man pushing a stroller, though? Now that's a little more uncommon—especially if something happened between him and Tim!"

Vindi nodded. "True. Now you've got a middle-aged white guy pushing a stroller and possibly interacting in some way with a one-legged man and his dog."

"Exactly: much more memorable," Stella said with a determined frown. "Let's split up again. I'll meet you at the end of the block. Call me if you find anything good."

Vindi tossed her empty coffee cup into a recycling bin and crossed the street. They were going up the strip from the opposite direction this time, and Stella stopped in each store—even the ones in which no one had remembered anything before, thinking new employees might have arrived since she was last there.

It wasn't until she hit the sunglass store again, however, that she made any headway with her new theory.

"You again?" said the woman wearing multiple pairs of sunglasses. "I'm Dixie. What did you say your name was?" After a quick introduction, Stella asked about Tim and Sawyer. "Oh, that," she said, her friendly smile waning slightly.

"I'm not here to get Tim in trouble. I'm more interested in what made him so upset that day. Joe Jones told me it had to do with a baby—or, I guess, not a baby, to be more exact."

Mentioning Joe had been the right thing to do.

"Joe's a good man to take care of Tim like he does."
The woman sucked on her bottom lip and then
squinted up at Stella. "You're not with police?"

"No, not at all. I work for NBC News. I'm just
interested in what happened the day Tim got
arrested."

"Damn rookie cop. Everyone in town knows
Tim, but that new guy acted like a gunslinger in
the Old West. Fool. No, no, hon," she called to a
woman in the middle of the store, "you want
round—not square. The square lenses don't do a
thing for your face!" She picked up a pair from the
closest rack. "Here, try these." She smiled when
the woman put them on, and then turned back to
Stella. "So, Tim bumped into the stroller right outside my door. It was his crutch, actually, and I
think the guy bumped into Tim, not the other way
around, but he put up a real fuss about it. I could
understand why, at first, since the stroller nearly
tipped over, but I'll tell you what, for only having
one leg, Tim has reflexes like a cat! His hand
snaked out and caught the edge of the stroller
right quick."

"The baby was okay?" Stella asked.

"There wasn't a baby! The guy was pushing a
stroller full of dirty rags."

"Wh—what?"

"Yup. Made some excuse about heading to the donation center, and that's when I rolled my eyes. I've been in a bad way before with nowhere to live, and let me tell you, homeless people don't want your stained, dirty, gross, old rags! Gently used or brand new—that's what they need. Lord knows they'll be hard enough on the clothes, so they'd better at least start out nice, you know?"

"Wait a minute, back up. Was this the man pushing the stroller?" She held up Sawyer's picture.

"Hmm," Dixie squinted and leaned in close. "It could have been. Maybe with darker hair? Looks about right."

It wasn't terribly convincing as a witness identifying Sawyer, but Stella pressed on. "So, a stroller full of dirty rags and no baby. When did Tim get upset?"

"Well, I'm not exactly sure. It was right after he righted the stroller. The man was telling me about his big donation plan," she rolled her eyes again at the memory, "and I guess it might have just been the stress of the day. We had police surrounding the office building next door, over that poor man's murder. All those cops just made poor Tim nervous. I guess he was bound to crack at some point. Well," she said with a short laugh, "crack more than he already had."

"I don't suppose you have surveillance cameras anywhere?"

The woman put her hands on her hips. "No, thank you—not for me. I don't need someone hacking into my system to watch me pick my nose when the store's empty, no sir-ee."

"Wow. Okay, then, thank you so much. You've been very helpful," Stella said, leaving the store. She saw Vindi disappearing into the store across the street and decided to try the next shop over before connecting with her. If Dixie had seen the incident between Tim and Sawyer, maybe someone at the grocery store next door had, as well.

The doors to *Palm Springs Eats and Meats* were propped open, and Stella headed directly to the counter. The same man from earlier was still there, and he crossed his arms when he saw her.

"I've got nothing more to say, so unless you plan on buying an energy drink or a hot dog that's been rolling on that heater for the past five hours, it's time to pack up and go, miss."

His accent was heavy, but even if Stella hadn't understood him perfectly, his tone brooked no argument with his dislike of her being there. She opened her mouth to apologize, but before she could get a word out, she happened to glance at the hot dog roller and said, "Uhh... there seems to be a situation there. One maybe... exploded?"

The man jumped up. "Dang it. Steven! I told you to put the machine on medium! High is too much for these dogs. We don't need customers getting hit with exploding bits of meat product!"

As he whipped around the counter with a spray bottle and towel, Stella crossed her arms. "Do you have an accent or not?" His last round of words had sounded as if he were a Palm Springs native, not a transplant from another country.

From his profile, she could see him grimace as he cleaned splattered bits of meat off the wall behind the heater and between the slats.

"I come from Somalia, but I guess I'm soaking in the culture here," he said, his full, heavy accent back.

Stella crossed her arms. "Now wait just a minute. I need some information and I think you might have it. I'm looking for Tim, because I want to ask him about an incident that happened right outside your store two years ago. I can't find him, though, and now Joe's worried, so you'd better step up."

He swiped one last time at the hot dog machine and then brushed past Stella. "No, miss," he said, his voice thick with the harsh accent. "I'd better get back to work, that's all." He then added, almost as an afterthought, "I don't work with cops."

"I'm not a cop. I'm a reporter, and I—I'm worried about Tim, too."

He took his time putting the spray bottle away and rinsing the rag out in the sink. He finally turned around. "Not a cop?" he asked in an American accent.

"No!" She slid the picture of Sawyer across the counter. "Joe Jones at the bodega told me he tries to protect Tim, and I don't want to change that. I think he might know something about a murder, though, and I don't want him getting hurt. If you know anything, now would be a good time to share it."

He stared down at the picture, really looking at it this time, and when he looked up at Stella, he called, "Steven! Get that video cued up—the one with Tim and the stroller."

Behind him, a boy about twelve years old stood from a table, silently opened a door behind him, and disappeared. A few minutes later, his thin, warbling voice called out, "Okay, Papa. It's ready."

"Would you like to see what happened?" he

asked, motioning for Stella to walk behind the counter.

"Yes," she breathed, hoping to finally get some answers about what happened two years ago that had left Tim in a frenzy and a killer on the run.

40

Before Stella walked behind the counter, she tapped Vindi's name on her contact list. "I think I found something," she said when her friend picked up.

"Where are you?"

"I'm in that little grocery store—" She felt someone standing close behind her and turned to find Vindi, her phone pressed against her ear, grinning.

"I struck out on my side," she said, dropping her cell phone into her purse. "What do you have?"

"Vindi, I'd like you to meet..." She looked at the store owner, her eyebrows raised. "I guess we haven't officially met."

As they all shook hands, he said, "I'm Steve Lightner."

"Steve?" Stella asked with a smile. "Sounds very American."

He bit his lip and then smiled a toothy grin. "You'd be amazed at how fast most people run when they think they're talking to a foreigner. I use it to my advantage when I need to. Come on back; I'll show you what I've got." As Steve led the way back to the small office behind the counter, he rubbed his head with one hand. "Joe got in touch right after it all happened—said he was worried police were going to twist the facts to lock Tim up. I didn't want to be part of that—everybody here knows Tim, and his mom comes in to give us money all the time so he can eat, drink, and generally stay alive. So, I told the cops I didn't see anything, but I kept the video just in case Tim needed it down the line. You never know what cops are going to do. If he gets arrested two years from now, they might bring this case back up to show he has an existing record."

"What video?" Vindi asked, tapping her foot impatiently as Steve spoke. "What are we doing back here, anyway?"

Although she cringed a bit at Vindi's tone, Stella couldn't help but wonder the same thing.

They stood in a small, claustrophobic room, each wall covered from floor to ceiling with cramped, overstuffed shelves. Steve's son, Steven, sat in a small chair facing one of the shelves with a fold-down counter. It wasn't until Stella focused her attention on that wall that she realized, in the middle of books and stacks of everything from paper cups and towels to toilet paper, a small monitor perched with a long cord attached a laptop.

"All queued up?" Steve asked his son. The boy nodded and Steve said, "Hit play."

The video started with surprising clarity in full-color. Tim and Hope walked right in front of the camera by the store's front entrance with Hope's tail wagging as she pitched along next to Tim. He was mid-wave to someone across the street when a man walking in the other direction, clearly Sawyer but with slightly darker hair, pushed a stroller into Tim's crutch. The impact jolted Tim, but he recovered quickly and caught the stroller just before it hit the sidewalk.

From the camera's vantage point, it was impossible to make out anything inside the stroller, but after righting it, Tim leapt back, nearly losing his balance as he ran into Hope. The dog's hind quarters hit the sidewalk, but she jumped up just as

Tim managed to steady himself. He looked at Sawyer and stumbled backward again. In the meantime, Sawyer quickly adjusted whatever was inside the stroller and appeared to say a few angry words to Dixie, who'd just entered the frame to investigate. Tim hurried away with Hope close behind, and Steven paused the video on a haunting shot of Tim looking over his shoulder, a terrified expression on his face.

There were a few moments of silence while the four of them processed what they'd seen on the video. Vindi was the first to speak. "That's definitely Sawyer," she said, tapping her lip with a finger. "You said he had kids, right?" she asked Stella.

Stella nodded, "Yes, but they are nearly teenagers now. Two years ago, they wouldn't have been anywhere close to needing a stroller."

"So, what was in the stroller," Vindi asked, "if it wasn't a kid?"

"The owner of the sunglass store next door—"

"Dixie?" Steve offered.

"Right, Dixie said it looked like a bunch of old, dirty rags." Stella stared at the video screen, hoping that, if she focused enough, some spark of insight would come through. "It sure looked like Sawyer was using them to cover something up, though, didn't it?"

"Tim might as well have seen a ghost for how he acted," Vindi said.

"Makes you wonder what else was in there. Something really shook him up," she said, frowning again at the monitor. Stella looked at Steve, who frowned at them. "No one knows about this video, is that right?"

Steve nodded. "I'm not looking for trouble, okay? Police came knocking a couple of days after they arrested Tim. They were pretty overloaded with that Chambers murder, so it took a bit to look into Tim's arrest. By then, Joe had already been in touch, so I told them I didn't know anything—hadn't seen anything. I was only trying to protect him, though, you understand?" Suddenly, Steve's bravado was gone, and he looked concerned, wondering now, two years later, if he'd made the right decision.

Stella patted his arm. "I don't think it would've made a difference. It only matters now because we know things nobody knew then." Vindi walked out of the room and Stella followed, stopping at the counter to turn and thank Steve.

"Here, take one. Please, I insist," he said, forcing a hotdog into her hand. "I'll have to throw them away, otherwise."

She stifled a chuckle, certain she'd never had a

less appealing offer. "Where are you from, any-way?" she asked.

"San Jacinto, about twenty minutes away, but my grandad was born in Mogadishu."

"I'd work on the accent," Stella said with a smile. She turned toward Vindi and they walked out of the store, coming to a stop once they were on the sidewalk.

"What now?" Vindi asked, looking up at the camera that had captured the incident between Tim and Sawyer. "We know Sawyer was here around the time of the murder doing something suspicious with a baby stroller, of all weird things. That gets us all of nowhere when it comes to Preston's murder trial."

Stella linked arms with Vindi and started walking back to her car. "Now we find Tim. Tim has all the answers. Let's head toward the fountain —Joe said he sometimes hangs out there."

"What are we going to do when we find him, though? I don't speak the language of country song titles."

"Nor I," Stella said with a sigh, "but maybe we'll get lucky and find one of his moments of lucidity. We have to at least try." She looked in vain for a trash can to get rid of the hot dog and finally saw one across the street. As she stepped off the curb to cross, however, she caught sight of a mane of fuzzy, matted fur darting through foot traffic on the other side of the street.

Stella froze, one foot still on the curb behind her. "Hope?" She shrugged off Vindi's hand and raced into the middle of the intersection, stopping traffic in all directions—and just in time.

The dog galloped unevenly into the street. Hope was alone and in a panic as she zig-zagged between cars, the whites of her eyes showing her alarm.

"Hope!" Stella called, louder this time. The light turned and several cars honked, unaware that an animal was running free.

As she stood there, arms wide, trying to keep any cars from moving, a distressing thought entered her mind. She scanned the sidewalks, searching in vain. Joe had once said that even death wouldn't separate Tim from his dog. So, if Hope was here, where was Tim?

41

The hotdog saved her.

Hope hobbled by close enough for Stella to grab the fur at her neck, and before the dog could panic even more, Stella shoved the hotdog under her nose. Hope's nose worked overtime as she struggled between the fear of whatever had sent her running and her desire to eat.

The smell of meat won.

Stella led Hope away from traffic, tearing off small bits of hot dog along the way. At the sidewalk, a woman getting into her car saw Stella's predicament and pulled a spare leash out of her trunk. Stella took it gratefully and threaded the end through the loop, making a slipknot. She gave the final chunk of meat to the dog, and while she was distracted, slipped the opening over her head.

"Ew," Vindi said, finally appearing at Stella's side. "What is that?" She pointed at Hope.

"This is Tim's dog," Stella said, leading the animal away from their car.

"What are we going to do with it?"

"We're going to the fountain," Stella said, adjusting her stride to the dog's, "as fast as we can. Come on, girl. Let's go."

They made an odd threesome with Stella murmuring in that funny, sing-song voice people reserve for animals and small children, Vindi walking several paces behind, looking disgusted by the mangy mutt, and Hope, tail wagging unevenly as she hop-walked nearby, occasionally poking Stella with her nose, looking for more hotdog.

As they approached the town square, though, Hope tried to turn back. She pulled on the leash and finally planted her hindquarters on the ground, turning her face away from Stella when she tried to cajole her forward.

"What's that?" Vindi asked, pointing to a crowd forming near the fountain.

Stella looked up from the dog and saw an ambulance pull up on the opposite side of the fountain. Its lights were flashing, but the siren was ominously quiet. The crowd parted to let the medics pass, and through the new gap, Stella saw an officer standing guard. A pair of legs sprawled out on the ground nearby and the kelly-green pant leg stood out like a lightning bolt at night.

She shoved Hope's leash into Vindi's hand and rushed forward, stopping at the edge of the crowd when her worst fear was confirmed.

Tim's body lay alongside of the fountain, a sapphire red lake of blood pooling underneath his wavy hair. The medics only confirmed what the officer surely already knew: that Tim was dead. Before long, more officers were on site, cordoning off the area with yellow crime scene tape.

By then, Vindi had called in the story to her news desk. When Stella got back to her, she pushed Hope's leash into her hands and immediately flipped open her bag to pump hand sanitizer into her palm. She disconnected the call and said, "My boss wants a live shot on the homeless murder."

Stella wasn't surprised. "I'm going to take Hope... somewhere. Call me after you talk to police, okay?" She walked the dog away from Tim's body and the fountain square—away from whatever horror the dog had surely witnessed.

"We're going to see Joe," she said. She then added for herself, "Maybe he'll know what to do with you." As they made their way back through town, the late afternoon sun cast long shadows and their side of the street was completely shaded and cool.

As they crossed into sunlight toward the bodega, a scuffle broke out just ahead at the corner.

A group of high schoolers circled a girl, pecking at her sweater, the mass taking turns hurling insults. As Stella and the dog approached, some turned their vitriol onto Hope.

"Hey, Tripod!" one girl said. She would have been gorgeous, if not for the mean, scrunched expression on her face. "Hey, over here. I'll give you a leg up, you dumb dog," she screeched. As far as insults went, it didn't even make sense, but her posse of friends jeered and laughed. Baffled, Stella looked for a way around the group, but they were standing directly in front of the entrance to Joe's store.

A wailing siren pierced the air, and an unmarked police car with a small, portable light on the roof sped past with Trish McDonald behind the wheel. The detective was heading toward the murder scene, so it made sense that she'd look serious, but more than that, the cop looked genuinely distressed.

Before Stella could turn back to the storefront, the group of mean girls turned their sights back on their original target: the girl in the frayed cardigan. The lead mean girl was saying, "...you dressed better, we wouldn't have to say anything, at all, Liv."

Liv stood stoically in the center of the circle of hell, and a hardened set to her jaw made it clear she'd withstood worse—probably from this very group of tormentors.

The sight was enough to jar Stella out of her single-minded focus on Tim's murder. She whipped her reporter notebook out of her bag and, pencil poised, asked, "Where do you all go to school?" The mean queen said their school name, and then Stella asked, "What's the name of the principal there?"

Interested looks turned suspicious, and their fearless leader suddenly looked less bold. "Mister Neavins. Why?"

"Well, bullying is such a hot button topic these days, and we're always looking to feature the perpetrators, but it's hard to find bully volunteers. Everyone likes to be the bully, but no one likes to be called a bully, you know what I mean? Now, however, I can go right to Mr. Neavins with a list of names, see? It'll save me days of research."

"Bully! What do you mean?" their leader said, her swaggering confidence back. "We were just having a little talk with our friend, Liv. Right, Liv?"

The girl with the frayed, white cardigan shrugged, not making eye contact with anyone, and Stella seized the opportunity to separate the girls.

"Can you help me, Liv?" The girl shrugged again. "Can you hold onto this leash for a moment while we go into the store?" She turned to the mean girls. "I'll be in touch. Maybe the principal can set up meetings between you, me, and your parents, and we can discuss how much fun Liv was just having. I look forward to it."

The head-mean-girl's expression remained cocky, but the rest of her possee started to fade into the dwindling crowd in the sidewalk as Stella and Liv walked into the store.

"Thanks," the girl said, still staring at the ground. "I know what you were trying to do, but it'll probably only make it worse next time."

"Worse?" Stella asked.

"They'll latch onto anything. It's usually best if I just sit there and take it quietly, and then they move onto their next target."

"How often does that happen?" Stella asked in dismay.

"Once or twice a week. It depends. This time, they didn't like my sweater. Next time, it'll be my hair, or a zit, or a grade on a test." She looked up hopefully at Stella. "Mom says I can homeschool next year if things don't get better. I'll miss choir, but it'll be worth it."

"Worth it to escape daily persecution," Stella said grimly.

"Huh?" Liv asked.

"Nothing, sorry." By then, Joe had spotted them from the back of the store and was making his way toward them. Still several aisles away, he seemed to recognize the girl.

"Not again, honey?" he said, and the kindness in his voice almost broke Liv.

"No big deal, Joe, right?"

He steeled his expression. "That's right. Someday, you'll be signing their paychecks and they won't mess with you, then, will they, girl?"

Stella froze, his words sinking far deeper into her consciousness than normal. Wasn't that every bullied kid's thread of hope—that, someday, they'd be in charge of their tormentor's fate? Was Trish McDonald living that reality now? Had she taken things too far?

42

The hours dragged on painfully and terribly slow. Tim's mother waited in the bodega for police to confirm what they all already knew: that Tim was dead, likely killed while he fed the pigeons he so loved watching.

When Joe had seen Hope by Stella's side, he'd known without asking that something bad had happened. He'd called Tim's mother, Jane, and now Stella was stuck in a kind of morbid vigil inside the store.

The network wasn't interested in a homeless man's murder, although Sher mentioned they might want to bookmark the crime for an upcoming piece on wounded warriors and mental health care for returning vets.

The words "bookmark it" had sounded hollow to Stella's ears, as if Tim was just a footnote—an afterthought in the world of breaking news and current events.

Liv, the jittery high school target Stella had tried to rescue on the street, was long gone, although she'd mumbled uncomfortable thanks before she left.

Now, at five thirty on Sunday night, Hope leaned against Stella's leg while she sat in a chair just inside Joe's small, cramped office. She was waiting for some opening to leave the dog with Joe or Jane and leave the store for Vindi's hotel.

When her phone rang, she jumped for it, glad to have something to do besides stare at the dog.

"Stella, how's it going?" Lucky drawled. "Are you at the, uh, the house right now?"

"No," she murmured, "I haven't been there all day." She explained how she and Vindi had canvassed the strip and what they'd found.

"The country song guy you knew, Tim, is dead?" His voice, usually low and sexy, was hard and almost linear by the end of his question.

"I mean, I wouldn't say I *knew* him," Stella said, rubbing the spot between Hope's shaggy, fluffy ears. Before Lucky could answer, a breaking news graphic flew across the tiny screen in Joe's office.

"I've got to go, Lucky. I'll call you soon." She disconnected over his objection and reached for the volume knob, turning the sound up.

The anchor at the San Diego station had just tossed the newscast over to Vindi.

Although it was supposed to have been a day off of work, Vindi looked like she'd dressed specifically for the live shot. She had managed to apply full makeup in the last hour and had a live interview ready to go.

"Katherine, thank you. Police have just cleared the scene after medics removed the body of Tim Price, a familiar fixture in this luxury community known just as much for his special friendship with a stray dog as for his friendly demeanor and strong morals, despite struggling mightily with PTSD and depression after coming home from three tours of duty in Iraq.

"Joining me live is Palm Springs Police Detective Trish McDonald. Detective, we have a lot of concerned people out there, wondering if there's a killer on the loose. What do you want to say to them?"

As the detective gave a calming sound bite, Stella stared at her with a critical eye. Was the other woman paler than normal? The usually calm, collected cop fidgeted, her hands fluttering at her sides and then twisting together in front of her. Although her sound bite extolled calm and restraint, her appearance gave off the opposite vibe.

Vindi said, "Tim Price was a homeless veteran and by all accounts a beloved figure in a community that embraced him despite his battles with unseen demons. Where does the investigation stand? I understand there are cameras surrounding the crime scene. Will they be important as your investigation continues?"

Was it a trick of the light, or did Trish pale further? "Of course. Our officers will scour the scene, and we'll rely on citizens to come forward with any information pertaining to this crime. That's all I can say at this time, as the investigation is ongoing."

As Vindi tagged out, Stella turned back to Hope leaning woefully against her leg.

"It's going to be okay," she crooned, and Hope rested the side of her face against Stella's leg.

As she tried to comfort the dog, her mind was stuck on one theory of what might have been happening over the last two years. It seemed too fantastical, though—too ridiculous to believe—but she couldn't stop thinking about it. The longer she sat there, the more sense it seemed to make.

Trish McDonald was paying back her high school tormentors using a high-profile murder case. The detective wanted both Maria Garcia and Gail Abingdon fired, publicly shamed and universally reviled, just as she had been in high school.

Although it seemed unimaginable to suspect a grown woman would resort to framing an innocent man to succeed in her goal, Stella thought that was exactly what she'd done.

First, she'd withheld key evidence in the case from prosecutor Gail Abingdon, also known as mean girl number one from their high school days. Trish knew Sawyer Harrington was in the area on the day of Drew Chambers' murder, but she'd kept that information buried in a mound of seemingly unrelated paperwork. Her goal was clear: get Gail Abingdon to convict the wrong man. When the truth came out that Sawyer Harrington had motive and was seen near the scene of the crime, that would surely be a black mark against an otherwise rising star at the prosecutor's office— one that would stay with her for years to come.

Trish had then staged that perp walk with a Dr. Ruiz lookalike. She must have planted a fake note from Gail to Maria, assuring the CNN reporter that she had the exclusive on a major arrest. When Maria had run with it, Trish had gone to Stella, giving her the real story, making a mockery of Maria's immediately debunked "facts" and getting the other woman pulled from her job.

Now, though, another man was dead because of Trish's vendetta against her high school tormentors. In her haste to get back at Gail and Maria, she'd let the real killer walk free, and now he'd struck again. Trish was just as liable in Tim's death as Sawyer.

The biggest question of all now faced Stella: what was she going to do about it?

43

It had been several years since Stella and Vindi had pored over paperwork together, and now it felt surreal to be diving into another investigation with Vindi Vassa.

After her live shots, Vindi had driven Stella to the hotel. She would stay with her through tomorrow at least; after that, only time would tell. The network would either fly her to New York with a first class ticket or fire her on the spot.

"I'm ordering Chinese... or do you want pizza?"

"I could do either," Stella answered, not taking her eyes off the paperwork in front of her.

"Chinese it is," Vindi muttered, picking up her phone to find the nearest restaurant that delivered.

After she placed their order, she shuffled through the arrest reports and court documents. "I can't believe John helped us out here," she said. "I mean, he's basically shooting himself in the foot by giving us his contact's cell phone number."

They'd called his contact at the police department, an adorable, tiny woman named Wendy, who'd agreed to copy the police reports relating to Tim's arrest two years earlier. Stella had so many questions for the officer. How did she know John? What kind of source was she? *Would she do house calls for the handsome TV anchor?* She, however, only muttered, "Thanks," when she took the papers.

Now she looked at Vindi, feeling philosophical. "Yeah, but I think he realizes it's a fight for truth and justice now and not about beating the competition."

Vindi frowned. "It's always about the competition, Stella. Always."

She shrugged and held out a sheaf of paper. "I think this is going to be key." She pointed to a line in the report from Tim's arrest two years earlier. "Right here, it says McDonald was called to the bodega after Tim was arrested. That means she would have seen the video from Joe."

"That doesn't mean she would have known it was Sawyer," Vindi said reasonably.

"Yes, but look here!" Stella flipped to the next page. "It says right here, 'store owner, Dixie Danger—'"

"Dixie Danger?" Vindi interrupted. "Stop it." She grabbed the paper from Stella and barked out a laugh. "That must be an alias!"

"Nevertheless," Stella said, taking the papers back, "'Dixie Danger said the stroller was full of dirty, bloody blankets.' With a fresh murder just hours old and a block away, that should have raised alarm bells."

"Agreed, but that's easy to say in hindsight. It's also easy to explain away as an *over*sight. We need to prove that Trish *knew* Sawyer was guilty and intentionally hid that evidence from prosecutors."

"You're right," Stella said, tossing the papers onto the bed and rubbing a hand over her forehead with the back of her hand. "We need a smoking gun." She thought about Preston's real, airtight alibi that he and Tanya refused to go public with. She'd agreed to talk to Tanya off the record, but she regretted it immensely.

"Or we need Trish to *think* we have one," Vindi agreed.

Their food came, and while they ate, Stella

thought back over all the clues—false and other-wise—they'd managed to assemble, and ticked them off with her fork to Vindi. "So... Preston has an airtight alibi—"

"I wish you could tell me what it is," her friend said, an unusual whine in her voice.

"I can't, though," Stella said. "Sawyer found out his wife was having an affair with Drew Cham-bers. He stashes a butcher knife in an old baby stroller so he can sneak the weapon in and out of the office building, attacks Drew, and has practi-cally made his escape when he bumps into Tim."

Vindi took over, "Tim sees the bloody knife, freaks out, and there's an altercation. Before police arrive, Sawyer disappears, Tim tries to tell Joe what he saw, but instead he's arrested, and the business owners unite to keep him out of jail. So, really," she said, taking a moment to eat a forkful of rice, "by all accounts, the store owners pro-tected Tim. Trish—or any of the cops in Palm Springs—wouldn't have known anything about any man with a stroller, right?" Stella chewed on her food—and Vindi's comment—for a few min-utes, and then Vindi muttered, "I feel like I climbed in a time travel machine and we're back in Montana."

Stella leaped up from the bed and slammed

her carton of sweet and sour shrimp down on the dresser.

"Where are you going?" Vindi asked when she grabbed her jacket.

"I just need to find—there it is!" She triumphantly pulled her cell phone out of a coat pocket. "I just want to be sure of one thing..." Although John's contact had given them copies of several internal police reports, Vindi's comment about being back in Montana made her realize she definitely wasn't a newbie reporter, anymore. She was working for a major network and she needed to use the might of the company to help her with this case.

Two switchboard operators and a disgruntled sounding shift commander later, she and Vindi stared at her cell phone, waiting. After five minutes, the screen lit up, the vibration setting sending the device dancing about an inch across the table.

"Chief Taylor?"

Authority seeped across the phone lines as Palm Springs Police Chief Nick Taylor answered. "Yes, is this Stella Reynolds?"

"Thanks for calling."

"I can't say I'm happy to do it. It's Monday night, and—" kids yelled in the background and he hushed them before continuing, "I'm having a very rare bit of family time. What do you need?"

"I—we," she said, including Vindi, "have found some inconsistencies in the Drew Chambers investigation, and I wanted to give you and your department a chance to respond to them before I go on national TV tomorrow."

"What kind of inconsistencies?" he said, not sounding too concerned.

"Missing evidence, missed suspects, arresting the wrong person... that kind of thing," Stella said, cringing at how casual she sounded.

When he spoke again, he was more focused. "What's your deadline, Stella?"

"Tomorrow afternoon at one o'clock Pacific Time." She wanted to give herself plenty of time to write and edit her story.

Chief Taylor blew out a sigh and said, "Okay, let's meet tomorrow morning. We'll get to the bottom of these alleged inconsistencies, and hopefully you won't have a story to run by the end of our interview."

"Thank you, Chief," she said before disconnecting. When she turned to Vindi, she was smiling at her.

"Remember back when you didn't even want

to call the chief, because you thought he'd get mad?"

"Well, I got over that, didn't I? It's kind of his job to answer our calls."

"You're going to blindside him with this information, you know. He's not going to have any answers."

Stella nodded in agreement. "I think Trish managed to keep most of the relevant details a secret, but the goal is to make him suspicious—make him start asking questions, too."

"The jury will probably have a verdict tomorrow," Vindi added.

"It's going to be a long day, isn't it?" Stella asked. "A sit-down with the chief, a potential verdict, live shots from morning 'til night for you, and then what? Back home to the daily grind on Wednesday?"

"Yup. Jury selection starts in San Diego for another murder trial, so if this wraps up, I'll be there by Wednesday morning. You?"

"I don't know," Stella said, stacking papers on the desk and removing takeout cartons from the bed. "I guess it'll depend on how things go tomorrow." She picked up her phone and tapped in a number. "Does this place have a fax machine?"

"Yes," Vindi answered, her eyebrows drawn together as she looked at Stella. "Why?"

"We'll need one more thing tomorrow," she said, shifting focus when a woman answered her call. "Hi, Maria? It's Stella Reynolds. We need to talk."

44

It sounded like a generator was chugging loudly nearby, but it was just Woz's labored breathing. Terry had to wait to get mic checks until the other man sat down and put on his headphones. Even then, Terry fussed with the camera for a few more minutes, waiting for Woz's rattling breath to stabilize. They were in the conference room at the Palm Springs Police Department. The room was stark, stuffy, and dim, and Woz and Terry had spent the better part of an hour setting up lights with gels and filters for their interview.

Chief Nick Taylor was stiff and unsmiling while they waited, and after the first few failed attempts at small talk, Stella fell quiet, too.

"Mic check, Chief?" Terry asked.

"What do you mean?" he snapped.

Terry said, "Perfect, thanks. Stella, whenever you're ready, I'm rolling."

The chief resettled into his seat and Stella looked down at her notes. "Can you tell me, Chief, since there's no hard evidence tying Preston Harrington to Drew Chambers' murder, how your investigators narrowed in on him as the suspect?"

The door behind the chief opened, and just as Woz started to push himself up to stop anyone from interrupting, Detective Trish McDonald poked her head in.

"Your admin asked me to come see you, Chief?" She squinted at the cameras and lights hovering over the room, and then her eyes drifted down and locked onto Stella. Her expression hardened.

"Yes, Trish, come in. Stella, you've met Detective McDonald? I asked her to join this interview. As the lead detective from day one, she has more information on the case than I do. I thought she could help answer your questions. Can somebody get her a chair?"

After much rearranging and adjusting of lights, they were finally ready to go again.

"So, Chief, I was just asking how Preston Harrington came to be a suspect."

He cleared his throat. "Sure. I know the CSI effect is in full force in many courtrooms, and people think every case can be solved with incontrovertible DNA proof of a suspect's guilt. Often, however, that's not the case, but that doesn't make our case weaker." He looked over at Detective McDonald. "In fact, our on-the-ground detective work is more important than ever before, and that's exactly how we were able to solve this case. Detective McDonald, here, was the first one on scene and had to actually hold the scene for several minutes until medics retreated. That's when the clock started ticking. Right, Detective?"

She jerked toward her boss and nodded woodenly. "That's right. You only have one chance to get things right in a murder case, and we were fortunate to have a great ground crew spread out and start asking the right questions."

Chief Taylor clapped a hand on her shoulder. "Don't be modest, Trish. You took the lead on this one, and I couldn't be prouder of how it all ended up. We'll see soon how the jury responds, but I think we built a solid case, and Gail and her team have done their best. Now we wait."

"Chief, I want to talk about how some people were excluded from the suspect pool."

"Excluded?" His eyebrows rose almost comically high. "It would be inappropriate to—"

"Did you know that, at the time of Drew Chambers' murder, he was having an affair?"

"We know a lot of things about the victim that aren't going to be litigated in public—"

"Did you know one affair, in particular, only ended because he was killed?"

"Trish, do you want to—"

"I guess I'm asking," Stella pressed, "because it seems like both the woman he was sleeping with and her husband, at the time, would be just as likely suspects and have just as much or even more motive as Preston Harrington. I'm wondering if their alibis were ever checked out."

Chief Taylor looked at Trish, cleared his throat, and said, "We simply won't re-litigate the case before the trial is even over."

"What if I told you that the man—the ex-husband of the woman having an affair with Drew Chambers—was identified in store surveillance videos from that day just blocks from the murder scene?"

When it was clear that Trish wasn't going to say anything, Chief Taylor attempted to cover her silence. "You can rest assured that we investigated and confirmed everyone's whereabouts, except

Preston Harrington, who, I'm sure you'll recall, has refused to tell us where he was at the time of the murder."

She held out a note. "Do you recognize this?"

Confused by the change in questioning, the chief took the paper and unfolded it into a square that was half the size of a notebook page. "No, what is it?" he asked.

"Can you read it for me?" Stella asked.

The chief blew out a sigh. "I'm getting tired of this game, Stella. I'm not going to—"

She interrupted him. "It says, 'Ruiz in cuffs, courthouse hallway, 1:30.' Do you recognize the handwriting?"

"No," he answered tersely.

"Oh, sorry, Chief, that question was for Detective McDonald." Trish refused to look at the paper, and Stella asked again. "Detective, is that your handwriting?"

"No."

Stella had been expecting that. "Detective, who are you dating?"

McDonald bit her lip, losing her angry facade for just a moment. "I don't think—"

Stella turned back to the chief. "Chief Taylor, does that look like Detective Matt Skokie's handwriting?" He brought the paper closer to his face, and then his eyes darted to McDonald before he inspected the paper again. "Maria Garcia faxed that over to me last night. She says somebody slipped her that note during the trial. She thought it was from Gail Abingdon, who'd become a great source for her throughout the trial, but Gail had nothing to do with the note. Do you recognize it?"

"N-no, I've never seen it be—"

"Would it surprise you to learn, Detective, that a court bailiff says you asked him to pass it to Maria one day last week?"

"Trish, what's going on?" the chief asked, turning toward his detective, his mouth shaped like an upside-down crescent moon. "Turn the cameras off—"

"Th-this is," McDonald tried to stutter out a rebuttal. "I-I don't know—"

Stella's heart pounded through her ribs. This was it. If she didn't get McDonald to confess now, she wouldn't have another chance. She leaned forward again and felt the pressure from the unblinking eye of camera lens that faced her.

"Detective, what has been your primary goal with this case? Solving a murder, or getting back at your old high school tormentors?"

"Now wait just a moment—that's absurd!" Chief Taylor said.

"Detective," Stella said, ignoring him, "did you intentionally lie to prosecutors about Heidi Harrington's affair? Did you intentionally withhold information about Sawyer Harrington being seen near the murder scene, so Gail Abingdon would convict the wrong man?"

"Outrageous!" Chief Taylor spluttered. "Trish, I don't believe—" Whatever he was about to say died on his lips, however, when he glanced at his detective.

McDonald was pale and wiped tiny beads of sweat from her brow, but she seemed glued to her seat.

"What has been your main goal in this investigation?" Stella repeated.

"Justice," the detective answered, wiping her hands on her pants.

Stella narrowed her eyes. "Justice for whom?"

McDonald's expression steeled. "Justice *for the victim.*"

Stella leaned forward and lowered her voice. "Which victim, Trish? Which victim?"

"What are you talking about?" Chief Taylor asked, looking between the women. "Trish, what's going on?"

"Another man is dead," Stella said urgently, "and it's because the real killer is out there. You know that, right? Tim is dead because Sawyer wanted to tie up the loose ends."

"Tim Price?" the chief asked, now staring intently at his detective. "What is she talking about?"

"I-I... I was going to make sure it all came out in the end, I swear it!" McDonald tore her gaze away from her boss and looked down at her shaking hands, as if she couldn't bear the way he was staring at her. "We had already arrested Preston when we got a tip on the hotline from Heidi. She was worried... worried that her husband had done something rash.

"We spoke—she told me about her affair with Drew, but by then we'd already convinced prosecutors that Preston was the guy. I thought—I just thought—"

"You thought you'd let Gail convict Preston and then come forward with new information? It would ruin Gail's career," Stella said.

"The way she ruined my life for so many years," Trish bit the words out through pinched lips before looking back down at her hands. "It would all be okay in the end. Preston would go home and Sawyer would be arrested. It would all be right, don't you see?"

"But then Sawyer struck again."

"We don't know that."

"Oh, come on," Stella snapped. "He killed Tim in broad daylight. Someone saw something; some camera caught something."

Chief Taylor had sat back in his chair, stunned by the revelations coming from his lead detective, but when Stella mentioned cameras, he sat up and looked at McDonald with a cold, steely glint in his eye. "There is someone—we were going to put out a notice on local TV today for the public's help identifying the killer." He paused, but Trish refused to meet his eye. "Do we already know it? Do you know who killed that man?"

McDonald nodded, her miserable face belying her role in the gruesome crime. "It looks to me like —like Sawyer Harrington."

"Why did he care if Tim Price was alive or dead?" the chief asked.

Trish fell silent, so Stella said, "Because Sawyer knew Tim could identify him as Drew Chamber's killer and Sawyer didn't want to take the chance."

While her final words still rang in the air like a speech bubble in a cartoon, the door opened.

"Chief?" A beat officer in uniform winced when he saw the cameras. He squinted through the bright lights and said, "Sorry, sir, but we just got news that the jury's back. They have a verdict in the Preston Harrington trial."

45

The courtroom was buzzing, the energy palpable, as Stella walked in just behind Chief Taylor and Detective McDonald. The gallery was full, but she was the only reporter on hand. She'd left Woz and Terry in the media room and snuck in behind the top law enforcement officers, so she could witness the jury's verdict in person and not through a video monitor.

Ignoring a look by the court bailiff, Chief Taylor headed directly to Gail Abingdon, pulling Detective McDonald somewhat reluctantly behind. Before the chief could do more than say a few words, though, the bailiff's voice rang out.

"All rise. The Honorable Judge Catherine Jenkins presides."

As Judge Jenkins sat down, she leveled a sharp, unblinking stare at Chief Taylor. "Mrs. Abingdon, are we ready to begin?"

It was a partial rebuke, and Gail Abingdon's face flushed as she said, "Yes, your Honor, ready here." Chief Taylor looked uncertainly between the two women before sitting directly behind Gail.

"Mr. Yarley?"

Preston Harrington's lawyer stood. "Yes, your Honor, we're ready." His client, for the first time in days, looked pale and nervous—hardly ready.

The judge called the jury in, and Chief Taylor, now crouched behind Gail Abingdon's chair, spent the few minutes it took for them to file in whispering frantically into the prosecutor's ear. Gail's slack jaw tightened as Chief Taylor's story continued, and soon her eyebrows were mashed together, her pale face colored with bright red spots on her cheeks.

By the time Chief Taylor took his seat again, Gail Abingdon stared blankly at the jury, her mind clearly working overtime as she tried to decide what to do with a mountain of new information about the case.

Just as she cleared her throat, though, perhaps ready to make a last minute request to the judge, the lull ended. She'd missed her chance. Judge Jenkins began questioning the jury.

Once the judge was satisfied that all members of the jury agreed with the verdict, she asked the forewoman to stand.

"Wait!" Chief Taylor stood. "Your Honor, I'm so sorry for the breach in etiquette—"

"Chief Taylor, you are out of order. Please sit down before I have you removed from my courtroom."

The pool cameraman stuck his head out from behind the camera for a moment and then pressed a button on the side of the lens to zoom out the shot wide.

"Gail," Chief Taylor looked critically at the prosecutor as he sat, "Now. Say something now, before it's too late!"

His words seemed to unfreeze her, and the stunned prosecutor stood slowly, like a deer in the woods coming unexpectedly into the high beams of an off-road ATV. "Your Honor, may we approach?"

"This better be good," Judge Jenkins said. She turned her microphone off and motioned both Abingdon and Yarley forward.

The minutes crept by, an occasional outburst from the judge and Yarley the only sounds in the room. Not a stray sniff or cough could be heard as everyone strained forward, hoping to catch a snippet from the trio gathered at the front of the room.

Finally, after nearly fifteen minutes, during which the judge called Chief Taylor and Detective McDonald to the bench, she dismissed the entire group. With a click, her microphone was live again, and she waited for all the players to take their seats, rubbing her knuckles until the court-room was still again.

Preston whispered frantically to his lawyer, who only held up a hand, asking for patience. The man had none to give, though. He looked ready to leap up and attack his own lawyer, until Tanya reached out a steadying hand.

"Dad, wait," she said. His shoulders didn't relax, but he sat back stiffly.

Judge Jenkins turned to the jury. "Ladies and gentleman, we have hit road bumps in this trial from the beginning and, I'm afraid, even here at the bitter end, we are still spinning our wheels to ultimately find justice in this case. New evidence —weighty, important, and shocking new evidence—has come to light at this late hour, mere minutes before you were to hand down your verdict."

A tittering broke out amongst the jurors, and Judge Jenkins held up her hand.

"The case is still technically pending, and that means I have three options. I can let you deliver your verdict, knowing that key information has been willfully withheld by investigating officers. Alternately, I can tell you to set aside your verdict and let you hear this new evidence and go back to the jury room to deliberate again. Finally, I can call a mistrial and make the state start from scratch with a whole new jury pool in a whole new trial." The general groaning that had broken out amongst the jury escalated to an all-out riot of noise. "Ladies and gentlemen, I know how frustrating this must seem," the judge spoke over the jury, and after another moment of grumbling, they quieted. "Ultimately, my only concern can be that true justice is carried out today." She turned from the jury and frowned past Gail Abingdon at Chief Taylor and Detective McDonald. She then looked down at the bench and silence fell over the courtroom.

After a long, spellbinding minute of quiet reflection, the judge looked back up at the police officers in the room and frowned. "Preston Harrington, please stand." Preston and his lawyer stood, supporting each other as they waited for her decision. She took a visible breath and then picked up her gavel. It hung over the sound block just as justice hung in the balance for Preston Harrington. "I declare a mistrial. The defendant will be immediately released without bail. I will hold a hearing in this courtroom tomorrow with all parties at nine o'clock sharp. Detective McDonald," she raised her eyebrows, "your testimony will be first." With that, she banged the gavel and stood, leaving the courtroom with a flourish.

The courtroom erupted like a pop-up thunderstorm over an ocean beach. Preston Harrington sagged against his lawyer, and Yarley guided him into his seat.

Directly behind Preston, Tanya crumpled forward against the rail that separated her from the lawyers and her father. She heaved a few sobbing breaths and then turned to lock eyes with Stella. Tears spilled down her cheeks, and she mouthed, "Thank you."

As the jury filed out of the courtroom and the gallery began to empty, Gail Abingdon turned to the two officers. Her lips turned down and she jabbed a finger at the pair. "My office, now."

Stella left the courtroom and hurried down the hall. "Woz!" She tore the door to the media room open.

He slung the camera over his shoulder. "Let's go."

Vindi joined them with her photographer and they waited for the elevator together.

"You called Steve?" Stella asked.

"He's meeting us outside at your satellite truck," Vindi said, holding up her phone. "I said, 'don't bring the hotdogs, only your memories from that day.'"

"Great—and he's bringing the surveillance video?" Stella confirmed.

"Yes. We'll take it when you're done."

"Stella?"

Tanya stood behind them, her face set and her eyes bright. "I'm ready—t-to go on air—to do an interview. Whatever it takes to make this right."

"Are you sure?" Stella looked at Preston's daughter doubtfully. She didn't want Tanya getting lost in the moment and regretting an interview later.

"I'm sure. I've been selfish, and after everything Dad's done for me, I... it's time."

"Where is he?"

She laughed without humor. "Apparently, being 'released immediately' does not, in fact, mean immediately. The jail has to process him out, so he's technically still an inmate, but he's not in handcuffs, anymore, at least."

Stella nodded. "Come with me. We've got," she looked at her watch and her stomach lurched, "forty minutes. Oh my God, forty minutes to air! We can make it, but only if we hurry!"

"Can you tell him it's an emergency?" Stella lightly gripped Tanya just above the elbow. "Oh, great, thanks." She held the phone out. "You'll have to tell him it's okay to talk to me," she said.

Tanya took the phone and gulped, visibly nervous, even with her newfound resolve to come clean, come out, and come through for her father. "Hi, Doctor Munver? Yes, it's Tanya Harrington. I guess it's time—it's time to... mmm-hmm. Well, I wanted you to speak to a reporter and just confirm a few... Oh, okay. Sure. Yup, here she is."

She handed the phone to Stella, who introduced herself to the doctor on the other end of the line.

"With Tanya's approval, I'm happy to confirm that she and her father were here, at my office, for a three-hour appointment the day Drew Chambers was killed. They were in the waiting room from around nine in the morning until nearly fifteen minutes past their scheduled appointment of nine thirty. We wrapped up just after my assistant left for lunch—she's very punctual—so right around ten or maybe a quarter after noon."

"How can you be sure?" Stella asked. She only had one chance to get this right and she didn't want to go the way of Maria Garcia.

"Tanya contacted me the very next day and told me about the murder and her father's arrest. I take detailed notes as a rule, but with the looming situation with her father, I wrote down everything I remembered from that day and kept it both in my personal journal and in our online office system." He blew out a breath, and then added, "Marg was here, too, and can confirm the times. Marg, come here."

There was some fumbling and then a woman came on the line. "Hi, this is Marg Ruhner, officer manager."

"Oh—hi, Marg. You were working the day Tanya and Preston were in?"

"Yes, I have it down in my journal, too. Both the patient and her father were here until I left for lunch, and when I came back, they were gone. Oh, and before you ask, I had a tuna melt with chips and a diet soda to drink."

Stella hadn't been about to ask, but it was very thorough and convincing, just the same. Marg put her boss back on the line and he said, "We thought it might come down to this, but Tanya didn't want to become a punchline in her father's case."

Stella's adrenaline, which had been pumping double time since the judge declared the mistrial, faltered. "I don't think—"

"You have no idea the stigma still attached to people going through this, Stella. Tanya is an injured soul still coming to grips with her own identity. Her inner suffering is something you and I could never imagine. Do your best to take care of and protect her. There's no coming back from something like this."

He hung up, but Stella continued to hold the phone to her face. How could she protect Tanya *and* Preston? If she wanted the truth to come out about his innocence, the easiest way to prove he was nowhere near Drew Chambers when he was killed was to lay bare the truth about his daughter.

"Ready?" Tanya asked. She looked fragile, her skin sallow and pale, and despite the defiant set to her jaw, her hands fluttered down at her sides, a small line of sweat forming at her upper lip.

"Yes," Stella answered, drawing out the single syllable.

Terry turned the lights on and handed her the stick microphone, and Woz appeared in the door of the satellite truck. "About twenty-five minutes, Stella," he said. "Sher wants you on the phone now."

Stella squared her shoulders and took the cell phone he held out toward her. "Let's do this."

46

Her phone call with Sher ate up more than half of the remaining time before the start of the newscast, so when she finally hung up, she had less than ten minutes until her report would be broadcast live to millions of people across the country.

She looked critically down at her notes and then said to Terry, "I need—"

"Me. You need me and you don't even know it." Gail Abingdon strode out from between two parked cars and emerged in front of Stella. "You," she pointed to Tanya, "out. There's no need to take the focus away from the onerous miscarriage of justice that has transpired. I'll take over; you take cover."

Stella turned to Tanya with an I-thought-no-body-knew-about-you-but-me expression, but she only shook her head and shrugged. Stella's gaze then shifted to Gail Abingdon. "What are you pre-pared to say?"

"I'll tell your audience exactly what happens now—what my office plans to do now that we know what Detective McDonald has kept hidden for the last two years."

Stella's eyes narrowed. Just as Detective Mc-Donald had an axe to grind against Gail Abing-don, so, too, did the prosecutor have baggage. "My executive producer doesn't want a playground fight breaking out on our airwaves. We will only air *facts* tonight—no allegations. Do you un-derstand?"

"If anyone understands what's legally allowed, it's me," she said imperiously.

Stella's lips bunched on one side of her face, but she couldn't argue with Gail's superior knowl-edge of the law. "Terry, get a microphone on Gail Abingdon."

"Five minutes. We need mic checks!" Woz called from the truck. "Put your IFB in, already!"

"Sorry!" Stella found her earpiece at the bottom of her bag, clipped it on, and then shoved the tiny, rubber part into her ear. She dialed into the IFB line and gave the camera a thumb up.

"Finally," Woz said. His exasperation only made her smile; he was such a pain in the butt.

"Stella," Sher's commanding voice came over the IFB line, "Hank has decided to lead with your exclusive. I hear you have the head prosecutor with you?"

"Terry?" Stella motioned to Gail. The photographer pressed a button on the camera to make the shot zoom out. "Sher, this is Gail Abingdon. She's going to walk us through what happens next."

"We're all on tenterhooks," Sher said. "You've got twenty seconds, and you're off the top."

Stella shook out her tense shoulders and gave herself a quick pep talk. She was going to nail this live shot and never look back.

"Standby, Stella." She and Terry locked eyes. He winked, and she bit back the urge to grin as *Hank-freaking-Smith's* voice filled her earpiece.

"Tonight, an unprecedented situation in a Palm Springs courthouse as a judge stops a case just minutes before the jury hands down the verdict. Stella Reynolds is live with exclusive details about the case in Palm Springs, California. Stella?"

"Good evening, Hank. Just as the jury told the

judge that they had reached a unanimous verdict in the Drew Chambers murder trial, new evidence of possible police misconduct in the investigation came to light, stopping the trial in its tracks.

"Lead Prosecutor Gail Abingdon is joining us now. Gail, is Preston Harrington innocent?"

Gail nodded. "New information came in at the eleventh hour, and my office has now confirmed that Mr. Harrington is innocent, as he has claimed all along."

"If Preston Harrington is not the killer, who killed Drew Chambers?"

"Our investigation is ongoing, and tonight we're not prepared to release any information about—"

"Are any new charges pending in this case?"

Gail hesitated, her lips pursed, and then she said, "Detectives arrested Sawyer Harrington in the courtroom."

"On what charges?" Stella asked, subconsciously taking a step toward Gail Abingdon.

"First-degree murder, manslaughter, and obstruction of justice." She paused, and then added, "As the investigation continues, more charges may be coming."

"Will anyone else face charges?"

"We will determine at a special hearing tomorrow the criminal culpability of the police detective involved who either misplaced or ignored key evidence in the case."

"Gail Abingdon, thank you for your time." Stella turned away from the prosecutor and said, "I want to show you a video clip we uncovered, which has not been seen before by prosecutors investigating the homicide, that we believe proves Sawyer Harrington was near the scene of the crime the day Drew Chambers was killed."

The video started, and Stella hoped Woz was ready at the control panel in the truck.

"Okay, stop it right there. Take a look at the man with the stroller—the man we believe is Sawyer Harrington. I also want to draw your attention to the man next to him, Tim Price, a well-known fixture in the Palm Springs community. He might have had information for police about the crime, but we'll never know, because Tim Price was killed in cold blood yesterday."

Hank broke in with a question. "Stella, obviously we want to talk to Preston Harrington. What did he know about his brother's involvement? Do you think he was protecting his brother, willing to take the fall for him in a murder case?"

"Based on my interviews with his family members, I don't believe Preston knew his brother was hiding anything like that," she said honestly. "Certainly, however, we'll try to talk to Preston as soon as he's released from jail."

She tagged out and ran up the steps to the satellite truck. As soon as she opened the door, Woz handed her the surveillance video, which she handed to Vindi.

"Will you make it?" she asked.

"Just barely," Vindi answered, hustling off toward her own satellite truck.

Gail was waiting for Stella back by her camera. "How did you find that video?" she asked.

"An exploding hot dog," she said, smiling past her at Steve from *Eats and Meats*. "Thank you!"

He nodded. "Whatever I can do for Tim, you know? He didn't deserve to go like that."

The prosecutor tilted her head and said, "I don't know who you are, but I think we need to talk."

Before they walked away, Stella called, "Gail, with Preston free, what happens to Luna C Engineering?"

"As per Drew Chambers' will, his shares of the company go to his wife, Dr. Sloan Chambers. Last I heard, she wants to sell to Bionic."

"To Dr. Manuel Ruiz's company?"

Gail nodded. "Yes, apparently they're hung up

on negotiating what percentage of the company will be used for charity. Sloan's priority is to donate ten percent of their manufactured product to the VA."

"The Department of Veterans Affairs?"

"That's right. Sloan grew up with Tim Price. Apparently, she was really advocating for him to be in one of their clinical trials but he would never agree. It was important to her—maybe even more so, now that he's, well...."

Gail beckoned to Steve and then ushered him to a nearby bench at the edge of the parking lot.

A throaty voice broke in. "Stella?" Tanya Harrington looked small and uncomfortable standing next to Terry, and with her arms crossed over her stomach, Stella didn't know whether Preston's daughter wanted to throw up or sit down. "I—I guess I wanted to say thanks."

"You can't keep who you are a secret, Tanya," Stella said. "You're still hiding, until you let people in on who you are. I just didn't want you to have to tell everyone at once."

Tanya's lips fluttered tremulously as she attempted a smile. "Well. You're... thank you. For—for everything." She then turned and walked back to the courthouse.

Stella watched Terry break down the equipment, but instead of feeling relieved or victorious, a nagging feeling of doubt pulled at her brain like a nail at a sweater.

She still didn't know who'd broken into her room or why. Would she ever find out?

47

Days later, Stella frantically packed her bag. She was running late, and the maid service waited impatiently outside her door while she shoved things into her suitcase.

"I'm sorry!" she called over her shoulder. "I'm almost done. Come in—I'll just be a second."

The maid propped open the door, and after Stella swept her belongings off the bathroom countertop, she collected the towels and dumped them into her cart, then stood, looking at her wristwatch every few seconds, as Stella threw clothes, makeup, and electronics into her suitcase.

She dove to the far side of the bed when she remembered a shoe had fallen there the day before, and in her haste to move quickly, she knocked her bag off the chair, spewing the contents sloppily to the floor.

"Let me help," the maid said, just as much to get on with her job as to be helpful.

"Thanks," Stella said, clutching the ballet flat in her hand and standing tall.

The maid's fingers closed around a sheet of paper she'd picked up and she froze. "Do you know this man?"

"Who?" Stella walked closer. The maid held up the picture of Sawyer Harrington that Stella had used with Vindi when they were searching for information on him downtown. It felt like years earlier, but it had only been days. "Do *you* know him?" Stella asked.

"No, but I saw him coming out of a room downstairs a few days ago," she said. "Boy, was he mean! He had this nasty glint in his eye. I thought —" She laughed depreciatingly. "Well, it sounds silly to say now, but I thought he was going to kill me. I've been watching too many scary shows, I suppose. Another door opened down the hall and then he rushed past."

Stella repacked her bag and wheeled it down the hall to the elevator, hardly remembering to press the down button.

Sawyer Harrington had come to her room, but

to kill her or to talk to her? She shivered with the realization that she might have missed death by minutes. She'd been delayed coming back to her room that night because she and Lucky had been making up after their fight. With a snort, she realized she'd have to thank John for saving her life. If he hadn't lied to Lucky about his night, she and her boyfriend wouldn't have fought and she would have likely gone back to her hotel room earlier, perhaps to find Sawyer Harrington waiting for her.

In the lobby, Vindi sat on a club chair, reading a magazine. "Took you long enough," she said without looking up. "Manager said he's going to charge me a late check-out fee."

"I'll pay you back."

"Are you kidding? I'm not paying it, my station is. We'll call it even, I think." Vindi stood and the two women stared at each other.

"I'm going to miss you, Vin," Stella said, reaching out to pull her friend in for a hug.

"Yes, you will," she said, but her smile was lopsided, and she sniffed loudly when they pulled apart. "Hank Smith is stealing your exclusive sit-down with Preston?"

They walked through the lobby as they talked, heading for the taxi stand outside.

"Well, not stealing, really. Preston said he wanted the largest audience possible for his exoneration interview, as he's calling it, and I told him Hank had a much bigger draw than I ever could. Plus, he's flying eight of the jurors out to New York. They'd voted unanimously to convict Preston, and Hank thought it would make for a nice little segment to have them all together."

"So, you gave it away?" Vindi asked, her eyes narrowed, a hand on her hip.

"To help Preston, yes. He deserves it."

Vindi handed her key to the valet service and then turned back to Stella. "Any update on Jolene Colburne?"

"She called me yesterday after my exclusive with Heidi Harrington. She said doctors ran some blood tests and she had Vaiestrela in her system— the official name of Luna C's Wondred drug."

"So someone slipped her a large dose—"

"To drive her insane," Stella nodded. "I guess the reaction was so swift that Jolene got confused and stopped taking her other meds cold turkey. All of it happening in twenty-four hours was too much for her body."

"Who did it?" Vindi asked. "Not that many people have access to the drug."

"I don't know how it will ever be proved, but she said she had lunch with Sawyer Harrington before the trial got underway—she was working on getting an exclusive with him. Maybe she said something that made him nervous? I don't know." She fell quiet, thinking of her own meal with Sawyer when he'd offered her a supposed vitamin. Had it been Wondred? When she hadn't taken it, had he decided to take things a step further by breaking into her hotel room to kill her? She'd likely never know.

Vindi barked out a laugh. "I don't think I'll ever forget Sloan's face when you asked her why she was late to that luncheon."

Stella felt a pang in the pit of her stomach, remembering the conversation. "How was I supposed to know she'd been talking with Tim about a new clinical trial? All I knew was that she wasn't accounted for during the time of her husband's murder and her alibi was shot."

Vindi snickered again. "'Where were you when your husband was killed, Sloan? Answer the question!'"

Stella's cheeks flushed. "It was a simple question. I don't know why she threw her phone at me."

"Wow." The other reporter pawed at a line on

the sidewalk with her toe. "Well, I'm glad Jolene's doing better."

"Tanya told me that Jolene is the first reporter she told—she'd planned on putting it all out there. When Jolene took ill, though, she said it felt like a sign that she should stay quiet."

"It almost cost her father his freedom!"

Stella shot a look at the valet and pulled Vindi close. "Keep your voice down—that's top secret! Hank doesn't want that information out until his story runs tonight."

"Still," Vindi said, her eyes wide. "Can you imagine? Dirty cop, motivated prosecutor, a man with secrets, and bam! He would have spent the rest of his life in jail while the killer walked free. Prosecutors had their conviction."

"Yeah," Stella said with a scowl, "and it would have been based on faulty and missing evidence!"

Vindi's car pulled up and the Valet got out and handed her the keys. She rocked back a step and turned away from her car. "I still don't understand why Trish gave you that taped interview with Rita Perlman. What was she doing?"

"I think she was worried when she found out I was checking alibis and tried to stop me in my tracks. So, she gave me Rita's interview, hoping I'd believe that police had done their jobs and move on."

"Well, that backfired, didn't it?" The women smiled at each other and Vindi said, "So, just one last question: where's Hope going to stay?"

Stella grinned. "Tim's mom took her. From what I've heard, she's already had a thorough medical evaluation and been completely de-bugged and bathed."

"Well, that's that." Vindi looked down at the sidewalk then back up at her friend. "Where to now?"

"Dinner with Lucky in New York tonight, and then I have to go through training at the office and fill out a bunch of paperwork, so I can get paid." She looked down at her friend and both women burst out laughing.

Vindi opened the door to her car and waved. "Go get em, Stella."

"See you soon, Vin," Stella said as she climbed into the backseat of her taxi.

"Where to, ma'am?"

She looked up at the familiar voice. "Penny?" The woman tucked an unlit cigarette behind her ear and a wide smile stretched across her face as Stella said, "Take me to the airport."

"Following another criminal?" Penny asked, recognizing her from the other night.

"Always," Stella said, sitting back against the leather seat with a small, contented smile on her face. "Always."

####

ABOUT THE AUTHOR

Libby Kirsch is an Emmy award-winning television news journalist. She draws on her rich history of making embarrassing mistakes on live TV, and is happy to finally indulge her creative writing side, instead of always having to stick to the facts.

Libby grew up in Columbus, Ohio and now lives with her husband and children in Ann Arbor, Michigan. Yes, Thanksgiving weekend* is tense.

For more information, check out her website at www.LibbyKirschBooks.com
*Also known as College Football Rivalry Weekend.

www.LibbyKirschBooks.com
libby@libbykirschbooks

facebook.com/LibbyKirschBooks

twitter.com/LibbyKirsch

goodreads.com/LibbyKirsch

bookbub.com/authors/libby-kirsch

ALSO BY LIBBY KIRSCH

The Stella Reynolds Mystery Series

The Big Lead

The Big Interview

The Big Overnight

The Big Weekend

The Janet Black Mystery Series

Last Call

Last Minute

Last Chance

For updates on new releases or to connect with the author, go to www.LibbyKirschBooks.com

Turn the page for a preview of *Last Call*.

LAST CALL

LIBBY KIRSCH

LAST CALL - A JANET BLACK MYSTERY

Janet slammed the drawer of the cash register. By the time Cindy jumped at the noise, Janet had her phone out to make a call.

"Hey, Darlin'," Jason said when he picked up the line. "I was hoping I'd hear from you."

Janet smiled, in spite of her foul mood, and pushed wisps of light brown hair away from her face. Her hand came away damp. She'd been sweating in the Knoxville summer heat since before she even rolled out of bed, and the ancient air-conditioning unit behind the bar couldn't seem to keep up with the soaring temperature. Then she remembered the reason she was calling and frowned. "I just counted—and then I re-counted. Money's missing again." She walked toward the back of the room, away from Cindy and Frank, her bouncer, who'd just arrived for his shift. "This time we're short eighty-two dollars." She couldn't stop herself from turning back to look at her employees suspiciously.

"And?" her boyfriend asked.

"*And* Elizabeth was working last night." She watched Cindy disappear into the back cooler with an empty bucket.

"Anyone else?" Jason asked.

Her lips puckered. Why did he always sound so irritatingly reasonable? "Well, yeah, but I don't think—"

"I'm just saying. Don't fly off the—"

"I can keep my cool, okay?" she snapped, then flushed. She hadn't meant to shout. She lowered her voice to a whisper. "Jason, can you please just check the video? I gotta go." They disconnected, but before she could shove her phone back into her pocket, the screen lit up with a delayed notification telling her she'd missed two calls overnight from the very employee she suspected of theft. She glared at the walls, then realized it wasn't the poor reception *here* that was the problem. She'd been home all night with Jason, and for some reason the incoming calls from Elizabeth were only now showing up.

She tapped a few icons and shook her head. Her youngest staff member hadn't left a message, but the timing seemed suspicious. She learned just days ago that money was missing, and then last night, for the first time ever, Elizabeth tried to call her on her cell phone? Did she know, somehow, that Janet knew about the missing money?

Cindy hobbled out from the walk-in cooler, her gait awkward as she wrestled the full bucket of ice behind the bar. As usual, she was dressed to kill—or at least maim. She had poured herself into a bright pink tube top that ended just above a shiny green belly-button ring. Her tight jeans rode so low that Janet could see her hipbones jutting out, and Cindy had tied her bleach-blond hair back with a teal bandanna. Body parts were spilling from every piece of her outfit.

"You gained a set there." Janet motioned to Cindy's chest. Something had happened when she dumped the ice bucket into the freezer drawer, and her two boobs had turned into four.

"Oh my gosh! They musta come unstuck!" Her twang made the words musical. She bent over and reached into her tube top to rearrange things.

"Come on!" Frank turned away from the bar in disgust and headed for the far side of the room.

Janet watched him walk off before asking Cindy, "What's under there?"

"It's a silicone push-up thingamajig. Sticks right to my skin and pushes the girls up—but I'm so dang hot, they must've slipped down." She wiped beads of sweat from her brow and then smoothed the fabric of her tube top over her restored figure. "You know, I didn't used to need all this business under here, but after Chip, everything just kind of . . . fell."

Chip, Chip, Chip. It was all Cindy ever wanted to talk about. Janet plastered on a smile when her bartender looked up. "Kids, huh? How old is he now?"

"Seventeen, going on forty," she smiled indulgently. "He leaves for college this fall." She turned back to the bar, a towel and spray bottle in her hands, the goofy grin still on her face.

Frank slammed two chairs down from the table in the corner, still scowling. He might not have liked Cindy's methods, but he took his share from the tip jar every night without complaint. Janet only paid minimum wage, but they all cleared more than thirty dollars an hour on a good night, thanks in some part, perhaps, to Cindy's ramped-up double-Ds. Their nice hourly wage made it even more frustrating to discover someone had been stealing money from the register, and if Janet's new accounting program was right, it had been going on for weeks. That's why she'd had Jason install the state-of-the-art surveillance system. She was ready to catch a thief.

"Damn gum," Frank muttered, scraping the tabletop with a flat-edge razor.

He fit the job description for a bouncer—tall and strong—but his light brown hair was smashed flat on one side, as if he'd fallen asleep while it was wet, and his eyes were red and puffy.

Was he the sticky-fingered employee? Though Elizabeth, Janet's other full-time bartender, was her prime suspect, Frank was no prize, so if Jason saw him stealing in the surveillance video from the night before she wouldn't be shocked.

But Elizabeth still seemed the most likely culprit, although Janet couldn't articulate why to Jason. She just had a feeling the other woman was hiding something.

"Anything unusual last night?" she asked lightly as she walked back behind the bar.

"Oh, you know," Cindy said without taking her eyes off the two bottles of top-shelf vodka she was combining, "same old, same old. We had to throw poor Ike out just before midnight, bless his heart. Other than that, it was the usual."

"Did he make a fuss?" Janet already knew the answer, since she hadn't been called.

"Nah." Cindy placed the full bottle of vodka back on the shelf and set the empty one in the recycling bin.

Frank cleared his throat. "No fuss?" He hefted two more chairs off a table and dropped them to the ground with a bang. "He shouted the whole way out the door, 'The man will always find you— he knows,' not to mention the hail of curse words he spewed at Elizabeth."

Cindy shrugged as she took two bottles of well vodka from the bin and unscrewed the caps.

Janet looked shrewdly at her bartender. "Did we call him a taxi?"

"Yes ma'am, we sure did, and didn't kick him out until it arrived," Cindy said, unconcerned.

"Well, shit," Janet said with a shrug that mimicked Cindy's. Really, you couldn't ask for a better outcome.

Cindy raised her eyebrows and looked pointedly at a jar on the counter.

Janet grinned. "Aw, hell, Cindy," she drawled, making a show of pulling not one, but three one-dollar bills out of her back pocket and pushing them into the oversized, washed pickle jar. The swear jar already had five bucks in it from the last hour alone. "I keep forgetting to watch my damn mouth."

Her good humor was tested, however, by Frank, muttering in the corner.

"That's not how you'd have handled it on the force?" she asked.

"It's not a police issue. I just don't know why he's welcomed back time and again." Frank turned his back on the women and kept working.

Janet had hired him a few weeks ago, impressed by his pedigree. She figured a former cop would surely know how to handle the door of her small bar. So far, however, he'd been a disappointment, always ready to escalate a situation and challenge the status quo.

"I suppose you think that kind of behavior is fine?" he asked over his shoulder.

"No, but this is a bar, not a bookstore. It's going to happen." Janet crossed to the back cooler and emerged minutes later with a white plastic bin full of lemons and limes. She looked up at a sudden clattering at the front door. A gray and grizzled man with greasy hair and dirty clothes pulled at the handle. She could practically smell his days-old sweat through the glass.

"Door's broken!" he called, cupping a hand over his eyes so he could see into the bar. "Ma'am? It won't open." He jiggled the handle again, and then, as if he'd expended too much effort, he leaned in, leaving a streak on the glass with his forehead. Janet and Cindy exchanged amused looks, but Frank crossed his arms and stared daggers through the glass.

"We're not open," Frank said, looking at the man like he was the leftover foam at the bottom of a pint glass.

"Not open?" The man smiled, revealing several missing teeth. "How'd you get in?"

Janet chuckled and looked at Frank. "Take care of it." She pointed to the number for the taxi company nailed to the wall behind her, then waited until Frank picked up his cell phone before she took the empty fruit bin to the back room.

There, Janet caught a glimpse of herself in the mirror on the back of the door. She turned to the side to check her boobs. At thirty-one years old and without kids, they were right where they were supposed to be. She smoothed her black T-shirt with the bar's logo on it and tucked it into her jeans before heading to the desk.

She spent a few minutes going over the books. It was Thursday, which meant they could expect a big college crowd thirsty for deals. She squinted through the window into the back parking lot. If the beer truck didn't show, she'd have to change her happy hour special, as her inventory of cheap, crappy beer was low.

Janet looked at the clock on the wall and blew out a sigh. She'd check the cooler to see what would make a good replacement.

But first, she decided to call Elizabeth. The call went straight to voicemail, so she left a message, asking her bartender to call in; she wanted to ask directly about the missing money. Her phone chirped—the battery was low—so she laid it on the desk and called Jason on the landline, leaving him a long, detailed message about her plan for Elizabeth.

Despite the missing money, she liked being in charge. It was freeing to think if there was a problem with an employee, she could fix it.

Buying The Spot a year ago had made her a boss for the first time ever, and she was on a mission to be unlike any crappy boss she'd ever had. She wanted to be calm, be unflappable, and stay the hell out of her employees' personal lives. With a final nod to herself, she logged out of her computer and left the office.

As she cut through the main room, however, her step stuttered and her heart slammed into her chest. What was it about seeing cops that made you feel instantly guilty?

The man and woman in uniform were chatting with Frank by the front door. Cindy was behind the bar, not making eye contact, but Frank looked up defiantly when she cleared her throat.

"Hello, Officers," Janet said. "What's going on?"

Last Call, A Janet Black Mystery, Available now!

www.ingramcontent.com/pod-product-compliance
Lightning Source LLC
Chambersburg PA
CBHW051934240626
47153CB00005B/1492